Newpor ... & In... Service

Gw... ...

...nes Wilcox's stories have appeared in the *New Yorker*, *Avenue* and *Louisiana Literature*. He is the author of *Modern Baptists*, *Miss Undine's Living Room*, *Polite Sex*, *North Gladiola*, *Guest of a Sinner* and *Sort of Rich*. He is a graduate of Yale University and a recipient of a Guggenheim fellowship.

Also by James Wilcox

Modern Baptists
North Gladiola
Miss Undine's Living Room
Sort of Rich
Polite Sex
Guest of a Sinner

Plain and Normal

*

James Wilcox

FOURTH ESTATE • *London*

This paperback edition published in 1999
First published in Great Britain in 1998 by
Fourth Estate Limited
6 Salem Road
London W2 4BU

1 3 5 7 9 10 8 6 4 2

A catalogue record for this book is available from the
British Library

ISBN 1-85702-981-X

Typeset by Palimpsest Book Production Limited
Polmont, Stirlingshire
Printed in Great Britain by
Cox & Wyman Ltd, Reading, Berkshire

Chapter One

Any minute the volunteer might arrive, and Dr. Bennet was still in the shirt he had worn three days in a row. Joe Pollock, his roommate, had ironed a clean shirt for him, but Dr. Bennet was too upset to put it on. Using that starched, formal tone of voice he reserved for special occasions, such as when a cigarette had somehow burned a hole in his sofa, Dr. Bennet had informed Joe Pollock that he would not permit any species of volunteer into his apartment. He was not a charity case.

Joe Pollock, in fact, hated the word 'charity' just as much as Dr. Bennet. Never in his life had Joe accepted a handout from anyone. Even during the depression, he had managed to stay afloat without once setting foot inside a soup kitchen. As for today, all you had to do was ask Dr. Bennet's doorman and you'd find out that Joe Pollock never borrowed a cigarette without paying back, two bits each, as soon as his Social Security arrived.

Maybe it was because he was straight about these little things that Joe Pollock got along so well with folks like Nicky, the doorman from Estonia. Not a day passed without Nicky learning something useful from Joe, maybe a new expression in English (Cat got your tongue?) or the reason why this country was going to hell in a handbasket (the Democrats). Now, the Korean who sold those measly plum tomatoes on 181st Street, this was a tougher nut to crack. But Joe Pollock had so many other pals in the neighborhood that he didn't mind the brush-off from the Korean so much. The cops, they knew Joe. He gave them tips about lunch, where they could find the best bargain. And the guy who sold pretzels, he was a pal, too – even let Joe watch the cart once when nature called.

In his own way, Dr. Bennet was a little like that Korean, Joe figured, polite but remote, wrapped up in his own world. The Doc's problem was too much education. You couldn't blame a Yale man for not wanting to hobnob with a doorman who had never heard of Old Faithful, thought it might be a horse. That was why Joe Pollock had called up the agency. He was hoping they might be able to send someone with a college education up to Washington Heights, someone to help the Doc snap out of his funk. It was wearing Joe down, living with a man who did nothing all day, wouldn't go out for a walk, much less for a movie or a good square meal. Just stared at the TV all day – and not even a decent TV. Black-and-white, that's all it was, no color, and it fuzzed up everything but Channel 2, the one station Joe Pollock couldn't stand, what with that *60 Minutes*.

It was the counterman at Dunkin' Donuts over on Broadway who had told Joe about Manhattan Cares, how they had sent a *chica* for free to visit his mother-in-law once a week. Joe Pollock had got the number from Diego and made the call to the agency. He specified right up front that he didn't want just anyone. It would have to be someone really on her toes to satisfy Dr. Bennet's requirements, a Phi Beta-type female, not too young, but definitely not over forty-one – say, forty-two max. And she should have some meat on her bones, someone more like Jane Russell or Ava Gardner than these scarecrows who pass themselves off as women nowadays.

When the intake woman at the agency insisted on interviewing

Dr. Bennet himself, Joe Pollock resorted to a tactic he had learned in basic training – camouflage. Since Dr. Bennet would never submit to an interview, Joe shouldered the burden himself. He pretended he was the one who wanted a visitor.

And so, after Joe Pollock had taken the subway down to the Village for a meeting with the intake woman, it was arranged that a volunteer would be sent to Washington Heights on Saturday at 2:00 p.m. Joe might have been a little miffed at first that the volunteer the agency came up with was sixty-two and of unknown weight. (No snapshot was provided in advance for Joe's perusal, and they absolutely refused to tell him how much she weighed.) But when he reminded himself that the visitor was for Dr. Bennet, Joe felt better. The Doc didn't seem to care how a dame looked. In fact, he had made Joe take down a *Penthouse* calendar from their bedroom wall.

'You are not to open that door,' Dr. Bennet insisted with remarkable vigor after the volunteer's arrival was announced over the intercom. 'She is not allowed in this apartment, understand?'

Joe Pollock was pleased to note that already, even before her entrance, the volunteer was having a good effect. Dr. Bennet had never seemed more alive, so full of spunk. It was the first time in the six or seven weeks since Joe had moved in that the man seemed to really care about anything.

'Just say hi to her, Doc. You might find she's quite a gal. If you don't cotton to her, no one says you have to keep her. Just toss her back, and they'll fish out a new one for you.'

With an injured look, Dr. Bennet retreated to the bedroom. 'You have no right to do this to me, Joe.'

From the very beginning Dr. Bennet had suffered misgivings about allowing Joe Pollock to move in. Yes, the man had a heart of gold, solid as a rock, but then again, the same could be said for his head. Try to discuss anything serious with him – Dr. Bennet had once attempted to explain evolution – and he would fidget and squirm like a three-year-old, then start spouting some nonsense about how Mozart proved there was no such thing as evolution. Everything had gone downhill since Mozart, Joe claimed – not only music, but art, manners, morals, even looks. People just looked dumber these days.

Of course, if Dr. Bennet had not taken him in, Joe Pollock would have been homeless, out on the streets. After years of legal red tape, Joe's landlord had finally managed to raise the rent on his West Eleventh Street apartment from the $77 a month Joe had been paying to $845, totally beyond Joe's means. To be fair, despite the fact that Joe was only paying a hundred a month now for room and board, Dr. Bennet did not think of himself as his benefactor. Ever since his wife had died, Dr. Bennet had suffered from an unrelenting anxiety, which he supposed could be called a broken heart if the words didn't sound so trite and tame. Joe's very presence in the apartment was somehow comforting, particularly at night when his doglike snuffling in the other twin bed – Hermione's – would give Dr. Bennet something to be irritated about. After so much angst, irritation seemed almost welcome, a cozy, housebroken emotion. And then, too, Joe made the best pancakes in the world, when he was in the mood.

'He's in the bedroom, won't come out,' Joe Pollock said, as he ushered the volunteer into the living room.

The sixty-two-year-old dame Joe had been expecting turned out to be bald, a man. Standing out there in the hall, the guy had apologized for not being Mrs. Lucille Wheeler. The agency had tried to phone this morning about the last-minute change – Mrs. Wheeler's husband did not like the idea of her traveling so far uptown by herself – but no one had answered. So the guy – S. Lloyd Norris was his name – decided to keep the appointment anyway. He hoped Mr. Pollock didn't mind that he just showed up like this, without a proper introduction from the agency.

'You don't mind?' Mr. Norris repeated, since Joe Pollock had only shrugged when he let him in. 'You can call them if you like, to verify I'm, you know . . .' The muted elegance of the living room distracted Mr. Norris from attending to what Joe Pollock muttered in reply. Mr. Norris thought he was supposed to be visiting a needy old man. That was the whole point of signing up with the agency, to help the poor. Yet that picture on the wall, a stick figure in red crayon, looked inept and childish enough to hang in the Whitney.

'. . . and like I said, won't come out. Thanks to Yale, turned out stubborn as a mule, that man.'

'What man?'

'You hard of hearing? The Doc.'

Mr. Norris ignored the slur. He was adept at not taking things personally. And besides, he was indeed a little hard of hearing today. From cleaning too conscientiously with a cotton swab, Mr. Norris had impacted the wax in his left ear, which was scheduled to be removed, the wax, by an otorhinolaryngologist a week from Tuesday.

'I'm sorry, are you ill?' Mr. Norris asked somewhat hopefully. Ill would help make up for rich. 'Is your physician in the—'

'Fifty push-ups every morning and a hundred sit-ups,' Joe Pollock said, his annoyance at such a stupid question giving him a license to exaggerate, 'and you ask if I'm ill.' Slapping a crumb from the damask sofa he had lowered himself onto with a groan, he added, 'I'll have you know, fella, you're looking at a man who's never had a cold, not once in his eighty-eight years.'

Eyes on high beam, Joe Pollock waited for the volunteer's astonishment – *No, you can't be eighty-eight!* Actually, Joe was only seventy-nine, which was astonishing enough for most folks. Joe himself could hardly believe it, he looked so young and fit. But this S. Lloyd Are-You-Ill needed some help, the large-print version.

'Did you hear? Eighty-eight, can you believe?'

'No.'

'You calling me a liar?'

'No, no, I meant you look so young.'

Gratified, Joe Pollock motioned for him to sit. Mr. Norris descended upon the faint unicorn woven into an ottoman.

'I would say you were eighty-three, -four at most.'

'What's that?' Joe Pollock cocked a hand behind his ear. 'Anyway, want to know my secret? I'm going to tell you my secret. See, I never wear a tie. That thing you got on' – he gestured toward Mr. Norris's tie – 'it makes you look a good ten years older. Same goes for that suit. Me, I wouldn't be caught dead in a suit like that, brings out all that gray in your hair, see. So what's with the suit today, anyway? It's Saturday!'

'We had a meeting this morning at the office and—'

'Never mind. See this here?' Joe Pollock leaned closer, holding out a wiry arm. 'Go ahead, feel.'

'Feel?'

'Go on,' he prompted, and Mr. Norris, with an inward sigh of resignation, touched a protruding vein on the wrist.

'The shirt, you numbskull!'

'Oh.' The sheepish grin on Mr. Norris's face was a fitting accompaniment to the older man's curious barks of glee. But then when these turned into a coughing fit, the grin faded. 'You OK, Mr. Pollock?'

Joe Pollock hacked into the starched, three-pointed handkerchief offered to him, then wiped his mouth. 'He feels me up, can you believe?'

Mr. Norris shrugged. 'I thought—'

'You're a character, you know? Now go ahead, feel.'

Between thumb and forefinger Mr. Norris tested the baggy short sleeve that reached to the man's forearm. 'Very nice.'

'Hundred percent silk. You want to know something? I'm going to tell you something. Can't wash this baby in no machine. I got twelve of them, one for every type of social occasion, and I do them all by hand. A female visitor, see, that means I wear chartreuse.'

Mr. Norris blinked. 'But isn't that sort of flesh-colored?'

Indeed, from even a moderate distance, Joe Pollock seemed half naked.

'What?'

'Your shirt.'

Joe Pollock looked down at himself. 'Yeah, well, the chartreuse has got this button missing, and you know as well as the man upstairs' – his twenty-five-cent cigarette jabbed the air for emphasis – 'that you got to match. I've been looking all over hell and high water for a chartreuse button.'

Mr. Norris tried to wave away some greenish smoke that lingered in his vicinity. 'Could I ask you a favor, Mr. Pollock? The cigarette . . .'

'Want a drag?'

'No, the smoke. See, at my office, it's smoke-free. That's the rule.'

'And you bow down to it?'

'Actually, it was my suggestion.' The ottoman squeaked as Mr. Norris crossed his legs. 'My secretary makes it a habit to go out on the sidewalk to smoke.'

The cigarette dangled from Joe Pollock's thin, leathery lips as he said, 'Yeah, and what if it's raining?'

'Well, it's the rule.'

'Neither rain, nor sleet, nor snow, huh? Nothing stops you, out they go to catch their death of cold. Well, excuse me, mister, but for some reason I thought this was America, the land of the free.'

'I just thought I'd ask.' Mr. Norris's smile was wan. 'It's OK, I guess.'

Joe Pollock had heard enough. With a grunt he heaved himself to his feet. This S. Lloyd Boss had some nerve telling him it was OK-I-guess to smoke in his own home. As soon as he got this volunteer out the door he was going to call the agency and give them a piece of his mind. And if they didn't come up with a female forty-two max, they'd better plan on explaining themselves to the Better Business Bureau.

'Mr. Pollock, I don't really mind the secondhand effect and all, but—'

'Well, fella, looks like he's not coming out.'

'Who?'

'Don't say nothing to the agency about this, but it's really not me you're supposed to visit. It's my pal in there. Stubborn as a goddamn mule.'

'But, Mr. Pollock, I'm assigned to you.'

'Yeah, well . . .'

'I'm supposed to stay two hours.'

This last was said at the door, where Mr. Norris had been herded.

'Don't worry about it, bub. I'll tell them you were here two hours – make it three, four if you like.' Joe Pollock's eyes teared from the rising smoke. 'See, Saturdays they aren't so good for me. They got these here concerts at Juilliard—'

'Hey, that would be great,' Mr. Norris said with a touch of desperation. What would Manhattan Cares think of him if he were rejected on his very first assignment? 'I love classical music.'

'You do, huh?'

'It's one of my favorite things,' he lied again.

'Crumb – you like George Crumb?'

'Absolutely great.' Who? The X-rated cartoonist?

'Elliott Carter?'

'Genius, sheer genius.' Sounded more like a lawyer.

Joe Pollock blew a smoke ring into the stale air of the corridor. They were walking toward the elevator. 'Me, I can't stand those fellows. You listen to one measure of Mozart, see, and you got more going on than in – Hey, almost forgot.'

Joe Pollock drew the soiled handkerchief from his drooping shirt pocket. 'Here, take it,' he said, trying vainly to thrust it between the closing doors of the elevator.

'No, no, you keep it, Mr. Pollock. I'll get it next time.'

'Crumb,' Joe Pollock muttered on his way back to the apartment, the handkerchief stuffed back in his pocket. 'They send me a deaf bald male who likes Crumb . . .'

Chapter Two

The new vacuum Joe Pollock had selected after an exhaustive study of *Consumer Reports* was supposed to be off-limits to Dr. Bennet. But as he surveyed the valance over the French doors that led to the terrace, Dr. Bennet decided that the rule was senseless. If he wanted to use the vacuum to touch up the fabric, which looked dusty to him, what was wrong with that? Feeling bold, he went to the closet and with only minor vexation managed to screw in the proper attachment. A few minutes later the valance was presentable and the vacuum returned to the special hooks Joe Pollock had installed in the front closet.

Not a thing more needed to be done in the living room. Joe's *Penthouse* had been weeded from the magazine stand, and his ivory belly dancer – ivory might offend some people these days – exiled to the bedroom. On second thought, though, Dr. Bennet decided that the hydrangea on the butler's table was too fussy and old maidish. The pale corymbose blossoms were transported to the study, where a more suitable replacement was found. With their beige petals veined in ochre, the orchids in their antique cobalt planter had an understated masculine elegance. Once he had set them on the butler's table, Dr. Bennet could not help admiring them for a moment or two. Then he repaired to the kitchen to make sure Joe Pollock had bought the proper biscuits for tea.

Next to the tansy, a herb Dr. Bennet grew to discourage ants, a silver tray was laden with a tea service that his late wife had inherited from an uncle, a Danish count who bred ill-tempered corgis on Staten Island. Dumped on top of the Wedgwood drabware was a package of Fig Newtons, half consumed. Dr. Bennet smiled at Joe Pollock's childishness. Apparently, his friend was miffed because he had not been allowed to call back the agency and demand another volunteer, a female. 'You just don't go sending people back as if they were defective merchandise,' Dr. Bennet had explained with great patience.

The previous Saturday, with his ear pressed against the door, Dr. Bennet had shuddered at the mannish voice coming from the other room. The volunteer, Mrs. Wheeler, sounded like a toad, which was exactly what Joe Pollock deserved. But when, after her rather sudden departure, Dr. Bennet had emerged to gloat, Joe Pollock stumped him by declaring the visitor actually *was* a man. Not just a man, but one of the most uptight, boring specimens Joe had encountered in all his days on earth. On and on Joe went about how the guy just sat there in his pinstripe suit and tie, made Joe do all the talking. He might as well have been Korean. What kind of agency would pick someone who liked Elliott Carter to be a visitor, Joe would like to know. The more Joe griped, the more Dr. Bennet realized how much he was yearning for some decent, intelligent conversation, something neither Joe Pollock nor any woman – not since Hermione had passed away – had been able to provide. The problem was, though a woman might have a certain native intelligence far surpassing a man's, she invariably went haywire whenever Dr. Bennet was around.

Dr. Bennet had suffered this affliction, being far too appealing to the opposite sex, for as long as he could remember. He had thought that turning seventy might bring some relief, but to his horror, the housekeeper he had tried out before Joe moved in had made a pass at him. She was inspecting a suspicious mole on the nape of his neck when a curious sensation swept over him, as if he had been licked. Of course, Mrs. Bledsoe denied it. Nonetheless prudence required that he relieve her of her duties. It was a most unpleasant scene. She claimed she was being fired because of her age – she was sixty-seven – and her mustache. Fearing a lawsuit, he slipped her a far-too-generous check as she departed, and he vowed never to permit another woman in the house.

But the volunteer was not a woman. And furthermore, it dawned on him that the volunteer was not really for him, anyway. Joe Pollock was the one who needed one. He didn't have a single relative who stayed in touch, not a single friend, either. The poor guy was just too proud to admit how lonely he was. Well, if Joe wanted a visitor, he was going to get one. You just didn't meddle with people's lives the way Joe did and get off scot-free.

He had still not found the biscuits preferred by the Queen Mother when the intercom buzzed.

'Mr. Norse here.'

'All right, Nicholas. Send him up.'

'Mr. Pollock?'

For a moment, as he stood holding the door, Dr. Bennet was inclined to be outraged. Couldn't this volunteer tell the difference between a six-foot-two gentleman who was often mistaken for fifty and an eighty-year-old runt with a mashed-in nose? But then it occurred to Dr. Bennet that Mr. Norris was simply asking where Joe Pollock might be.

'Mr. Pollock went out for some cigarettes. He should be back shortly.'

'Oh.' Mr. Norris was relieved. It was the right apartment after all, 8G. He needn't have worried so much about his short-term memory – though he had gone to the wrong building at first, the one next door. They all sort of looked alike in this neighborhood.

'Won't you come in, sir?'

The treaded soles of Mr. Norris's running shoes squeaked over the tiles Joe Pollock had scrubbed on hands and knees that morning. Dr. Bennet winced. The sound was like nails on a blackboard to his sensitive ears. 'May I take your . . .' He wasn't sure what to call the thing Mr. Norris had on. 'Your wrap?'

'My what?'

'Your . . . jacket.'

'Actually, it's my shirt.'

'Of course. Well . . .'

Sorely disappointed by this man's appearance – he was not wearing the pinstripe suit Joe hated, and he was certainly not as old as Joe had led him to believe, probably just somewhere in his forties – Dr. Bennet showed him into the living room.

'Perhaps you might want to wait here for Mr. Pollock,' Dr. Bennet suggested, wondering how a shirt could look so much like a windbreaker. And, for that matter, how a business executive – a boss, as Joe had put it – could look so totally bereft of any air of authority. Was it any wonder that the economy was in shambles, if such men were in charge?

'Please don't—' Dr. Bennet began as Mr. Norris plopped uninvited onto the tapestry ottoman, the one piece of furniture in the apartment that was off-limits to everyone, including Dr. Bennet himself.

'Pardon?'

'That unicorn.'

'Oh, sorry.'

Mr. Norris transferred himself to the sturdier Queen Anne chair indicated by Dr. Bennet. His late wife had salvaged the chair from a thrift shop whose proceeds helped fight illiteracy – or was it the Metropolitan Opera it fought by funding a less privileged Brooklyn company? In any case, there was nothing in the apartment that was not battling something or other – especially that ottoman. Dr. Bennet had nearly collapsed when Hermione had informed him that she had paid $9,000 for it at an auction that was intent on wiping sexism from the face of the earth.

'In case Mr. Pollock didn't mention it,' Dr. Bennet said, after an awkward silence, during which he himself couldn't decide whether to be seated or not, 'I'm Dr. Bennet.'

'Oh, are you his son or something?' Mr. Norris hoped he didn't sound too fatuous, but he wanted to make up for sitting on the unicorn.

'Oh, no, no, Mr. Norris, we're not related at all,' Dr. Bennet explained as he finally settled onto the sofa. Joe Pollock's volunteer's face, though bland and undistinguished, did betray a certain perspicuity, a native intelligence. 'Was the trip satisfactory?'

'What trip?'

'Uptown, here.'

So many of Dr. Bennet's friends had to excuse themselves from traveling this far north, to a neighborhood that they confused with Harlem, particularly after the recent riot staged by his Dominican neighbors. Hermione would have condemned the police, not the illegal immigrants, had she lived to witness the uprising. Indeed, her socialist streak was so pronounced that she had tried to persuade him to live in Spanish Harlem shortly after they were married. But Dr. Bennet had put his foot down. Washington Heights was as heterodox as he was going to get.

'I hope you didn't take the tube up here, Mr. Norris.'

'The subway?'

'There are stretches one must pass through that are far from desirable, if you know what I mean.'

'Actually, I drove down from Yonkers.'

'Oh.' Dr. Bennet had heard of Yonkers, but like Mars, it seemed somewhat improbable that it was actually inhabited. 'You commute to work?'

'Every day. My office isn't far from Times Square.'

'Times Square?' Dr. Bennet wondered if this volunteer had something to do with pornography. If so, it was intolerable. He would have to be dismissed. 'What sort of business do you conduct, sir?'

'Labels.'

'I beg your pardon?'

'We specialize in developing and designing labels for personal care products. You'd be surprised how hard it is to get the exact color and wording and punctuation to complement the shape of the label, which has to enhance the shape of the container itself. Like shampoo. "Apply liberally, rinse, repeat."'

After brooding for a moment or two, Dr. Bennet looked up and said, 'Why must one repeat? That's something I've never understood.'

'So you'll use more shampoo.'

'Isn't that dishonest, Mr. Norris?'

'I don't write the copy myself. If I did, the directions would say, "Return this bottle to place of purchase and buy a generic brand that's half as expensive and does the job just as well."'

'Mm. And just what is it that you do?'

'All the computer programs for cost analysis, market-research breakdown, client indices, viscosity.'

'Viscosity?'

'The glue, what type of glue you need for certain labels. But this also applies to the inks that go right on the bottles as well. The software I've developed makes it possible for our artists – that's what we call our creative staff at NyLo – for the artists to know the parameters without being technically proficient themselves. Also, I've refined a warning device, something like a car alarm, that goes off when one of our artists gets a little careless with grammar. You know how your PC has a spell check.'

'My what?'

'PC. Well, my grammar alarm goes off if an artist authors a mouthwash label that says, for instance, "Don't let anything come between your lips and she." The artist also receives a slight shock, as well, through his mouse.'

'His what?'

'Just a joke. I'm not allowed to use behavioral conditioning in the office. Anyway, you might notice that the spell check on your

PC is often mistaken. So I've urged our artists, when they author copy . . .'

Too polite to administer a shock to Mr. Norris for his barbaric verb, Dr. Bennet let the man drone on while his own mind wandered to other matters – more specifically, to the legs he had just crossed. Long and shapely, Dr. Bennet's legs were somewhat notorious, thanks to an ode celebrating their perfection that appeared, to his complete and utter mortification, in the Vassar alumnae magazine some years ago. The poetess, a classmate and former close friend of Hermione's, had been banned from Washington Heights as a result of this tribute. Hermione never forgave the poor woman, a widow, who insisted her subject was an imaginary set of legs. If only Dr. Bennet's unique birthmark had not been so vividly mapped, Hermione might have relented. The irony, of course, was that even though they were indeed his legs, Dr. Bennet had never touched the author. She was a horsey woman, given to riding to hounds, definitely not the type of woman one wished to be linked to in scandal – particularly when one had a wife who was ten times more attractive, whom one adored.

'. . . and there's a program as well to show our employees how much money they waste when they don't read the directions correctly on our copy machines or when they send personal faxes or leave the water running in the restrooms. In fact, my secretary thinks this particular program could be turned into a web site,' Mr. Norris went on, wishing he would stop talking about himself. He knew he was boring the old man half to death – not to mention sounding like a self-centered jackass. But he was afraid that if he didn't talk there would be a horrible silence, proof that he was unfit to bring cheer and goodwill into the lives of shut-ins – or whatever they were.

'Web site?'

'My secretary has a friend whose son-in-law made almost a million on a web site he started up. She thinks my ideas about efficiency management, how small economies turn into big savings, well, she thinks they might attract a lot of executives. The trouble is, she doesn't know the first thing about marketing such a project. I mean, who would want to go to a web site that urges you to turn off the copy machine when you're through?'

'Mm.'

'But she gets all worked up, says I could be the next Bill Gates. I tell her, even if I could – which I couldn't, of course – even if I could I wouldn't want to be the next Bill Gates. This country has enough celebrities as it is. Why would it need yet another? What we need now are plain, normal people who do their jobs and are grateful and content that there's enough food on the table.'

'Mm.'

Mr. Norris stole another glance at the old man's chin. Was that dried yolk or some sort of growth, a fungus?

'Yes?' Dr. Bennet prompted.

Mr. Norris had opened his mouth, but because of the yolk – not something he would dare mention to such a polite and proper gentleman – he forgot what he had been talking about. Though he was only forty-three, there were times when Mr. Norris feared the onset of senility, when all the chores and responsibilities that made life such an intolerable burden were lapped by a brief oblivion. 'I was just wondering,' he said, casting about for something, anything to say, 'you know, uh, about Mr. Pollock. Last week I got the feeling, like, did I do something wrong?'

Dr. Bennet shrugged. 'Mr. Pollock is a difficult man.'

'You sure he wants to see me again?'

'I'm sure of nothing Mr. Pollock wants – or thinks.'

The fir on the terrace, a single branch drooping in sight just below the valance, shimmered as the dull plumage of a sparrow – or was it a thrush? – burst upon the sky.

'Have you known Mr. Pollock long?'

'Not really. He used to be my sergeant. We were stationed together in Texas during the war.'

'World War Two? But that's a long time to have been friends, isn't it?'

'We lost touch after the war, Mr. Norris. It wasn't until three or four years ago, that's when I ran into him again, backstage at Carnegie Hall. The Pittsburgh Symphony was playing, and we both had friends in the wind section.'

'How strange.'

'Not strange at all. Mr. Pollock conducted the band I was in at the base down in Texas. A lot of his players went on to good jobs all over the country. Mr. Pollock himself was quite a clarinet player, a real natural. If he had just gotten himself a proper education, he could have played in any orchestra he wanted. But he was afraid to leave the army. Stayed there till he was forced to retire.'

'Does he still play?'

'No, sir. Busted his fingers up with his damn boxing, years ago.'

'What about you?'

'Me? Haven't touched the bassoon in ages. Not since college.'

'Yale, right?'

'How did you know?'

'You have that look,' Mr. Norris said, just before remembering that Joe Pollock must have mentioned it.

Dr. Bennet frowned. 'And what else did Joe say about me?'

'Nothing, honest.' Wondering if he had sounded like a liar, but unable to explain his innocence, Mr. Norris babbled something about how wonderful he thought Yale was, how he wished he could have gone there himself.

'Well,' Dr. Bennet said, his feathers smoothed, 'there are plenty of fine colleges in this country. You did go to college, didn't you?'

A nod.

'And where was that, Mr. Norris?'

'Harvard.'

The long legs uncrossed as Dr. Bennet scrutinized the bland, unreadable face opposite. Was he being mocked? Surely a Harvard man would have better things to do with his time than visit someone like Joe Pollock. What was this world coming to?

'Actually,' Mr. Norris added, 'it was only for a year. Things didn't work out too well for me in Cambridge, so I transferred to Loyola down in New Orleans. That's where I'm from, Louisiana, this town called Tula Springs, not far from—'

'Take any physics?'

'No, I majored in economics.'

'Never had a single course in physics?'

'In high school, yes, but I—'

'Well then, sir, surely you must know what Aristotle said about bodies in motion.'

'Bodies in motion?'

'A body in motion has a natural tendency to what?' Dr. Bennet prompted. 'To come to rest, correct? Plain and simple Aristotle.'

'I guess.'

'But he was wrong, of course.'

'He was?'

'Well, didn't Newton say just the opposite?'

'Oh, right. Things keep going – inertia and all that.'

Though the clap was subdued, barely audible, Dr. Bennet's hands did express the curious feeling that coursed through him – hope. How many times had he tried to have a similar conversation with Joe Pollock, something scientific, real, filled with solid data, facts, only to have Joe start taking everything personally, refusing to be corrected, and then dragging in Mozart to prove a point. It just wasn't possible to talk to Joe without Mozart peering from the wings, waiting to march onstage and take over the whole show.

'Wait here a minute,' Dr. Bennet said, as he rose with surprising ease from the sofa. Where was the pain in his leg, the chronic ache? 'I've got something you might find interesting. Be right back, sir.'

Heading for the study, Dr. Bennet retrieved his glasses from the pocket of the rumpled tweed jacket that Joe wanted to throw out, like trash. The volume Dr. Bennet was looking for was right next to the bound copies of the *American Journal of Physics* – or no, was it the *Physical Review*? The longer he searched, sliding the built-in library ladder from one end of the room to the other, the more he realized Joe was right – the books should be catalogued.

But he wasn't going to let Joe himself do it, not according to the system of key signatures he proposed.

When he was just about to give up, Dr. Bennet came across the morocco-bound volume his late wife had presented to him on their first anniversary. Purloining the typescript of his dissertation for Boston University, she had snuck it off to a printer and binder with a nineteenth-century letterpress. The result was a masterpiece, so noble-looking it was almost embarrassing.

Before returning to the living room with the book, Dr. Bennet savored the smell of the goatskin and turned a few pages. The quiet authority of the Garamond typeface almost made the solecisms he encountered seem deliberate, like eccentric genius. And the title page – well, nothing could outdo the elegant design of the words *Presocratic* and *Victorian Misconceptions*, not even the first-edition *Felix Holt* his late wife had given him when he went to work for her father's real estate firm.

'Here, I found it,' Dr. Bennet said as he emerged from the study. 'My disser— Oh, Joe.'

Joe Pollock was back, and the Fig Newtons that Dr. Bennet had put away were now strewn across the coffee table.

'What's that?' Mr. Norris asked.

'For Pete's sake, Doc. You're not going to make the poor guy muck around in that, are you?'

'Well, I thought . . . Why are you pointing? Stop that.'

'You got egg.'

'What?'

'Egg all over your chin.'

Dr. Bennet palped where Joe Pollock indicated, and then, with a slight tremor, peeled off the yolk.

'How about a brew?' Joe Pollock said to no one in particular.

'I was planning on tea.'

'Tea would be great,' Mr. Norris chimed in. 'I'm not wild about beer.'

'Don't like beer?' Joe cuffed one of Mr. Norris's rather large, protruding ears. 'What are you, some kind of fruitcake?'

'Joe,' Dr. Bennet admonished.

'Get a load of this,' Joe Pollock went on. 'This boss man here, a real genius, he wanted to know if me and you was a couple of fairies. I nearly decked him, better believe. Good thing you came out of that study.'

Mr. Norris ducked to avoid another blow. 'I didn't say that. I just wanted to know . . . You did say you slept together, Mr. Pollock.'

'In the same *room*, knucklehead,' he said, as Dr. Bennet adjourned to the kitchen.

With a grim smile he filled the kettle from the tap. Leave it to Joe to ruin his chance for a decent conversation. And of all things to discuss, their sleeping arrangements. Used to be that two men could live together without an ounce of suspicion. Now it was almost impossible for men to be roommates, straight men. As the kettle heated, Dr. Bennet's smile became less grim, more rueful. Deep down, he really couldn't believe that men actually found other men attractive. Yet he did not consider himself a bigot. He tried his best to believe everything these men said of themselves, and when Hermione's best friend used to show up for dinner – Chet dropped by at least once a week – no one could have been more gracious than he, Dr. Bennet. By reminding himself over and over again that Chet really could not feel any romantic interest in Hermione, Dr. Bennet squashed the jealousy and envy that for some reason simply refused to cry uncle.

'Do you take sugar, Mr. Nor—? Where did he go?' Dr. Bennet asked, as he carried the tarnished tray into the living room.

'The john,' Joe Pollock muttered.

The cups trembled as the tray was lowered onto the harewood commode. Dr. Bennet was smiling again. If he were going to be hung for being gay, surely it was ludicrous that this dried-up piece of mutton, eighty years old practically, was the only evidence. It was really quite insulting that Mr. Norris would think he, Dr. Bennet, could do no better if he were—

'What's so funny?' Joe Pollock demanded.

'Nothing.'

'Son of a bitch.'

'Joe, you don't have to drink tea. Go get yourself—'

'Never mind that. It's that goddamn agency. You won't believe the way they've loused things up. I ask for a dame, and what do those numbskulls at Manhattan Cares send over? A fag, that's what. Can't get nothing right.'

'Just because he doesn't like beer . . .'

'Beer schmeer.'

'Joe, I will not have you insulting a guest in this house, your own guest, by the way, the one you insisted on having.'

'He told me so himself.'

'What?'

'Just now, when you were in the kitchen. He wanted to explain why he thought you were that way yourself. I tell you, Doc, you and your tea, it was bound to catch up with you someday.'

'Me? What about you? He meant you too.'

'Yeah, well, that's the risk I took moving in here with you. I like my independence, you know. I'd much rather live on my own. If I weren't such a sucker, didn't feel so sorry for you—'

'Sorry for *me*? I beg your pardon, Joe, but you know darn well that if it weren't for me, you'd be out on the streets, a charity case.'

Joe Pollock squinted hard at the lighted cigarette in his hand, then flung it down on the herringbone parquet.

'I'm sorry, Joe. I didn't mean – What's this?'

The handkerchief Joe Pollock had handed over was stiff as a board, starched within an inch of its life. 'Belongs to the fairy. Give it to him.'

'Where are you going? You give it to him.'

'For your information, I'm heading back to West Eleventh Street, my apartment.'

'But—'

'Where's my belly dancer, my ivory belly dancer?'

'Joe, how can you go back when—'

'That cock-and-bull story about my rent going up, you believe that? I just said that so you wouldn't feel guilty. The apartment's there, waiting for me, and I won't be spending an extra hundred a month on you anymore, better believe.' At the door, Joe added, 'Sayonara, Doc. You can pack up my things and send them down to the Village. And make sure that ivory is in there, understand?'

The door didn't slam. It shut quietly. Dr. Bennet poured himself a cup of tea. But when he tried to sip it, he burned his crotch with more than a few spilled drops.

Mr. Norris, though, fared better. After finishing up in the bathroom, where his spastic colon was acting up a bit, he accepted the cup offered to him, along with the carefully folded handkerchief. Dr. Bennet explained that Joe Pollock had gone out to buy some cigarettes – and groceries. Then for a few moments they discussed Aristotle and inertia. Acceleration. Angles of incline. Mr. Norris pumped two more cups of caffeine into his system to keep from yawning.

The boredom, though, made him feel even more virtuous. If he actually enjoyed talking to Dr. Bennet, where would the merit be? As he descended in the fresh, immaculate elevator, Mr. Norris decided that he really enjoyed doing good for others. It was a shame, though, that these two gentlemen didn't live in some sort of tenement.

'A proud gay man with lots of integrity, that's what. And if those creeps don't like it, tough titties.'

Mrs. Norris was not one to let anyone think ill of her ex-husband. They had gotten married at seventeen, when they were both still seniors in high school down in Tula Springs, Louisiana. Pearl Fay was pregnant at the time, thanks to a second-string linebacker who quit school and ran away to the Coast Guard. Severinus Lloyd Norris was her very best friend in all the world – they had known each other since kindergarten – and he had done the gentlemanly thing, not only marrying her but also keeping quiet about the linebacker. Of course, it nearly killed his own parents, who were strict Catholics, the kind who ate tuna casseroles on Fridays, not something good like shrimp. But Pearl Fay had a way with older people and soon won them over. They would have made the best grandparents, too, if only she hadn't miscarried – and they hadn't died. But such is life.

It was Mrs. Norris herself who had wanted the divorce. Although she had known from sixth grade on that Lloyd was 'one of those,' he himself was never man enough to look himself square in the face and acknowledge the truth. Instead, he went to Mass every day and somehow got her to stop being Baptist and turn into an RC herself. That was how she had met Herbert, who was also converting at the same time in order to please his mother-in-law. By then she and Lloyd were living in Yonkers, a place she never thought she'd end up in, mainly because she had never heard of it before. But it turned out to be the only town near the city where they could afford a real house. Pearl Fay, of course, had had it up to here with apartments. Ever since they'd been married, Lloyd and she had been crammed into one rental after another while he finished high school and went on to college. Then there were all those jobs he quit because he thought the companies were too racist. Why invest in a house when they both knew his current boss was bound to make some comment that would upset Lloyd? He was sensitive not just about African-Americans, but Jews, Arabs, and Asians. Which was the reason they finally moved up North, to get away from all that prejudice down there.

In any case, Pearl Fay's nesting instinct had been repressed long enough. She let him know that Yonkers was the end of the line for her. Nothing – not even if he found out his boss was the Grand Wizard of the KKK – would uproot her again. This was why, when she asked as politely as she could for the divorce so she could marry Herbert, she had to have the house as well. Lloyd was the one who would have to move out, a fact he didn't comprehend at first. But after taking her to court and losing, he found an apartment in Manhattan over a shop that sold nurses' uniforms.

Then, wouldn't you know it, Herbert began to have some qualms. Though he had promised to divorce his wife once Pearl Fay was free, Herbert discovered he was far more moral than he had suspected. He simply couldn't go through with the divorce. On the day Herbert informed Pearl Fay that he was going to quit Mary, Queen of Heaven and join a parish in White Plains, Pearl Fay decided her house needed a thorough cleaning. When she got around to the upstairs bathroom, she was disgusted by the mess in the medicine cabinet. In moving out, her ex-husband had not only ruined her alphabetical arrangement of pills, but had also left behind bottles she didn't want cluttering up her very limited space. Those prescription diarrhea pills, they should be under 'P' for paregoric, not 'C.' Of course, Lloyd really loved these pills. She shouldn't just dump them into the garbage. They were opium, he claimed, some sort of opium derivative that made him feel like he had died and gone to heaven. Yes, he was the only person she knew who looked forward to getting diarrhea. To think she had actually been married to a man like that. Herbert had shown her that what she had known with Lloyd wasn't love at all, never had been. The passion she and Herbert had shared, the rapture, how could she go on living without it? Instead of dumping the pills into the flowered wastebasket, she opened her mouth.

A Sears repairman, who had an appointment to see why the Deluxe RoboSprinkler in her refrigerator's vegetable bin smelled

funny, drove her to the hospital in his van. There her stomach was
not pumped. The repairman had found one of the pills she had
dropped, and handed it over to a resident in the emergency room.
Pearl Fay had swallowed a handful of vitamin C. Mortified, she
was sent home with a few curt words about wasting busy people's
time. On the phone to her mother that same day, she broke down
and wept at what a failure she was, even at suicide. (Of course,
she didn't mention her failure at homewrecking.) She begged her
mother to come up north and stay awhile so she wouldn't do
anything foolish again. Mrs. Holsum, a widow, tried to get Pearl
Fay to move on back to Louisiana, where she belonged. But Pearl
Fay was adamant. Her house was her home now. She was too worn
out to start over again anywhere else. So Mrs. Holsum promised to
come for a long visit as soon as she possibly could.

When the doorbell rang the very next morning, Pearl Fay
wondered what she had ever done to deserve such a good, selfless
mother. Her eyes welling with tears, she flung open the door with
a 'Mama!' and saw Severinus Lloyd Norris standing there. As he
explained, once he had lugged in his suitcases, Pearl Fay's mother
had given him hell on the phone for nearly causing her daughter
to do away with herself. She told him it was his duty to look after
her until she, Mrs. Holsum, could find someone she could trust
to run her gourmet popcorn stand at the mall while she was in
Yonkers.

Pearl Fay told her ex to go back to his apartment; she didn't need
him underfoot at a time like this. But Mr. Norris was genuinely
worried about her. Yes, it might have only been vitamin C this
time. But who knows what might come next? He simply couldn't
have anything like that on his conscience, even though he knew it
wouldn't have been his fault at all. Not really. Pearl Fay agreed.
She said plainly, mincing no words, that if anything happened to
her his conscience could be clean as a whistle. And yet, he pointed
out, it was his fault that he had made her so insecure about being
a Baptist. If she had never converted, well, she never would have
found herself in such a mess, falling in love and all. Hearing this,

Pearl Fay realized he was right. His conscience should bother him just a little.

'I don't know why you have to volunteer for straight people anyway,' Mrs. Norris was saying a few days after Mr. Norris was rejected by the old men. He was still moping around the house, wondering why Manhattan Cares hadn't come up with another assignment yet. 'What have straight people done for you, Lloyd? They've made your life one big lie, a living hell.'

'My life isn't a living hell.'

'Sure it is. Why don't you join a gay organization, help the gays? It'd be a good way to meet someone. You're always complaining about not meeting anyone. Here you had practically a whole year to yourself in Manhattan, complete freedom, no responsibilities, and you couldn't come up with a single boyfriend, not one?'

'I'm not going to join a volunteer group to find a boyfriend.'

'Then just how do you plan on finding one?'

Certainly not by eating this, he thought as she forked another banana-macadamia waffle onto his plate. Already bloated, Mr. Norris wondered what would happen if he just said no, no more. The trouble was, Pearl Fay considered leftovers an affront to her dignity and worth as an individual. And after all those vitamin C's, she needed all the dignity and worth she could get.

'These are so delicious, Pearl Fay, but please don't fix another.'

'It's no trouble. I've got the batter right here.'

'No, I'll never make it to the bus on time.'

'Maybe the bus, Lloyd. Did you ever think you might meet someone on the bus?'

'Honey, they're all straight people on the bus.'

'You should smile, start up little conversations with the nice-looking men.'

'Right, six A.M., everyone's eager to chat.'

'If only you looked more gay yourself.'

'Let's not go into that again. I don't want you buying me any more wild ties or whatever.'

'I thought you liked that shirt I bought.'

'Pearl Fay, it looks like a jacket, a woman's jacket.'

'So? If you don't sound gay and you don't flap your hands around when you talk – can't you at least learn some mannerisms?'

'My briefcase . . .'

'Right by the door.'

'Oh. Well, bye.'

'Wipe your mouth, Lloyd. No, don't dirty that handkerchief. Here.' She ripped off a paper towel decorated with geese and whisked a speck of macadamia off his pursed lips.

Chapter Four

'Thirty-four.'

Bruce Powers, Mr. Norris's boss, looked skeptical. 'You had a thirty-four-inch waist, Norris?'

'Just about. When I was living alone, I was down to thirty-four – and a half.'

Mr. Norris was explaining why he didn't think it would be wise to join Mr. Powers for lunch that day. He mentioned the waffles he had consumed for breakfast and the pork roast that was scheduled for dinner that evening.

'Don't!' Mr. Norris yelped, as his boss grabbed a love handle.

'Don't!' Mr. Powers mimicked.

Happily married with four sons, Mr. Powers was so heterosexual that he hadn't any of the usual qualms most straight men harbor about flirting with men, or whatever it was they did. Horseplay, Mr. Norris supposed was the term. In a way, he was flattered that his boss felt so comfortable around him. After his divorce, Mr. Norris had made a clean breast of it, telling Mr. Powers in a private conference that he was a homosexual, that he always had been one and was just too scared and confused to admit it until Pearl Fay forced him into it by being so honest herself and kicking him out of the house. Of course, he didn't explain to Mr. Powers just how honest Pearl Fay had been, how she had wanted to make everything legal and aboveboard after a year of ushering with Herbert by forcing Mr. Norris to admit that he, too, had been carrying on furtively, he must have been, since that was what all the gay married men on *Sally Jessy Raphael* confessed to. Except that Mr. Norris hadn't been carrying on with anyone. In fact, he had never had sex with a man – not once in his entire life. Pearl Fay was appalled, and her lawyer refused to believe it could be true. The only evidence they could find against him was a box of muscle magazines – which, in fact, had been left behind by the former owner of the house in Yonkers. Pearl Fay had thrown them out when they had first moved in, but Mr. Norris had retrieved them from the garbage and stashed them behind some glass wool in the basement. If they hadn't shown up in court, every single last *Strength and Health* and *Mr. America*, he might have put up more of a fight for the house. But it was deeply humiliating, the way the lawyer had used them, saying how shameful it was that Mr. Norris could not even have the manly gumption to go out and buy some real pornography himself rather than resort, in secret, to these secondhand, completely and utterly nonpornographic representations of obviously nonhomosexual men, some of whom had gone on to Hollywood stardom where they continue to represent all that John Wayne had fought and died for, all the family values that this S. Lloyd Norris had betrayed when he forced himself upon the innocent, seventeen-year-old Pearl Fay Holsum with a straight-A average in home ec and got her pregnant. (Apparently, either Pearl Fay or the lawyer had forgotten the part about the linebacker.)

In any case, Mr. Powers got the thumbnail version of the divorce, in which Mr. Norris made it clear that he was through with lying and deception for the rest of his life. And he wanted his boss to know that since he had been hired at NyLo as a straight married man, he would be willing to resign if Mr. Powers would give him a little time to find another job.

Mr. Powers had assured him that this would not be necessary, that he valued Mr. Norris's computer skills and was indeed planning to recommend him for a raise. But when Mr. Norris declared – as his ex-wife had urged – that he was going to inform everyone working for him on the fiftieth floor that he was gay and proud of it, Mr. Powers cautioned him. The problem was Earleen Vigoris, the president and CEO of NyLo. Ms. Vigoris had a son who was chairman of the Campus Crusade Against Gomorrah at Putting Green State University. If word got back to Ms. Vigoris about Mr. Norris's proclivities, it could mean trouble.

Mr. Norris objected. He told Mr. Powers he didn't want to remain at NyLo if the president was a Neanderthal in skirts. But Mr. Powers argued persuasively, helping Mr. Norris to see that it was really none of Ms. Vigoris's business – or anyone else's at work – what Mr. Norris did in the privacy of his own bedroom. When Mr. Norris declared he had nothing to be ashamed of, that all he did in the privacy of his own bedroom was eat Fritos and sleep, Mr. Powers said no one would believe this. And if they did, then wasn't it humiliating for Mr. Norris to admit that in this day and age he was a big zero, couldn't score at all?

So Mr. Norris's views were somewhat modified, though he did tell Mr. Powers that if anyone asked him point-blank, he was not going to lie. He was not going to invent girlfriends or pretend he was still married or do anything whatsoever to make life more convenient.

'Want me to bring you something back?' Mrs. Kundaa, his secretary, said on her way to lunch.

'He's chowing down with me,' Mr. Powers answered for Mr. Norris.

'I can't, Bruce, really,' Mr. Norris said. 'It's not just the waffles. I've got to finish this new program.'

'What new program?'

From the door, where she was glaring at Mr. Powers's feet, which were parked on Mr. Norris's desk as he lounged in Mr. Norris's chair, Mrs. Kundaa said, 'The one that tells it like it is, how this place is going straight to hell because of all the waste and corruption.'

'No, no, it's nothing like that,' Mr. Norris said with a merry laugh, or what he hoped sounded merry. 'It's just some statistics I've been compiling about all the money that goes down the drain when people leave the water running, so to speak, the lights on, and all that. It's nothing, really.'

The furrows on Mr. Powers's massive brow deepened as he hoisted himself out of the chair Mr. Norris wished he wouldn't sit in. The man's 6′5″ frame was too much for the swivel mechanism, which no oil could assuage.

'Suit yourself, Norris. Go ahead and work.'

'Thank you, Bruce. I appreciate it.'

'What are you thanking him for?' Mrs. Kundaa said, as Mr. Norris gently shut the door behind his departing boss, whom he probably shouldn't call 'Bruce.' But 'Powers' sounded a little hostile. And 'Mr. Powers' – well, how could he call him that when he had been at NyLo longer than Bruce Powers, seven years longer, and was the same age? Yet his boss did look so much older, midfifties at least, mainly because he was so hefty, so tall. Mr. Norris, who didn't consider himself short, always felt as if he were in the first row of an Imax theater when his boss was around, so chronic was the strain on his nerves.

'He should be thanking you, S. Lloyd.'

'Mrs. Kundaa, I wish you wouldn't talk to him that way.'

'What way?'

'Do you want to get me fired?'

'Let him try. I wish that big ape would try.'

For some reason he couldn't fathom, his secretary seemed to thrive on conflict. When there wasn't a landlady around to sue for slander or a dog walker to drag off to small-claims court, she would come down with a cold or the flu, which would clear up immediately if she was unjustly billed by Sprint. Mr. Norris had never liked her. But as a gentleman, he felt it was his duty to protect her from this dislike, and so bent over backward to be courteous and give her the benefit of the doubt. Several times he had plotted with Mr. Powers to get her kicked upstairs to the fifty-first-floor corporate offices. But even though she had been offered a raise and the title of executive assistant, Mrs. Kundaa had refused to budge from Mr. Norris's side. She told Mr. Powers that S. Lloyd Norris was the only decent, honest man in the entire company and that not all the money in the world would tempt her away from him.

Although Mr. Norris had promised Mr. Powers not to discuss his sexuality with any coworkers, he did break down and tell Mrs. Kundaa the truth one afternoon. And didn't he have good reason? For one thing, he couldn't bear to hear himself described as decent and honest with such a secret weighing on his conscience. Then, too, there was the hope that Mrs. Kundaa might be so outraged by the revelation that she would refuse to work for him any longer. Though she was a self-proclaimed atheist, Mrs. Kundaa was as fierce as any Bible Belt preacher in her denunciation of Madonna and the pandering media that allowed such a creature to thrive. When the company newsletter had once referred to her as 'Ms.' Kundaa, she had demanded both a retraction and an apology in the next issue. Surely such a woman, one who still wore widow's weeds in honor of her late husband, an inspector for the Department of Motor Vehicles, who had gone on to his reward a good twenty years ago – surely she could not tolerate such a boss.

Yet all Mr. Norris's hopes were dashed. Instead of being denounced as an abomination, a lying pervert who was a good example of everything that was wrong with this country, he was subjected to a tearful embrace and reassured that she, Mrs. Serge Kundaa, would not let any of those filthy pigs like Bruce Powers touch a hair of his head. It was a dreadful moment, and Mr. Norris wished he had listened to Mr. Powers and kept his mouth shut.

'You understand that the program I'm writing, it's just about the money that could be saved if people didn't photocopy so much and—'

'And spend two hundred dollars on lunch like Powers does. Do you realize that that man's expense account equals what we pay some of our artists on forty-nine? And yet guess who's being downsized?'

'Yes, well, have a wonderful lunch, Mrs. Kundaa.'

'I tell you, Lloyd, if you'd just put in all this stuff I've been telling you about, like the helicopter Vigoris hired the other day, you think that was company business? It was for her son. He was invited to appear on *Firing Line* and—'

'Mrs. Kundaa, please, I've told you time and time again this is none of our business. I don't want to hear about it. Now if you don't mind, I have some statistics to go over.'

'You're hopeless, you know. Here you have a chance to really make it big – OK, OK, I give up. I'm going.' As she leaned over to retrieve a ball of yarn, she added, 'I'll bring you back a meatball hero.'

He peered closer at his spreadsheet. 'Please don't.'

'You had one yesterday. Didn't you like it?'

The day before, Mr. Norris had asked for a can of tuna in water. She was the one who had brought back the hero, which he decided shouldn't go to waste.

'You need red meat, S. Lloyd. Look at me, you wouldn't call me overweight, would you?' With her florid face and trademark panting, Mrs. Kundaa did exhibit a certain rude health, as if she had just raced a loaded grocery cart on *Supermarket Sweep*. Yet she was portly – indeed, quite overweight. 'All I eat is protein, red meat. It keeps the juices flowing.'

'Good, I'm glad. Now if you don't mind . . .'

She stabbed a knitting needle through her coiled, braided bun and left.

By the time six o'clock rolled around, quitting time, Mr. Norris was dizzy with hunger. He had taken a firm stand when Mrs. Kundaa returned from her hour-and-a-half lunch with a meatball hero. Yes, he would have loved to devour it, but it was a matter of principle. He might be gay, but he was not a wimp. No, sir, she had gone too far this time, claiming he had said he would be glad to have some red meat for lunch. He should know what he had said, thank you very much. Mrs. Kundaa had tossed the hero into his wastebasket, and then acted unnaturally efficient the rest of the afternoon, avoiding all small talk and eye contact and answering the phone in a cool, severe way that made him ponder how he might keep her in a state of mild offense on a more permanent basis.

'Good night,' he said on his way out.

'I don't want this.' She handed back the five-dollar bill he had put down on her desk for the hero.

'Please, take it, Mrs. Kundaa.'

She clicked her mouse past a Ninja game to a business letter, which she began to fiddle with, ignoring him. It was her practice to stay late in order to make up for coming in at 9:50. Mr. Norris wished she would come in at eight, as he did. But she had declared that she was not a morning person, and nothing could be done to change it, short of giving her new genes.

'Five dollars does not a jumbo meatball hero buy,' she said, after he tried once again to interest her in the bill. 'This is not the depression.'

'Here's a twenty. You have change?'

'I am not a change purse, Mr. Norris. If you don't mind, I have work to do.'

'Well, OK, don't let the bedbugs bite. I mean, uh, you know, don't stay up too late.'

Chiding himself for sounding so stupid – bedbugs! where did they come from? – he headed on to the glass doors with NyLo's logo, a minimalist hammer and tongs.

In the elevator going down, Mr. Norris was sure it would be one of those days when they shot straight past the forty-first floor. Three people got on at forty-four, then someone at forty-two. Mr. Norris sighed. Usually if someone got on at forty-two, it meant for some reason that the elevator didn't stop at forty-one.

But then it did, it stopped. And not only that, the Beak himself got on and poked 'L' with the tip of his tightly furled umbrella.

For the past six or seven years the Beak and Mr. Norris had descended from their respective floors in the evening without nodding to each other, much less saying hello. When he had first noticed him, Mr. Norris had bristled with contempt. Though he didn't like to think of himself as prejudiced, Mr. Norris found his patience tried by men who looked too Waspy – and this rather diminutive, silver-haired Beak was as Waspy as they came. Instead of the perspiration that afflicted Mr. Norris on even the mildest of days, arrogance and condescension seemed to ooze from the fine pores of the Bermuda-tanned – or was it Antigua? – skin. And the nose only enhanced this effect, a major proboscis that reeked of patrician airs.

But then one evening the door had opened on a talking Beak. As the man chatted with a colleague, a woman, Mr. Norris heard a peculiar timbre that reminded him of something that he had always assumed was totally unique – Ward's voice. Ward was the sophomore rugby player who had sat beside him in M. Jouet's French literature class at Harvard. They did not look alike at all, Ward and the Beak. No, Ward was ruddy as a farmhand, his reddish hair coarse as straw. When Mr. Norris, a freshman, had missed three 8 A.M. classes because his wife was so homesick she threw up, Ward not only lent him his class notes, but he also read aloud Racine's *Athalie* to show him how the rigid alexandrines could yield a supple, noble passion.

Soon they were going to Mass together – Ward was Unitarian, but loved Pascal – and then strolling back to Mr. Norris's off-campus apartment for bagels and mimosas, both of which Mrs. Norris hated almost as much as their French. She would sulk in the bedroom watching TV while they discussed Jansenism and the paper Ward was writing on *Phèdre*. It wasn't long before Mr. Norris realized that he would gladly give his life for Ward, literally. That autumn, his first in New England, burgeoned with dreams of self-sacrifice, Ward rescued from fire or the Charles by a Severinus Lloyd Norris who then expired, clasping his friend's hand. If Ward had only said the word, if he had given any hint at all of a certain inclination, Mr. Norris would have endured the biggest sacrifice of all – that of his own honor and self-respect. Yes, he would have left Mrs. Norris and devoted himself to Ward, heart, soul, mind, and body. But a remark Ward had made one afternoon, how Thomas Aquinas had proved sodomy was as much an offense against nature and reason as against God, dispelled Mr. Norris's foolish dreams. In a way, this was something of a relief. Perhaps it was enough to kneel beside Ward at Mass, to share those poppyseed bagels and the awful mimosas Ward made with a sparkling wine that came in pint bottles with no cork. In fact, just walking silently together along the Charles with the gold and vermilion leaves ripe, burdened with their splendor, this was a glory that nearly crushed him.

And then came the day Mr. Norris's stomach cramps got so bad that he had to sprint home from his noontime bursary job in the dining hall. As he swung open the rotting screen door to the apartment, Mrs. Norris lifted her head from the egg compartment of the refrigerator and let out one of those little shrieks she gave whenever a resident mouse appeared. Smiling at her absurdity, he hurried on to the bathroom, the privacy he had to have to deal with the cramps. But when he flung open the door, there was Ward in all his glory, without a stitch on. While the freshman gaped, the sophomore went right on toweling dry his hair, which seemed so oddly dark.

There were no words. Mr. Norris turned around, and on his way out of the apartment noticed that his wife, too, was just as pale and naked – and never more beautiful. He headed straight for the registrar's office, where he informed the administration that he would be transferring the following semester, leaving Cambridge. His girlfriend, you see, was too homesick for Louisiana. She missed her mother something awful. (Of course, only Ward knew that

Chapter Five

'Well, the big day has finally arrived.'

'Huh?' Mr. Norris said, as she held open the back door for him. The front door of their Yonkers brick split-level – or rather, since the divorce, Mrs. Norris's brick split – was used only for company.

'That call you've been waiting for, Lloyd.'

'What call?'

'The one you've been moaning and groaning about. Here, give me that briefcase. I don't know why you put it down there, right in front of the refrigerator.'

He leaned over but was too late. Mrs. Norris had already whisked the briefcase away.

'What have I been moaning and groaning about, Pearl Fay? My colon?'

'Manhattan Cares, they finally called. They've got a ninety-year-old man who's nonhomophobic.'

'What do you mean nonhomophobic? Did you tell them I was gay?'

'Not them, no, although I don't know why you don't tell them yourself. It would save everyone a lot of trouble.'

Mr. Norris sighed as he wandered shoeless into the den. He could have worn his shoes if the electric mud scraper outside the back door were fixed, but for some reason, none of the batteries he brought home did any good. The batteries, though, did work on the chair Mrs. Norris had given him for his fortieth birthday, back when they were still married. A floor model from a shop in the South Street Seaport mall, the sleek black lounger offered both shiatsu and traditional Swedish massage. Mrs. Norris could not stand the thing herself. It ruined her Early American decor and made the den off-limits to company. But if it helped Mr. Norris unwind, she guessed she was willing to put up with it. He himself was rather embarrassed by it at first. The comment he had muttered while trying it out at the Sharper Image – 'Gee, Pearl Fay, this is heaven' – was not meant to be interpreted so literally. He had simply meant it was great to sit in after all the walking they had done that particular day. But he had grown to like it after they found out it could not be returned. And when she had tried to donate it to the rectory at Mary, Queen of Heaven, he had protested with surprising vigor. The IRS was bound to be suspicious of a chair that cost $2279, and he had no desire to tangle with them about such a write-off.

'So how do you know he's nonhomophobic?' Mr. Norris resumed once the dials were adjusted.

'I called him myself. Don't look at me like that, Lloyd. Did you want to trot all the way down to Chelsea and find out then that the old man hated queers?'

Mr. Norris winced. Though his ex-wife used the term in a militaristic, Act Up way, he had told her that he would prefer to think of himself as gay, not queer. Actually, he didn't really like the term 'gay' either, which fit him about as well as a pair of thirty-inch-waist jeans would.

'Pearl Fay, I wish you'd let me handle this myself.'

'Sure, like you handled those horrible pigs in Washington Heights.'

'They weren't horrible pigs. They were perfectly decent pigs – and the more I think about it, well, maybe it had nothing to do with my sexuality at all. Maybe they just didn't like the way I dressed or—'

'Trust me, they can't stand queers, that's it. Straight men are like that, it's generic. You should've heard the things Herbert used to say about you. He didn't think you had any right at all going to Queen of Heaven. He was sure you were going to hell, because it said so in the Bible. He read all that to me, Leviticus and Romans, and it was all the same as what I learned in the Baptists. They're not so different, you know, the Baptists.'

'Look, I've already told you, Father McBride can give you some books to read. They'll help you understand how it's OK for me to go to church and all.'

'Please, I don't need any book to tell me that. You should have heard how I stood up for you with Herbert. I actually gave him a black eye once, he got me so pissed off.'

'You're kidding.'

'No, sir. I let him have it, both barrels. If anyone thinks they can tell me my Severinus is headed straight for hell . . .'

'But did you have to strike him, Pearl Fay? Don't you see how that might have been a perplexing experience for him? He might have thought you liked me better than him.'

'Don't be silly. After nine years, he knew damn well what the score was.'

'Nine years! I thought you told me a year or so.'

'It was, spaced out over nine years. He was always reforming a lot, vowing never to see me ever again, especially after he was elected a knight or something in Opus Dei.'

'Funny how none of this was mentioned in court.'

'I think now I should have.' Setting down her scotch on the control console, she tripped the massage from Swedish to shiatsu. 'It would have shown how serious I was about the divorce, how it wasn't a spur-of-the-moment thing. Nine years I waited, honey. I wanted to be really sure it was the right thing to do.'

He switched back to Swedish and then took a gulp from her glass, even though he despised scotch. It tasted like soap and gave him an unbearable hangover.

'No one can say you're flighty.' He took another gulp. No matter how hard he tried to forgive her, there was always a lump of resentment, undigested, blocking the way. Sure, she had made an honest man of him, yanking him out of the closet. But the truth was, he didn't want to be honest, not that honest. If it had been up to him, he would have been perfectly happy to coast into old age with a bland, respectable, sexless marriage. If most straight couples could get away with this, why not he? But no, Pearl Fay had to have romance in her life. She couldn't even be content with sinful romance. No, it had to be made respectable – sanctioned by divorce and remarriage. And so, by default, she was forcing him to look for romance at a time when all his deepest instincts yearned for the peace and quiet melancholy of a wallflower's life.

'That hurt, Lloyd.'

'What?'

She wiped away a tear. 'That crack. It's like something a straight man would say.'

'I'm sorry. It's just that – well, nine years, for gosh sakes.'

'Oh, please don't start getting all jealous and macho on me. I can't stand it.'

'But it hurts. I hurt, too.'

'I swear, sometimes you sound just like Herbert.'

'Me?'

'Yes, you. He used to start whining how it hurt when he suspected me of sleeping with you behind his back.'

'Behind *his* back? We were married!'

'Hon, he considered our marriage null and void. In fact, he wanted me to get an annulment, as you very well know.'

Mrs. Norris had at least spared him that humiliation. She could have easily got one on the grounds that their marriage had never been consummated, despite many tries. It was the reason he had agreed not to mention her affair with Herbert in court. Both of them were left with a few shreds of dignity that way.

'So he was jealous of *me?*'

'I've told you before, Herbert was insane.'

Mr. Norris shrugged and finished the scotch in her glass. 'Why did you have to fall in love with an insane man?'

'Because you get no choice when you're straight. They're all nuts, Lloyd. Once they turn forty, they all go bonkers.'

'Bruce is over forty and he's not—'

'Bruce who? Powers?'

'He's been very kind and considerate to me.'

'Hey, my scotch, did I drink all this?'

She had been gazing at the news while they talked. Floods, famine, and Valium for pets were highlighted by a perky anchor.

The glass now in her hand, she said to it, 'I'm drinking too much, I think.'

'Have another, dear.'

'No, better not.'

'You know, for all his bluster, Bruce certainly has a timid streak. I really wish he weren't so afraid of Mrs. Kundaa. He should lay down the law to that woman.'

'What'd she do now?'

'Oh, nothing,' Mr. Norris said, and then proceeded to retail everything about the meatball hero, a factual story spiced more by his guilt in telling it than the slight exaggeration he added to counter a yawn or two from her. After all, Mrs. Kundaa was alone in the world, getting on in years, and there was something unmanly about bitching behind her back like this. In confession last Saturday, he had asked for guidance on this matter, how to deal with such an impossible secretary, and Father McBride had told him that in the eyes of God we are all impossible.

'What's that man's number, the one in Chelsea? I should call and make an appointment,' Mr. Norris was saying a few minutes later in the narrow dining room. He didn't mean literally now make the call, with the roast pork still untouched on his plate. But this was how Mrs. Norris interpreted his remark, as a slight to her loin and glazed baby carrots and made-from-scratch biscuits. After a laborious explanation and several apologies and a truthful statement about how hungry he was, Mr. Norris changed his mind and retracted the apologies, since they weren't sincere. He had nothing to apologize for. This led to a monogrammed napkin being flung down, a tear being shed, and a sudden vulgar belch that made them both laugh. As a rule, Mr. Norris never belched. So distracting was all this fuss and bother over nothing that it wasn't until dessert, a banana cream pie smothered in a curaçao-pear sauce, that he remembered to ask again for the number.

'I wouldn't call if I were you, Lloyd.'

'Why not? You said he likes gays.'

'Tolerates. Anyway, that's not the problem.' With a graceful sweep of her arm, reminiscent of her days as a synchronized swimmer, she gathered in a few beige crumbs that had strayed from his plate. 'He's a Communist, an Italian Communist.'

Mr. Norris regarded her curiously across the lighted candelabrum. If her figure were not so stunning – even Mr. Norris could appreciate it, in an aesthetic way – her prematurely white hair might seem matronly. But no matter how conservatively she dressed, her lithe waist and magnificent bosom made even a sweater set, such as she wore this evening, seem ironic.

'Well? So he's a Communist. That doesn't mean anything in Italy.'

'Lloyd, don't you see, he can't let a Fascist into his apartment.'

'Who's a Fascist?'

'When he found out you went to Mass every day . . .'

'What did you have to go and tell him that for?'

'Are you ashamed?'

'It's none of his business.'

'What do you want with a ninety-year-old Communist anyway? I tell you, Lloyd, it's no good, this agency. You got to find yourself a gay thing, somewhere you'll fit in. You're never going to meet anyone this way.'

'For heaven's sake, this has nothing to do with dating.'

'Then what the hell *is* it about?'

'You never heard about the Corporal Works of Mercy? The Church teaches—'

'How about doing me a Major Work of Mercy? Stop hanging around the house like this night after night. It's driving me bananas. Go find yourself a bar, make some friends, get some phone numbers. And please, dear, put down that platter. You're going to spill grease all over the carpet.'

He had been trying to help, carrying the remains of the pork to the kitchen. Automatically, he set the platter down on the Ethan Allen sideboard. But then, filled with defiance, he picked it up again and followed her into the kitchen.

'As a matter of fact, I did meet someone today,' he said, while loading the dishwasher. At the sink she dealt with the Waterford glasses and Limoges gravy boat, too delicate for the machine.

'Almost,' he qualified.

'How can you "almost" meet someone?'

'In the elevator. I dropped my handkerchief and he picked it up and – What?'

'Dropped your handkerchief? Oh, sweetpea!'

'It wasn't intentional.'

'It wasn't intentional,' she mimicked, in a way that reminded him of Bruce Powers. They both made him sound so uptight, with a broomstick up his rear end.

'I wanted to tell him it wasn't what he thought, not a come-on or anything. But then he gave me this look, so spiteful and ugly you wouldn't believe. I realized right then and there, Pearl Fay, that I didn't like him at all.'

She snatched a fork from his hand. The Strasbourg pattern registered for their wedding did not belong in the dishwasher. 'You're too much, Lloyd. Miss Coy Starlet drops her handkerchief and then gets all ditzy and confused, "Ooooo, I just hate him."'

'Why do I tell you anything?'

'Come now, Miss Jayne, don't sulk.'

His jaw clenched. There was that preposterous tease again, Jayne Mansfield. Could anyone on God's green earth be less like Jayne Mansfield than he! And yet, ever since he had made the mistake of trying to describe his ideal man to Pearl Fay (he would be kind, polite, and gentle, yet very masculine, a devout Catholic, and OK, maybe a former Mr. Rhode Island or something, Mr. Delaware), she would from time to time call him this. Heaven knows, though, that he had never managed to date anyone even remotely tethered to this ideal. The closest he had ever come was when he had been living alone over the nurses' uniform shop and answered an ad in the *Voice* personals. In his letter he had nipped off several inches from his waist and added them to his chest and biceps. His theory was that by the time the bodybuilder who had placed the ad got to know him, how warm and loving and masculine he was and how he planned to go to the gym every day and eat right, the exact measurements wouldn't matter. But when he met the mature Gold's Gym Hunk, as the guy called himself in the ad, Mr. Norris was appalled. This hunk was about as far from Mr. Norris's image of Gold's Gym as . . . well, as he, Mr. Norris, himself was. In fact, there was a definite – and highly embarrassing – resemblance. Stocky, stolid, with a pained expression from a too-tight belt, the mature hunk seemed really hurt when Mr. Norris said he wouldn't be able to go to the ballet with him the following week. No, not even if they were orchestra seats, third row center.

'You know, you're sort of cute when you pout.'

'I'm not pouting. I'm just thinking how you never give me a chance to explain. The Beak—'

'Huh?'

'That's what I call that guy in the elevator – he's got this nose, real hoity-toity.'

'Shame on you, Lloyd. That's no way to talk about a Jewish person.'

'No, no, he's ultra-Wasp. Funny how no one seems to notice,

but those old Wasp families, the real patricians, they all have these huge, arrogant noses, just awful.'

'Come on.'

'I swear they do.'

'The pot and the kettle.'

'What? I don't have a big nose.'

'You got big ears, mister. They stick out a mile.'

'But not in a Wasp way. I don't look like a Wasp.'

'Hon, you couldn't look more Wasp if you tried, all pale and dried up, the end result of hundreds of years of Puritan inbreeding.'

'And you wonder why I can't get a date?'

She stood on tiptoes to put away the gravy boat. 'How old are you, Lloyd? Fourteen?'

'It's not easy, this dating stuff. You wouldn't believe how high the standards are, the way guys judge one another.'

'You look just fine to me.'

'You're a woman. Gay men—'

'Help me, will you. I can't reach.'

Forgetting he was shorter than his ex-wife, he took the gravy boat she couldn't put away on the top shelf and vainly tried himself. When he suggested that they put it on a lower shelf, she gave him such a look that he dragged over a chair from the dinette table.

'What's this?' he said, standing on the chair. In his hand was a plastic bag of gold sequins he had unearthed from the top shelf.

'Oh, my prayers are answered!' Mrs. Norris said. 'I've been praying so hard to find those things and practically accused Emma Dvorak of stealing them.'

'Oh, for the team.' He handed them down to her.

Mrs. Dvorak was the mother of one of the girls on the synchronized swimming team that Mrs. Norris coached. The sequins would adorn the girls' bathing caps, eight of which were upstairs in Mrs. Norris's bedroom. Mr. Norris could not help admiring his ex-wife for sticking with the team over at the Greenlawn Racquet Club. Neither an illicit affair with an usher, a contested divorce,

nor an attempted suicide had caused her to miss a single practice
session. Surely those young women could be more grateful. He
was always hoping that they would give Pearl Fay a testimonial
dinner – but they never did, year after year.

'I can finish the caps now. Praise Mary! I just couldn't bear the
thought of driving all the way to Tarrytown for another bag. Now,
sugar, I don't want you hanging around the house this evening.
You go out and find yourself a bar.'

'I'm exhausted, Pearl Fay. I can't go into the city tonight.'

'I'm talking about here, Yonkers.'

'You nuts or something? There're no gay men in Yonkers, much
less bars.'

'You know this for a fact.'

'Yes, it's a fact.'

'Well, good night then. I can't argue with such nonsense.'

''Night.'

In the den, he was in time for *Mr. Ed.*

Chapter Six

'This is the piano,' the woman said.

Joe Pollock thanked her for the information. But it didn't take an Einstein to see what it was.

'And that's her flute.'

The battered case had a velvet lining, midnight blue. Leaning over, he sniffed the instrument with a nose as finely attuned as a hound's. The flute wasn't platinum, nor the finest silver. Nothing to write home about. But it would do.

'You know, lady, she ought not to do this, your friend. Twelve-thirty, that's when the lesson's supposed to begin. I'm here on the dot and then I stand around twenty minutes waiting for someone to let me in.'

He had been ready to give up when this dame had shown up – not his pupil, but a friend of the pupil. Loaded down with shopping bags and an umbrella that she didn't need and couldn't close, the woman had let him into the apartment with a flurry of complaints about her friend. Mavis was so irresponsible. She shouldn't schedule a lesson during lunch hour to begin with. And now Mavis's boss wouldn't let her leave until she heard from some client in Far Rockaway.

'My time is valuable, you know,' Joe Pollock went on. 'I don't come cheap.'

The woman looked up from the outsized umbrella she was trying to close. 'Just how uncheap are you, sir?'

'Forty bucks an hour.'

'You've got to be kidding.'

'Look, lady, I usually charge sixty. Your friend's got herself a real bargain, a regular steal.'

The idea of giving music lessons had occurred to Joe Pollock only after he had moved back to his Village apartment. There he had brooded for days over what he could do to stop people from taping notices for carpet-cleaning services downstairs in the building's entrance. He was sick and tired of ripping them down and reporting this trespassing to the police. No one else in the building seemed to care what a mess the entryway was. It was him picking up the Chinese menus, the two-for-one taco fliers littering the floor – him with the lumbago nobody was ever going to find out about. And then out of nowhere the idea came to him. And like all genius, it was amazingly simple: revenge.

For twenty bucks Joe Pollock got five hundred copies of his own ad, which he dumped not only at the carpet cleaners and the offending restaurants, but for good measure in every apartment entryway on 11th Street he could get into. Feeling years younger, liberated, he taped the ad to public phones and light poles, all the places he used to tear sheets down from. He really didn't care if his ad for clarinet lessons got any response or not. In fact, since he hadn't picked up his instrument in twenty years or so, he was sort of hoping he wouldn't be bothered. Which was why he priced himself so high when a man called – sixty an hour. That had scared him off. But when a woman phoned, this dame's friend, he liked her voice, her manner. She had class, real class. So he was more accommodating, especially since the flute wasn't his first instrument, or second. He told her she could have a trial lesson first, and if she didn't like it (meaning, if she didn't turn out to be as attractive as her voice made her sound) they would call it quits, no questions asked.

'Oh, this thing.' The woman gave the umbrella a kick and with a look of disgust, delved into her alligator handbag. 'I was going to give up smoking today, but thanks to Mavis . . .' She inhaled deeply on the cigarette she had dug out of the capacious bag. 'I don't know why she has to take up the flute again. Forty an hour – think of the people that could feed.'

'This friend of yours don't exactly look like she's starving.' Turtle Bay, Joe Pollock knew, was not a neighborhood you starved in. Especially with French doors leading to a garden out back. And what could be a Ming vase sitting on your baby grand. 'How old is she, anyway?'

'What sort of question is that?'

From her voice on the phone, Joe had guessed Mavis could be in her late thirties, forties top. But this friend of hers made him uneasy. She seemed at least sixty. Yet sometimes younger women had older friends, didn't they?

Glancing at her watch, the friend announced she simply had to get back to her office. 'My boss is helpless without me. I've got so much I want him to do this afternoon.'

Joe Pollock grunted.

'Last week Mavis has me wait two hours here for the cable repairman. Now this. As if I don't have a life of my own. And why are you giving me a quarter?'

'I could use a smoke, lady.'

The quarter scooted back across the polished lid of the baby grand.

'Out of the question. You should not smoke, sir. It's a horrible habit. I lost a boyfriend because of it – just last week.'

Boyfriend! Joe Pollock couldn't believe a woman this hefty and old could have had a boyfriend. He hoped that she wasn't going to start talking about the funeral. Joe Pollock couldn't stand that kind of talk.

'Walked right out on me when he caught me sneaking a cigarette. He's a health nut and couldn't be reasoned with. Oh, Mavis, where are you? I've got so much to do.'

'Go, why don't you go?'

'And leave you here alone?'

This was the limit. Not only was he dying for a smoke – how could he have forgotten to pick up a pack for himself? – but now she was insulting his honor, implying he couldn't be trusted alone in the apartment.

'What? You're going?'

As he straightened the collar of his Ralph Lauren jacket and adjusted his Hermes foulard, he did not deign to reply.

'Why don't you wait another minute? She'll blame me, I know.'

'I'm outta here, lady. You can tell your friend to forget it.'

'Well, at least take your quarter.'

But Joe Pollock didn't. He left it sitting there on the baby grand, where he hoped it would teach her a good lesson.

'Me? I have to tell her?'

'You're her boss, aren't you?'

Mr. Norris should have known that this wasn't going to be just the friendly good-buddy lunch Bruce Powers had said it would. His boss had corralled him into it after Mrs. Kundaa had left the office to take care of an emergency for her friend Mavis, the woman whose son-in-law had his own web site. But it was only after Mr. Powers had cajoled Mr. Norris to be a sport, to at least taste the Grand Marnier he had ordered to top off the Mississippi mud pie, that the bombshell dropped. Mr. Powers was *ordering* Mr. Norris to fire Mrs. Kundaa – no ifs, ands, or buts.

'It's for your own good, Lloydie boy. Look at her, waltzing in at ten, giving herself a two-hour lunch, and then, what's this I hear about you picking up her dry cleaning for her?'

'Well, it was on my way to work.' And it helped make up for the meatball hero. 'And besides, who told you I picked up her dry cleaning? I resent all this gossiping that goes on in the office.'

'She did. She was bragging about how wonderful you are, how you pick up her dry cleaning and how you got some gum off her shoe once and stapled her hemline when it fell down and—'

'OK, OK.'

'She's got to go, buddy.'

'Yeah, but why me?'

'Because if you don't, you're fired.'

'Bruce.'

'I'm dead serious. No kidding around. You're history if you don't. I can't have this kind of waste and mismanagement in my department. Enough is enough.'

'But you know how litigious she is. Her landlady is being sued for slander, for saying this man she dates had carnal knowledge of her.'

'Kundaa dates?'

'A guy escorts her to lectures and stuff – her second cousin, I think. Anyway, I couldn't bear to be dragged into court again. The divorce nearly did me in. I've never been so humiliated in all my life.'

'She's not going to sue you, buddy.' Mr. Powers gave one of Mr. Norris's large, protruding ears a friendly twist.

'Ow!'

'Ooo, Mommy, he hurt me.'

Glances from neighboring tables in the steakhouse did not stem Mr. Powers's belly laugh. But he was such a commanding presence that he could get away with nearly as much as a former Super Bowl star, which he was mistaken for from time to time.

'What am I supposed to tell her, Bruce? I've got to give her a reason.'

'We're downsizing, company policy. You had no choice, et cetera, et cetera. She'll get a decent severance package – not that it matters. Her late husband left her sitting pretty.'

'You're kidding? How can someone who worked for the DMV leave her anything at all?'

Mr. Powers shrugged. 'Don't mention this, of course. Top secret.

She's very touchy about her privacy. I'm only saying this to make it easier for you now.'

'I wish you would've told me earlier. I wouldn't have picked up her dry cleaning.'

'Just found out myself the other day. Hey, Mario – check!'

The elderly waiter, who had once conducted *I Puritani* at La Scala, hovered. 'No cappuccino today, Mr. Powers? You always – Oh! Yes, the check.'

'Bruce,' Mr. Norris said, as the waiter retreated toward the cash register, 'that's not right. You shouldn't goose him.'

'Mario is my buddy. He loves it.'

Back in the office Mr. Powers lent Mr. Norris his key to the executive washroom. Mr. Norris could have had his own key, which came with his promotion last year. But he had declined the offer, not because he was upset that the promotion meant only this key, no raise, but really because he considered the idea of a separate fancy bathroom undemocratic and demeaning to the regular employees. Yet there were those times when his colon acted up and he needed the solitude.

An hour later, he emerged from the immaculate tiled room with a thoroughly examined copy of the *New York Review of Books*. The Grand Marnier had not calmed his stomach as much as he had hoped, but it had numbed his faltering courage, stiffened it a little. As Mr. Powers had said on the way back from the steakhouse, it was high time he claimed his manhood. He shouldn't let himself be pushed around by Mrs. K just because he was a switch-hitter. ('But I'm not a switch-hitter,' Mr. Norris had reminded him. 'I'm totally out in left field.' Mr. Powers had seemed not to hear this.)

'Where have you been?' Mrs. Kundaa inquired as he eased past her desk. 'I've been looking all over for you.'

'Stomach.'

'And look, you've got my book review all wet.'

'It's not all wet.'

'I've never known anyone to spend so much time in the john. Are you sure you're all right, S. Lloyd?'

'I'm fine. Listen, would you mind coming into the office a moment?'

'It *is* all wet – ruined.'

Though not large, Mr. Norris's office would have had a spectacular view of Weehawken across the Hudson were it not for a revolving souvenir emporium atop a Ninth Avenue skyscraper. Tourists on the slow-motion carousel peered dully through his tinted windows. But like a grouper in an aquarium, he had learned to go about his business undistracted.

'Sit down,' Mrs. Kundaa said, as she shut the door behind her. 'I want you to hear this.'

'Actually, there was something I wanted you to—'

'Shh. Not so loud. These walls are cardboard. Now, Lloyd, you remember my friend Mavis, the one whose son-in-law made all that money on his web site? Well, I just got back from her apartment, and she's promised to introduce you to him. When I told Mavis about the helicopter—'

'What helicopter?'

'The one Vigoris hired to get her son to the *Firing Line* taping on time, from La Guardia. It was a horrible show, too. Her son was on a panel—'

'Yes, I know. Bruce has already told me all about the show. That's none of our business, though. And I really don't think it should be something you're discussing with your friends. I don't want to meet her son-in-law, in any case. I don't want a web site about saving pennies.'

'But, Lloyd—'

'And speaking of saving pennies, you realize that all across the country, not just here at NyLo . . .'

She had pulled a knitting needle from her gray braided bun even though there was no yarn in sight. 'Yes, I know, Lloyd. We got to stop photocopying so much, turn out the lights.'

'No, it's more serious than that. You've read about all the

downsizing that's going on, one corporation after another forced to cut back, tighten the belt. I'm sure you understand that NyLo is not unique. We're caught up in the larger picture no matter how honorable our intentions may be.'

The knitting needle tapped impatiently against her dimpled chin. 'It's all nonsense, this downsizing. The only thing that needs downsizing are a few choice expense accounts.'

'Well, actually, Mrs. Kundaa, you must admit the economy is not healthy.' His heart hammered as fiercely as it had that morning when, genuflecting on his way out from the seven A.M. Mass at St. Patrick's, he had seen the Beak putting a few coins into the Poor Box. 'In any case, don't get me wrong. No one could value you more than I do. I understand how you've stuck by me all these years, even after you found out about my sexual preference and all. I mean, not that it's a preference per se, like choosing chocolate over vanilla, but anyway, here.'

She took the handkerchief he held out and dabbed at her blurred eyes. Then blew loudly. 'Lloyd, dear, you have no idea how much this means to me, to have you finally speak up like this. I've been feeling so paranoid lately, like everyone hated me, and now to hear you say this, well, I never thought you'd have the gumption to stand up for me, to be man enough to demand that raise I should have gotten last year.'

'Actually, that isn't exactly—'

'Oh, don't worry. I know it's not enough, but even a token from that ape, Powers. I just wish you hadn't waited so long.'

Before he knew what was happening, she was planting a moist smack on his forehead.

'Hey, Lloydie,' Bruce Powers said, as the door swung open. 'You got those keys? I – Oh, still friends, I see.'

'Still?' Mrs. Kundaa echoed. She folded the handkerchief and handed it back to Mr. Norris. 'Come hell or high water, this boy and I are joined at the hip.'

'Terrific.' Mr. Powers took a swig from a quart bottle of mineral water. 'So he's told you about the severance package, right? Not many outfits would do that for you. You've got a health care maintenance that will carry you over until you find another job, if it's within three or four weeks. And there's – Ow! Hey, Norris, you see that? She jabbed me with that friggin' needle.' He rubbed his rear end gingerly. 'Well, good riddance. Let her run off. Anyway, you got those keys to the john? Hurry, man.'

'Here.'

'Thanks, buddy. Well, see, it wasn't so bad after all, was it?'

'You shouldn't have – I mean I didn't get a chance to – Wait, will you?'

'Can't hold it any longer. Gotta run, boy.'

Chapter Seven

During the past six years it would not have been unusual for several months to go by without a sighting of the Beak in the elevator. Out of four elevators to choose from, such infrequency seemed statistically probable. With this history in mind, Mr. Norris was not surprised that, for two full weeks after the Grand Marnier lunch, their paths had not crossed. Whether this was a relief or not, he wasn't sure. As for the sighting in St. Patrick's, Mr. Norris began to doubt whether it had indeed been the Beak by the Poor Box. After all, not only was the Beak a Wasp – surely, he must be – but also the box had been a considerable distance from where Mr. Norris was genuflecting in the cathedral's uncertain gloom.

'Turn off that goddamn light!' Mr. Powers barked as Mr. Norris got off the elevator.

Mr. Norris looked blankly at his boss, who was holding open the door to the NyLo suite.

'It's eight-thirty in the morning. What do we need all these lights for?' Mr. Powers said to the receptionist. She smirked, and Mr. Norris realized then that he was being ribbed. The software program he had devised to remind employees of the money they were wasting was in place now. And this was the thanks he got. He did not think it was very funny.

'That's three cents down the drain,' Mr. Norris heard, as he paused at the water cooler. Bruce Powers again.

Mr. Norris turned to say something firm and reasonable.

'Lighten up,' Mr. Powers preempted. 'Don't look so glum, chum. Or is it cheaper? Get it?'

'Oof!' Mr. Norris said, as the fist grazed his belly. It hadn't hurt at all, so skillful was the feint. And so ridiculous was his 'Oof!' that he couldn't help joining in the little laugh.

'Ms. Vigoris wants to see you,' Mr. Norris's new secretary informed him as he rounded the corner to his office.

'When? Right now?'

'She didn't say.'

A dowdy twenty-three-year-old Republican, Penny, Mrs. Kundaa's replacement, was perfection incarnate. She came and left on the dot, ate a half-hour lunch at her desk, made no suggestions or emendations to his memos and correspondence, and evinced a complete lack of interest in both his diet and private life. Mr. Norris was thrilled with Human Resources for unearthing such a gem.

'I guess I better go up now, Penny – don't you think?'

In response, the secretary just sat there. Undoubtedly, she would come into her own at eighty or so, when her dim, weary gaze would suggest a lifetime of experience and wisdom.

'I was told Ms. Vigoris wanted to see me,' Mr. Norris said, after he had taken the elevator up to the fifty-first floor. There, instead of the industrial gray carpeting of forty-nine and fifty, custom-designed Norwegian rugs were scattered over a gleaming parquet. On the walls, instead of cracks (done on purpose on fifty, so the architect claimed, to suggest the decline of Western hegemony) were unposed scenes from a trailer park in Jupiter, Florida, blurred amateurish snapshots whose companion series, a trailer park in Orlando, was on a nationwide tour of business schools.

'Do you have an appointment?' Mrs. Kundaa inquired, fixing him with a bright, chilling smile.

Mrs. Kundaa was now Ms. Vigoris's executive secretary. Two weeks earlier, after Mr. Norris's attempt to fire her, she had stormed out of his office and straight up to the CEO for a private interview. An hour later she was back in Mr. Norris's office, where he was informed that Ms. Vigoris's current executive secretary had just been promoted to her own cubbyhole on the forty-ninth floor.

'Appointment? Penny just told me that she wanted to see me.'

'I wish Earleen would consult me first before she goes making appointments. She simply must finish her breakfast. I won't have her rushed.'

'Oh, of course, of course, let her finish. I'm sorry. I can come back any time.'

'I'll let you know.'

'Yes, Mrs. Kundaa, any time that's convenient for Earl – for Ms. Vigoris, any time at all.'

'Indeed.'

Back in Yonkers that evening, Mr. Norris was adjusting the shiatsu dial on his chair when he heard the front door slam. It was Mrs. Norris, home from the Racquet Club. With the remote he switched off *The Munsters*, which he really wasn't watching, and found his place again in *The Ambassadors*. From the hall, Mrs. Norris asked if he had remembered to take out the garbage. Before he could reply – he was puzzling over the appearance of the Munsters in the James novel – she was in the den. Her eyes bloodshot from the club's highly chlorinated pool, she announced that all her problems were solved. And it was so simple. Instead of submerging on the upbeat, her girls would corkscrew on the downbeat of 'You Light Up My Life.'

While she demonstrated with her hands, her voice eager, trembling with enthusiasm, he tried to look interested. Mrs. Kundaa was still on his mind, though. He could not stop worrying. Why hadn't she called him back that afternoon? Did she remember to tell Ms. Vigoris that he had dropped by to see what she wanted? Perhaps he should have spent a little more time chatting with Mrs. Kundaa herself. Did she understand that it had been Bruce Powers who had tried to fire her, that he, Mr. Norris, had only been carrying out orders? Yet every time he tried to go into all this with Mrs. Kundaa, she would cut him off. It was a painful subject, especially since he wanted to be honest about his own unwilling complicity. Forgive and forget, she would say. But a bitter revenge was in store for him. He could feel it in his bones whenever she aimed that bright smile at him.

'You're not listening.'

'I am, Pearl Fay.'

'Something's wrong, hon. What is it?'

'Nothing. I'm fine.'

She plucked a mesquite-barbecued chip from the bowl in his lap. Her teeth, even as a soap star's, bit daintily. So perfect were those teeth that most people assumed they were dentures. A bit of staining and yellowing by her dentist, a true artist, had helped. But she was still thinking of having a few imperfections drilled in.

'You sure, Lloyd?'

'I said I'm fine.'

'Good, because I got some news.' Perched on the arm of the electronic chair, she was crushing his James beneath her shapely loins. As he extracted the expatriate, she went on. 'You remember Dawne Schmidlapp, don't you?'

'How could I forget? She's the one who cost you the trophy, right?'

Mrs. Norris had had her heart set on winning the New York State Invitational for the Associated Synchronized Workshops of the Americas. But during the meet last summer, Mrs. Schmidlapp, who worked for Con Edison, had run out of breath and shot up out of the water three beats early. Devastated by the humiliation, Mrs. Schmidlapp had tendered her resignation from the Mermaidens.

But Mrs. Norris refused to accept it. Instead, she encouraged the forty-six-year-old part-time student to lose fifteen pounds. Which she did, on a banana and veal diet.

'Must you always bring up the negative parts, Lloyd? Why can't you say something nice about her? She did do the choreography for *The Rite of Spring*.'

'Mm. So anyway, what about her?'

'Well, she just told me this evening at practice that she and her mama had this huge fight about her mama's boyfriend. Dawne can't stand him anymore, the way he never vacuums and stuff. So she's moving out. She's going to come live here with me.'

'Whoa, hold on a minute.' The shiatsu droned to a halt. 'I'm not going to share a bathroom with our meter reader. There's not enough room in this house, Pearl Fay.'

'I know. Which is why you've got to move out.'

'Me?'

'Dawne's real excited about moving in. I'm going to let her redecorate this den here, put up some drapes she has.' Mrs. Norris frowned at the spinning-wheel pattern on the calico curtains framing the room's only window. 'I never did like those drapes we have now. I don't know why I bought them. I just can't understand it.'

'What about your mother? She's the one you really want to come live with you.'

Mrs. Norris flexed an elegant long leg clad in violet tights. 'Mama's been stalling for weeks now. She's never going to find anyone for her popcorn. As a matter of fact, she's been harping on how I ought to move back to Tula Springs.'

'Well, what's wrong with that?'

'Severinus Lloyd Norris, I *can't* go back home now. Don't you see, the whole town would be gossiping about how dumb I was to marry a queer. They wouldn't understand a thing. I'd be the laughingstock, everyone pretending to feel sorry for me. I got friends back there who'd just love to find out all the truth about me.'

'But no one knows, you said. You never told your mother I was gay, not even her.'

'Right. But I don't trust myself. If I moved back to Louisiana, I just know I'd start blabbing the truth. It's the way I am. I just can't help it. And if my poor mama ever found out you liked men, well, it would kill her, Lloyd. You know it would kill her.'

Mr. Norris sighed. Though half Cajun, his mother-in-law was a mainstay of her Baptist church, which had fired their organist for buying a *Playgirl* at a 7-Eleven. And the organist wasn't even a man. She was a chiropodist who claimed there was an article in it she had to copy for professional reasons. In any case, though Mr. Norris would have preferred to have his mother-in-law know the truth about him, he respected his ex-wife's belief that the shock would be too great. The divorce in itself had been shock enough. Still in mourning for her husband, Mr. Norris's mother-in-law had spent a week in bed refusing all sustenance when she learned that S. Lloyd had walked out on her baby girl. (Gallantly, Mr. Norris had not corrected this version of the divorce yet. Pearl Fay's theory was that her mother could only absorb small doses of the truth, administered at judicious intervals.)

'Can't you see, Lloyd? It's not right, you and I living here like this.'

'You'd rather live with someone who sits around and eats bananas all day?'

With astonishing flexibility for a forty-three-year-old, Mrs. Norris leaned from her perch and retrieved a crumb from the braided rug. 'If you must know, someone told Herbert that you and I are back together again. I can't have him thinking that.'

'Why not?'

'It lets him off the hook too easy, like everything's back to normal again. He's got to realize that he ruined my life – and yours, too.'

'Mine?'

'Hon, if it weren't for him you'd still be living a happy life in the closet.'

'I'm happy now.'

'No, you're not. You're a wreck, ruined. You just don't have what it takes to be a minority. You get too upset because everyone hates you for being queer.'

'Everyone doesn't hate me.'

'Your brothers won't speak to you. Four brothers, and not one of them sent you a birthday card last year.'

'They never sent me a card when I was straight, either.'

'Never mind that. What about your sisters?'

'Pearl Fay, what can you expect? They're both nuns.'

'I know a lot of nuns who wouldn't suggest electroshock treatments. It's just a good thing your parents aren't alive. You probably would have gotten wired up. And would you please sit still when I talk to you. Stop squirming around.'

'I've got to go.'

'Number one?'

'None of your business.'

'Hold on a minute.' Her hand gently restrained him. 'Before you run off, lovey, you got to promise me you'll put the seat up – and that you'll move out of this house by Friday.'

'Friday!'

'That's when Dawne's planning to move in.'

'Now look here, that's impossible. You're giving me three days to find an apartment in the city?'

'Find one? You've already got a place.'

'Yeah, but it's sublet for now – sort of.'

'You never told me that.'

He shrugged. 'Someone from the office needed a place. So she's staying there now, a young woman in Human Resources.'

'Well, she'll just have to leave, won't she.'

'I can't ask her to pack up by Friday.'

'OK, then find yourself another place.' She applied a glittery pink clothespin to the bag of chips.

'Look, Pearl Fay, even if I could find a place that fast, I may not be able to afford it.'

'Don't start poormouthing. I gave you a real bargain on the alimony.'

'It's not that. It's work. I wasn't going to tell you this, but anyway, I think I'm in serious trouble. Mrs. Kundaa has it in for me. My hunch is that she spilled the beans about me, told Vigoris I'm gay.'

'So?'

'So? I'll tell you so. Vigoris wanted to see me today. I think she's going to fire me.'

'Then you'll sue. You can't be fired for being queer.'

'Honestly, Pearl Fay. Must you say "queer" all the time?'

'Stop being such an old fart. Stand up for your rights. If those women threaten you, you threaten them back.'

'But—'

'Don't be a wimp, Lloyd. Do you think I want a wimp for an ex-husband?'

'You don't have to do that,' he said, after she started to pull out the sofa bed for him.

'I want to check the sheets.'

And she did, holding them up to her nose and sniffing.

'Put them in the laundry tomorrow.'

'But, Pearl Fay, you just did them yesterday.'

'It wasn't yesterday.'

'By the way,' he said, as she headed for her own room upstairs, 'don't buy any more of those mesquite things.'

'You don't like them?'

'No, they're too good, Pearl Fay. I can't stop.'

'You'll be buying your own from now on, big boy.'

'Yeah, well, fine. I'll eat them in the gutter.'

''Night, Lloyd. And don't stay up watching TV all night. I can hear it upstairs and I need my ten hours.'

Chapter Eight

On the way to the steakhouse, Bruce Powers did not speak. When Mr. Norris began to cross Ninth Avenue against the light, a ham fist grabbed him by the collar and saved him from a cab or two. But there was no admonition, no joshing. Bruce Powers simply sighed.

'Say, Bruce,' Mr. Norris said, after Mario had shown them to Mr. Powers's usual table. It was near the wall of raw steaks, aging somewhat indecently in public. 'You don't happen to know of any apartments, do you? Something real cheap.'

An eyebrow went up.

'Bruce?'

'Huh?'

Mr. Norris repeated his question. This time the eyebrow didn't even bother to go up. His boss just stared blankly at the gold-tasseled menu, bound in plush scarlet.

'Is anything the matter? Bruce?'

The answering smirk, more characteristic of Pearl Fay than his boss, was not reassuring. Mr. Norris pondered it while he pretended to study the menu. Then it dawned on him why Ms. Vigoris had not called again. She was putting it off on Bruce Powers. It was he who was going to wield the ax.

As they waited for Mario to bring the martinis Mr. Powers had ordered for both of them, without even bothering to ask his employee if he might not prefer a glass of milk – what Mr. Norris usually ordered – Mr. Norris wondered if he should begin thinking about suicide. After all, he was about to be fired, disgraced by the company he had served faithfully for almost fifteen years. Not only that, his wife – ex-wife – found him such a burden that she wanted him out of the house by Friday. If only he had a companion, someone to cling to at night, to share his sorrows with. But after all the personal ads, the dating services, the furtive visits to bars during the period he had lived alone above the nurses' uniform shop, he had come up with nothing. The awful truth was, if Mr. Norris killed himself, he would never know what it was like to have had sex with a man. It just didn't seem fair to him. According to Kinsey, even your average heterosexual male had had more experiences with men than he had. And yet he, Mr. Norris, would end up going straight to heaven, if suicide weren't a sin.

'Eat.'

'I'm not hungry, Bruce.'

The suspense was mind-numbing – or was it the martini? In any case, they had downed the liquor, a goblet each, with only occasional remarks about a movie neither one had seen. And now the food was here, two New York strip steaks with a side of fried zucchini, a veritable hillock such as Jane Eyre, the movie's heroine, might have wandered over, lost, somewhat dazed.

'What's with you, Norris? Dig in.'

Mr. Norris dabbed at his nose, which seemed to have enlarged, like a Novocained lip. He had never attempted a martini before, particularly one served in something a goldfish might have called home. With a napkin slick as a cardinal's robe, he dabbed at mucus and possible tears he could not feel on his benumbed face.

'You want all this to go to waste, Norris?' Bruce Powers's knife and fork were poised, but he himself had not yet taken a bite. And Mario, the elderly waiter, had come and gone unmolested. 'You realize how many lights you'd have to turn off to afford one of these? Eat.'

'I can't, Bruce. I'm sorry, but . . . I'm just too upset.'

The knife and fork settled down on either side of the majestic plate. 'I see. So she told you, huh?'

'No, not really.'

'But you know. Vigoris can't keep her word, can she? She was going to let me do this.'

'She didn't say anything yet. But I've known all along this was coming, ever since Mrs. Kundaa, you know. Just last night I was saying to Pearl Fay the ax was going to fall.'

An inscrutable look masked the full, handsome face contemplating Mr. Norris. 'I got to hand it to you – you had me fooled.'

'Pardon?'

'All these years, Norris, I've been feeling sorry for you. A little nebbish, that's what I thought, going to Mass every day, remembering your anniversary, turning off lights like Mommie's good boy. And all this time . . .' He smiled and shook his head.

'All this time what?'

'You knew what you were doing every step of the way, didn't you? And when it's safe to be gay, then suddenly you're telling everyone you're a little faggot, too.'

'Bruce, that's not fair. I—'

'You gays are taking over everything nowadays, aren't you? You strut around the locker room and dare anyone to give you a funny look. But let me tell you something, Norris. I call a spade a spade. I'm not going to be intimidated by all your so-called rights. You don't play straight with me, and I'm going to let you know just what I think. Take me to court if you like, but I'm not going to let any faggot lawyer tell me I can't treat you like I would any real man.'

The silverware jumped as the fist struck the table. But it wasn't the ham fist.

'I've had just about enough, Powers.'

'Sit down. Let me finish.'

'As far as I'm concerned, you're finished, mister. You and your racist pig friends, you're all finished.'

'Norris.'

'Don't Norris me. Go Norris yourself.'

And with that, he stormed past a bewildered Mario, who wanted to know if his steak was not medium enough.

Exultant as a martyr in a tumbrel, Mr. Norris made his progress through the commoners on the fiftieth floor. Some looked up with puzzled smiles as he urged them to put down their yogurt and go out for something decent to eat – French fries, cake. Other clerks and secretaries simply ignored him, even when he had to steady himself on a monitor or two. Feeling was returning to his cheeks, but perhaps it would be wise to have a cup of coffee in his office before venturing upstairs. He did not want to slur any words as he told Vigoris and Kundaa exactly what he thought of them. Imagine, Vigoris didn't even have the courage to fire him herself. She had to sic that pansy on him, that fat yes-man who couldn't even . . .

'Congratulations,' Penny murmured, as he scraped by her desk.

He paused, wondering if he had heard right. 'I beg your pardon?'

'Congratulations, Mr. Norris.'

Even though she was a Republican, his secretary could have been expected to have an ounce or two of compassion. This sarcasm cut to the quick.

'My good woman, if you don't have the decency, the common courtesy, to treat your – to treat *me* with some respect, then I suggest you get that big behind out of that chair and go work for someone else.'

'Oh, Mr. Norris, I'm sorry. I didn't mean anything.' Tears pooling in her dim eyes, she looked stricken, mortified. 'Please, I just wanted to say I knew. Mrs. Kundaa called while you were at lunch and told me.'

'She had no business blabbing like that. It's my job to let you know anything pertinent to your duties.'

'Yes, sir, I understand. But she wanted me to help move you right away.'

'The nerve.'

'We can wait, though, if you say so. I don't know how long it will take Mr. Powers to move out of his office, but Mrs. Kundaa said he should start right away, after lunch.'

'What are you talking about?'

'He's moving in here so you can have his office.'

'Huh?'

'Well, sir, since you're his boss now, it wouldn't make sense for you to stay here.' She sniffed delicately, then, at his request, repeated what she had just said.

'Oh, Lord, Penny, please don't tell me I'm going to be his boss.'

'But I thought you knew, sir. Mrs. Kundaa said I'd be working for him, and you'd get someone new. So, I – Mr. Norris, sir, are you all right? Perhaps you should sit down.'

Mr. Norris sat.

Chapter Nine

Since their street was on a slant, it made sense for the Norrises to walk uphill first – toward the Home for the Aged Blind, which crowned the hill – and then coast back when they were tired and short of breath. During these aerobic walks, which had been more common before the divorce, Mrs. Norris might speculate about breast-reduction surgery. If it would indeed put an end to her backaches and general depression, then Mr. Norris urged her to stop obsessing about it and schedule an operation. But she would argue that plastic surgery would be against Natural Law and say something about how fat Thomas Aquinas was. Only after the divorce did she admit that it had been Herbert who had put this worry into her head. He was an expert on Catholic doctrine – and loved majestic bosoms.

'So what's stopping you now?' Mr. Norris asked as they painfully ascended toward the Home. They were the only ones in the neighborhood who used the narrow sidewalk, cracked by age and sycamore roots. Though their street was a backwater with virtually no traffic, a constant roar from the six-lane parkway in the valley below could engulf their more languid remarks. Still not recovered from his liquid lunch, Mr. Norris could not summon up the extra energy to repeat his question, which went unanswered. He had come home early, by four, and was hoping a walk might clear the vapors from his head. He did not want Pearl Fay thinking he was drunk when he explained to her what had happened and why it would be impossible for him to accept the promotion. Although Mr. Norris knew he was innocent, technically speaking, it was still not right that Bruce Powers should get all the blame for Mrs. Kundaa's attempted firing. Besides, even if he did accept and become Bruce Powers's boss, how long would it be before Bruce let Vigoris know that he, Mr. Norris, was gay? The whole setup would be too precarious, trying to work with a man who had been so publicly humiliated.

'You could get the operation now, couldn't you?' he tried again a few blocks later. They were taking a breather at the sign that announced the Home, still not visible at the end of a long drive even steeper than the street.

'I mean, Pearl Fay, you did get your teeth stained,' he prompted. 'It's the same thing.'

'It's not either. I did that to look more natural.'

'But it was still—'

'Lloyd, honey, stop. Please stop.'

'Stop what?'

'I know you didn't come home drunk at three-thirty to talk about my boobs.'

'I'm not drunk. I had one martini. And it wasn't three-thirty.'

She took his hand and gave it a gentle squeeze. 'What is it? Were you fired?'

'Not exactly.' He needed more time. In an hour or so, after some coffee, then maybe he could explain.

But there was no getting around it. She wanted to know the facts now. As the color drained from the November sky and their faces became less detailed, more generic, she got them. And as he had feared, her reaction was totally inappropriate.

She was overjoyed for him. She hugged him. She even shed a tear.

'No, you're not listening to me, Pearl Fay. Don't you understand?'

'Of course I do. You've finally been given the recognition you deserve. That stupid company finally came to its senses. A little justice now! Yes!' Her fist almost connected with his nose as it was raised in a somewhat dated power-to-the-people salute.

'But I can't be his boss. It's impossible.'

'So let him find another job, then. It's not your problem, Lloyd.'

'But—'

'Don't you realize what this means? You can get yourself a nice apartment now. And I won't have to feel guilty about Dawne moving in and paying me rent. By the way, did they tell you what sort of raise you'd be getting?'

'I haven't talked to Vigoris yet.'

'Don't you dare accept anything less than what Bruce was getting, understand?'

'I'm not accepting anything, period.'

Unable to meet the look directed at him, he glanced away and found a car was upon them. As it headed up the drive to the Home, a child gaped at them from the rear window.

'Let's go back.'

'Lloyd.'

'It's getting dark.'

They were silent on the way down. Mr. Norris didn't know why, but he was thinking how sad it was that cars nowadays all looked alike. When he was that child's age, you could tell at a glance from a block away what make and model, what year was coming toward you. But now the Ford they owned didn't look that much different from a BMW.

'You OK?' she said, taking him by the arm. He had stumbled over a root in front of their next-door neighbor's, a run-down gabled cottage only a foot or two from the sidewalk itself. Fifteen years earlier the elderly couple living there had threatened to sue the Norrises, who had just moved to Yonkers, when a crab-apple branch had fallen on their roof during a storm. Mr. Norris had sawn down the tree, which was indeed rotten, and never heard from them again. He thought they might be Italian, but wasn't sure.

'Lloyd?'

'I'm fine.'

She did not release the arm, which prevented him from moving on to their own house – her own, the trim split-level.

'Please, hon, don't do this to yourself.' Gentle, sobering, the whisper somehow cut right through the steady roar from the parkway below, where a few lights danced. 'Something good has happened to you, Lloyd. Don't spoil it.'

'But—'

She touched his lips with a finger. 'Hush.'

'But I don't deserve—'

'Hush.'

A curtain parted in a darkened window. Feeling observed, he urged her on to the modest red-brick house, which seemed a veritable manor beside the cottage as the light failed.

Chapter Ten

A temp showed him into Ms. Vigoris's office the next morning. Mrs. Kundaa was downtown, being deposed about something suede, shoes or a jacket.

'She'll be here in a minute,' the temp said. 'Would you like a cup of coffee?'

'No, thanks.'

'Cream or sugar?'

'Just a little milk, skim,' Mr. Norris said, puzzled. The temp, a gray-haired man with a crewcut and gold earring, nodded on his way out.

'Ah,' came a voice a few minutes later, causing Mr. Norris, who was sipping a cup of tepid black coffee, to swallow down the wrong pipe.

With a patient smile, the CEO waited for her employee to recover from her sudden materialization. Though she was born and raised on an Ohio farm, Earleen Vigoris did not look very cornfed. A dark, svelte woman with hooded eyes, she had the reputation in the industry of being a despot. Yet in the few encounters he had

had with her – mainly at office parties – Mr. Norris had met with nothing but kindness and even a certain deference. She always apologized profusely for not remembering his children's names, and when told they didn't exist, she would look stricken, as if there had been some sort of tragedy. Perhaps if she were older he would have found it easier to tremble in her presence. But they were the same age, forty-three, somewhat young for a true despot.

When his coughing fit subsided, Ms. Vigoris asked the temp to supply him with another cup. Like his boss, the temp did not seem to enter a room, but rather to appear. If he were wearing slippers, he couldn't have made less noise as he glided over the parquet.

'Oh, no, no more coffee, please,' Mr. Norris said, worried about his spastic colon.

Her wide mouth crumpled. Pain flawed the zircon-blue eyes. 'You don't like my coffee, Mr. Norris?'

'Oh, no, it's wonderful, really great.'

'Another cup, Lewis. And bring a rag.'

The temp looked down at the beige spots on the Norwegian rug, where some of the coffee had been coughed. The goatee, which Mr. Norris hadn't noticed at first – it was so wispy and light – quivered.

'Don't worry, I'll get it.' Sinking to his knees, Mr. Norris ignored the CEO's protests and began to dab ineffectually with his own starched handkerchief. He stopped only after catching a glimpse of something odd and unnerving, which turned out to be her crotch. Did she not wear panties beneath that itchy-looking dress suit?

'Please, Mr. Norris, leave it, will you?'

Back on his feet, he was glad to see the temp had disappeared. For some reason, Mr. Norris felt constrained by his presence.

'Now, where were we?' she went on, after fielding a call that he tried hard not to listen to. She was saying something about a helicopter being late again.

'Well, Ms. Vigoris, it's about that promotion.'

'Of course, I've been meaning to congratulate you.' Leaning over her glass desk, she extended a limp hand.

It was amazingly soft, the digit he touched.

'I'm honored and all that, but the point is, see, I was wondering if I could go back to what I was doing. This would make me very happy, Ms. Vigoris.'

Her carmine lips fixed in a smile, the CEO appeared not to have understood a word of what had just been said, as if she were waiting for a translator to catch up. Indeed, beneath her bobbed silken hair, almost blue it was so black, tiny headphones lurked, such as a U.N. delegate might wear. But what hers hooked into, only the good Lord knew. Rumor had it that she listened to soy and pork futures while carrying on her business.

'You see,' Mr. Norris went on, 'I don't think – even though I'm very thankful and grateful to everyone here – I don't think it would be right to have Bruce Powers under me.'

'Under you?' She tittered in a most unseemly manner.

'I mean, he would be reporting to me,' he said, more earnest than ever. 'And since he's been *my* boss for the past seven years, you see how awkward this would be.'

'Ah, so what you are saying, you wish to make things easier for everyone concerned.'

Mr. Norris could now smile.

'You want to fire Bruce.'

'No, no, of course not. I couldn't—'

'Hold on. You're not going to get me to do your dirty work for you.' Under the glass, her satiny smooth, malnourished legs crossed. 'I'm not going to fire a man who has two sons at Yale, another at Groton, and a fourth on welfare.'

'Welfare? I thought he was at Princeton.'

'He dropped out to write screenplays.'

'Oh. Well, anyway, that's neither here nor there.'

'You're pretty coldhearted, Mr. Norris. Their education means nothing to you, I suppose.'

'Of course it does. That's why I can't take this job.' Discouraged but not defeated, Mr. Norris decided there was only one way to break through the language barrier. No more hedging about Bruce

Powers and his sons. What was called for now, the only thing this former farmhand would understand, was a blunt, unequivocal battering ram of honesty.

'Ms. Vigoris,' he interrupted, as she rambled on about tuition, 'I think I'll have to be more than frank with you. The fact is, I would not be able to accept this promotion because sooner or later you'd be bound to find out the truth about me. You see, well, I'm sort of, you know, men.'

'Men?'

'I'm sort of attracted to them.'

'You're gay, Mr. Norris?'

He blushed.

'We all know you're gay, Mr. Norris. What's your point?'

Baffled, he took a moment to find it. 'But I thought, I mean all this time, as I was told, they said you were prejudiced against them.'

The bright smile faded. 'Just who is this "they," Mr. Norris?'

'Uh, no one, no one in particular. Oh, my!'

A delicate china cup was thrust right under his nose. It was the temp again, sneaking up from behind.

'Thank you so much, Bruce,' Mr. Norris said coolly, trying not to appear spooked.

'It's Lewis, *Mr.* Lewis,' the temp said.

'Yes, I meant—'

But the man had already disappeared, leaving Mr. Norris with a cup and saucer in his lap and a matched pair in his hands.

'So it was Bruce, wasn't it? He told you I have a policy against gays, right?'

Mr. Norris should not have hesitated for a fraction of a second to defend his colleague. But he did. He wanted desperately not to tell a lie if there were a charitable way to do so. 'No, he never said you have a policy per se against them.'

'You admit, then, that he did say *something* about gays and I.'

'Me – gays and me.'

'You and gays, fine.'

'It was just something in passing, a remark. In fact, I'm not even sure it was him – he. It might have been Mrs. Kundaa.'

'Impossible.' Fidgeting, she tucked a leg under her. The girlish posture, though not unbecoming, was curious for a CEO.

'Yes, impossible,' he went on. 'But Mrs. Kundaa perhaps doesn't fully understand what a wonderful man Bruce really is. She's always had an innate hostility to him that isn't entirely fair. I've tried to explain to her that when Bruce blurted out that she was fired, I was also—'

'Enough.' She flashed him a look as chilling as his glimpse earlier of her nether regions. 'I won't have Mrs. Kundaa badmouthed in this office.'

'But I wasn't . . .' Common sense told him to back off. It wasn't for nothing that this woman was sitting in that tortuous chair sculpted by Louise Nevelson out of coat hangers. But yet something long dormant inside him refused to be quailed. He would have his say, whatever the cost.

'All right, forget about Mrs. Kundaa. It's really not about her or Bruce, even. It's me, Ms. Vigoris – I. I thought with your background, your father raising turkeys and stuff, you probably wouldn't understand about gay things and all.'

'Yes, I'm just a Neanderthal, Mr. Norris.'

'No, no, I didn't mean that.' A Paloma Picasso cup clattered in its saucer, but he couldn't tell if it was the one in his hand or the one in his lap. 'I was referring to something specific – your son, I mean, wasn't he on TV once, on a student panel? I believe it was *Firing Line*, and he was advocating that all gays be branded.'

As she cocked her head, quizzically, her dark hair betrayed unexpected tints – a mica-like red, some turquoise – like a grackle's plumage. 'Tattooed, Mr. Norris.'

'Oh. I didn't actually see the show myself.'

'No, of course not. He told you about it, right?'

'No, it wasn't Bruce, honest.'

But even as he defended him, Mr. Norris remembered that it had indeed been Bruce.

'Look, Ms. Vigoris,' he said finally, desperate for a gulp of honesty, 'you may smile, but it's not what you think. This isn't about my sexuality – though I can't help wondering if your son doesn't realize that tattooing is expressly forbidden by Leviticus. Anyway, it's about performance, Bruce Powers's. After all these years he's developed an amazing rapport with our accounts and—'

'And as a result our billings have dropped an amazing three and three-eighths in the past quarter alone. And is it any wonder? Just look at how dull and stodgy we've become.'

A cup tumbled to the rug as he tried to field the shaving cream tossed from the other side of the glass desk. He picked up the can and for a dutiful moment studied the artist's copy: NATUREs OWN: AllNatural ProtekShun.

With a shudder, he said, 'The spelling is beyond belief.'

'That was my idea, thanks. But it's the color I'm talking about.'

'Green? Well, it suggests nature, nothing artificial, I suppose.'

'Exactly – just like every other natural product under the sun. Mrs. Kundaa showed me toilet paper with the exact same shade. Bruce is about as original as Kmart.'

'Well, what do you want – pink? He's only doing what—'

'Fantastic. Pink for men. I love it. Just the right shock value, crossing boundaries.'

'You can't be serious!'

'Exactly – and Bruce is too serious, so literal. No sense of irreverence. Take a look at this. Tell me what it says.'

Mr. Norris reached for the folder she held out. A market research report. On the first page, respondents compared NyLo to 'potato salad' and 'Des Moines.'

'I ask you, Norris, why couldn't they have circled "sushi" and "Malibu"? Because of Bruce, that's why. He drags everyone to that obscene steakhouse . . .' She snipped the tip from an illegal cigar. Mr. Norris dearly wished Mrs. Kundaa had not told him, many months ago, that the CEO's cigars were smuggled. It troubled him greatly, supporting an atheist dictator who put gays in concentration camps.

'Actually,' he said, as a miniature cirrus drifted toward him, 'potatoes and steaks, they're sort of in style again, I think.' On the express bus from Yonkers he had overheard this while he tried to doze.

'No, really?'

'Yes, I did hear . . .' He coughed. The smell was horrendous. It was worse than coffee, as far as his colon went. 'Listen, I've got to go.'

'You know something, Mr. Norris – I think you have something there. Yes, brilliant. You gays, you really are the cutting edge.'

At the door he gave a sickly smile.

'Of course, it has to be done right, this retro stuff. Bruce doesn't have a clue. First thing you do, Mr. Norris, you hire one of your boyfriends as your assistant.'

'But I don't have a boyfriend.'

'I don't mean "boyfriend" boyfriend. Just one of your kind.'

A cramp soured the smile completely. 'But I like Penny.'

'Sorry. Bruce gets her.'

'But—'

There was no arguing. He had to run to the nearest restroom, which he did, depositing the Picasso cup in the temp's lap on the way.

Chapter Eleven

Mr. Norris was surprised when Bruce Powers accepted the invitation to dinner. It was meant as a gesture, something to reinforce the profuse apologies that Mr. Norris had been offering ever since the unfortunate scene at the steakhouse. But it turned out that Bruce's wife had been out of town for over a week on a sales trip to Chicago – she was in nonaluminum siding – and Bruce was in the mood for some home cooking.

'Home cooking?' Mr. Norris echoed. He had intended to take him out to a sushi bar in Hell's Kitchen.

'I've been eating out every night now, couldn't stand the sight of another restaurant. Besides, I hear the missus is quite a cook.'

Mr. Norris shrugged. 'She's OK, I guess.'

If Bruce had not looked so weary, so defeated, Mr. Norris might have tried to make sushi look more exciting than Yonkers. But he hadn't the heart to add any further disappointment to his ex-boss's life. And he certainly didn't want to seem in the least bit bossy himself. So after Bruce Powers set a date – that very evening – Mr. Norris called home and left a message on the machine that they would be having a guest for dinner. Fortunately, Mrs. Norris was out coaching the Mermaidens that afternoon, so there was no argument.

Although Bruce expected to take a cab all the way up to Yonkers, Mr. Norris could not bring himself to be so extravagant. His raise, it turned out, had not been quite as guilt-provoking as he had anticipated. Indeed, he was sure he was not making anything near what Bruce's salary had been for doing the exact same job. And with taxes taken out at a higher rate and Mrs. Norris's alimony increasing (the divorce agreement included a sliding scale based on his earnings), he somehow felt poorer than before the promotion. In any case, it might make Bruce Powers feel better if he saw how humbly Mr. Norris commuted.

The narrow seats in the Yonkers bus became something of a penance as the armrest Mr. Norris was squashed against gnawed cruelly into his side. Across the aisle was a free seat next to a slender gentleman. But Mr. Norris worried that if he scooted across, Bruce might take this as an insult. (He had gained fifteen pounds since being demoted.) And also, the slender gentleman – comely despite his scowl – might think Mr. Norris was up to something. So Mr. Norris smiled bravely and stayed put.

'And then I told Vigoris that I was gay. I thought for sure that would do the trick. But she—'

'Look, Norris, enough is enough. You don't expect me to believe you were up in her office trying to turn down a promotion, do you?'

'Honest, I swear. It's like I've been telling you—'

'So stop, will you? Day after day the same crazy story . . .'

Like air seeping from a tire, Bruce's exhalation seemed to deflate his solid, all-too-solid flesh. Yet there was still a certain nobility to the massive head, which for some reason seemed more leonine since his troubles had begun. Perhaps Bruce needed a haircut. In any case, Mr. Norris felt a lump in his throat as the bus rattled over the gangway of the Willis Avenue Bridge.

What Vigoris had said about Bruce Powers turned out to be

true. He really was trapped, unable to leave NyLo because of the impossible tuition he and his wife had to shell out to Yale and Groton. And there was no other job for him to move to, not at the moment. Mr. Norris was aware that Bruce was on the phone all day, networking every connection he could think of. Of course, this meant that Bruce was falling behind in the work he was supposed to be doing. But Mr. Norris covered for him not only by taking on extra responsibilities himself, but also by giving Penny, Bruce's secretary, a raise. While Bruce chatted with headhunters, Penny was run ragged with duties not in her job description.

On the Major Deegan the rush-hour traffic was viscous, threatening to solidify, which gave Mr. Norris plenty of time to explain again how innocent he was, how there wasn't any conspiracy between him and Mrs. Kundaa.

'Then why didn't you fire the woman yourself?' Bruce asked. They had covered this ground before during one of Mr. Norris's apologies in the office. It was amazing how much Bruce seemed to forget.

'I did, Bruce. I was in the middle of firing her when you came in.'

'What about since? Have you told her it was you, Norris – not me?'

'Well, I . . . She's very difficult to talk to these days. I really haven't had much of a chance to explain all the details. Besides, it really wasn't my decision, Bruce. You have to admit, you did make me try to fire her.'

'I like this. Revisionist history.' He chugged the rest of his spring water, straight from the bottle.

'It's not revisionist. It's the truth. I probably would have stuck with her until she drove me insane.'

'Exactly. And I saved you, didn't I? Now what's this? Why are we stopping?'

The arteries feeding into the expressway had clogged by the Bronx Terminal Market. Seeing that Bruce was beginning to fret and stew, Mr. Norris tried to distract him from giving any more advice to the bus driver. 'Funny how that's the Harlem River.'

'What's funny about it?'

'Because just a few blocks south it's called the East River. And over on the other side of Manhattan it's the Hudson. And yet it's all the same, one river. I mean, Bruce, you don't see nonsense like that going on anywhere else. What if they renamed the Mississippi every time it went past an island?'

'You're nuts, you know. Hey, driver, get into the right lane.'

'Bruce.'

'He's just sitting here, and I've got to pee.'

With an apologetic smile Mr. Norris glanced at the slender commuter across the aisle. The gentleman frowned and went back to his *Post* as the bus heaved into gear.

Normally, it was about a ten-minute walk from the bus stop to the house. But Bruce was so anxious to get to a bathroom that they made it in half the time – to the driveway, at least. In a sweat, Bruce tore open his collar and declared he could not make it up something that steep. Rather than walk up the driveway, then, Mr. Norris suggested the steps that led to the front door of the split level. But Bruce ruled them out as being even worse. 'What do you mean by building on a lot like this?' the ex-boss demanded. 'It's straight up and down.'

Mr. Norris felt suddenly protective of his – or rather, his ex-wife's – property. Yes, the lot was awfully steep and narrow. And the house itself did seem cramped, not full-sized, as if it were a beginner's model. But there was a certain quiet dignity to it, a poise that could be admired. And the bricks were real, not the faux limestone Mrs. Powers had tried to sell them.

'Go on, Norris.'

'What?'

'I need a breather. Go on, get.'

Taking the concrete steps two at a time, Mr. Norris steeled himself for a frosty reception. He knew Mrs. Norris didn't like surprises and planned dinner parties months in advance. But he had an opportunity now to explain why he had no choice in the matter. If she would only listen to reason, they might all have a fairly pleasant evening.

'I'm home. Pearl Fay? Hon?'

She wasn't in the kitchen. He took the carpeted stairs two at a time.

'Pearl Fay, what are you doing?'

In the master bedroom – hers now – she was peering through the gingham curtains. 'Come here.'

'What?'

'See what that man is doing?'

Bruce Powers was only partially obscured by a clump of rhododendrons in the Italian neighbors' yard.

Pulling the curtains to, Mr. Norris said, 'You shouldn't spy on a guest.'

'Some guest.'

'He can't help it. He drinks bottled water all the time.'

'You're lucky I don't boot you right out of this house, mister. Don't you ever surprise me again like this. I don't want any cute apologies on my machine. You talk to me in person. Now zip me up.'

'Where?'

'In back, Toad.'

She hadn't called him Toad in years, not since high school. Perhaps that was the reason they both started giggling. So foolish, he knew. Yet it was hard to stop.

'You'll have to forgive the mess,' Mrs. Norris said, as she handed Bruce Powers a scotch and soda. The men had been arranged in the front parlor so that Bruce could get an unobstructed view of the authentic spinning wheel that doubled as a CD rack. Mr. Norris, therefore, was seated on an unrelenting Shaker chair off to one side.

'I don't mind,' Bruce said, not taking the cue. Every surface gleamed with the unreal perfection of an airbrushed ad. Even the ferns, so carefully watered, seemed plastic.

'How long has it been since you two have seen each other?' Mr. Norris prompted after an awkward silence, during which Bruce had set his glass down on an immaculate *Family Circle*. Mrs. Norris could not seem to tear her gaze away from the offending Waterford.

'Must be six, seven years.' A belch was emitted. 'That company picnic, Norris.'

'What are you doing, Lloyd?' Mrs. Norris said. He had got up to move Bruce's glass onto the hand-knit coaster provided for him.

'What a fussbudget.' She rolled her eyes. 'I hope he's not Miss Prim at the office, too.'

Bruce stared blankly at her.

'By the way,' she went on, 'are you sure you don't want to wash up – your hands?'

'No, ma'am. I'm fine.'

'There's a powder room right around the corner, Bruce, under the stairs.'

'Huh?'

'Run along now.'

Looking a little baffled, Bruce hesitated a moment before getting up off the inauthentic settee he had been assigned to. It was too comfortable and well upholstered to be *echt* eighteenth century.

'What did he mean by "ma'am"?' she demanded, once Bruce was out of earshot.

'Nothing.'

'He was making fun of me – my hair.'

Mrs. Norris could be oddly sensitive about her prematurely white hair. Many times Mr. Norris had urged her to color it if it bothered her, if she felt people stared or talked behind her back. Then she would turn on him and say she had nothing to be ashamed of, that she was proud of the way she had been born, that God had made her hair that way for a reason – and then would burst into tears.

After hardly any time at all, Bruce returned with the cocky shuffle of a teen caught in a lie. For a moment, Mr. Norris feared that his guest's hands would be inspected.

'Now don't tell me that picnic was seven years ago,' Mrs. Norris said in her company voice, which was a little more Southern than her normal, everyday mode. 'Seems like just last summer. I remember it was so hot I nearly expired.'

'Remember that puck? I beaned your hubby good. He's the one who nearly expired.'

'That was you?' Mr. Norris said. While tending goal for the NyLo roller hockey team, he had been struck from behind by a puck. They had been playing in a parking lot on Bear Mountain.

'Yeah, I got you back good, boy.' Bruce took a healthy swig from his crystal tumbler.

'Got him back good for what?'

'Don't you remember, Pearl Fay? Your hubby here was misbehaving with my wife. I used to be so jealous in those days, a real nutcase. Anyone looked twice at Vanessa, and I'd want to punch him out.'

'Me misbehaving? I wasn't misbehaving.'

The good-natured smile on Mr. Norris's bland face stiffened. Misbehaving, indeed. He would have liked nothing better than to have ignored Vanessa altogether, snub her. After all, it was her husband, an outsider, who had taken the job he, Mr. Norris, had been hoping for. All the years of hard work, staying till nine, ten o'clock with no overtime, coming in on Saturdays, all this meant nothing. Mr. Norris had no social life to speak of, had sacrificed everything for the company, barely even had a chance to say hello to his wife. And yet management decided to give the job to Bruce Powers, who didn't know the first thing about labels, who was hired away from a telemarketing firm. Telemarketing! Wounded, angry, ashamed, Mr. Norris had nonetheless managed to put on a pleasant face at the annual company picnic on Bear Mountain.

Yes, he had actually congratulated Bruce Powers and given him his own NyLo hockey cap, which, of course, turned out to be too small for his fat head . . .

'What?' Mr. Norris said, recalled to the conversation by a girlish squeal.

'It's not true, Bruce Powers. I refuse to believe a word you're saying.'

'Refuse to believe what?' Mr. Norris asked mildly.

Bruce set down his scotch on the *Family Circle*. 'How I caught you sucking her toes. Boy, you're lucky you're still alive. Vanessa and I never had such a knockdown, drag-out brawl.'

'Her toes! I never . . .'

Even as he made the denial, Mr. Norris began to remember something about a yellow jacket that was hovering around the German potato salad. Somehow Vanessa had stepped on the yellow jacket and got stung.

'Fess up, Norris. I saw it with my own eyes.'

He had squeezed the stinger out of her heel, but never touched the foot with his mouth. 'Bruce, come on.' And Vanessa had started moaning – with pain, not pleasure.

'Look, Pearl Fay, can't you tell that boy's lying? If those ears of his got any bigger, he could flap himself right over to the nearest circus.'

Mr. Norris smiled. 'Pinocchio, the lying elephant.'

'What?'

'Bruce, I believe you're conflating—'

'You want conflating, I'll give you conflating.'

Mr. Norris yelped, jerking his knee out of range of the fat paw that had squeezed it. As Bruce chuckled, Mrs. Norris got to her feet.

'If you children will excuse me, I better check on the meat loaf.'

The spike heels left a trail of silent reproach in the broadloom.

'What did you have to bring that up for, Bruce? For gosh sakes.'

'What? What did I say?'

'Sssh!'

Even though she was in the kitchen, Mrs. Norris had preternatural hearing.

'What difference does it make now, Norris? You're divorced, aren't you?'

'I don't want her to think I was sucking anyone's toes. Is that asking too much, Bruce?'

The ex-boss swirled the ice around in his glass. 'I'm beginning to catch on, buddy.'

'Huh?'

'I always thought it was sort of weird, how you've moved back in with her.'

'I haven't moved back in. This is just temporary. She has a friend scheduled to move in with her next week – a woman friend.'

'Yeah, right. Good Lord, Norris, I forgot what a babe your little Pearl Fay is. You're a dog, Norris, one sly dog. The best of both worlds, huh?'

'Bruce, I resent . . . We don't, I sleep downstairs and she, she's not a babe. She's a grown woman who—'

'You can level with me, Norris. I won't tell anyone at work, I swear.'

'Why can't you get it through your head, Bruce. I'm not bisexual.'

'Good God, you mean you're straight? This whole gay thing, was it only to get my job, Norris?'

'Shhh! Hold it down, will you?' He leaned even closer to his ex-boss's downy ear. 'Read my lips, Bruce. I'm one hundred percent gay. I'm a homosexual, period. I have no interest in women whatsoever.'

Bruce Powers shook his head slowly. 'One sly dog.'

Chapter Twelve

Dr. Bennet had paid Nicholas, the doorman, to pack up Joe Pollock's belongings. The boxes had been carried down to the basement, where the UPS man was supposed to pick them up. As for the ivory belly dancer, Joe Pollock had let it be known – through Nicholas – that he wanted it insured and certified. All those forms at the post office, though, were too daunting for Nicholas. As for Dr. Bennet, he had gone to enough trouble and expense for that man. Let him come get the belly dancer himself. And furthermore, he told Nicholas that he wasn't going to pay for the boxes, either. Let Joe take care of UPS.

So the boxes still sat in the basement. And the belly dancer remained on a shelf in the bedroom closet.

'I can't quite figure it out,' Dr. Bennet summed up the situation for his parents. 'Why is it that everyone I know turns out to be crazy?'

'You don't mean everyone, son.'

'Yes, I do, literally everyone, Dad. There's not one exception.'

Edgar Bennet, who was sensitive about his age – he had just turned ninety – looked pained.

'Not you, of course, Dad. I was only talking about my friends.'

The sliding glass door opened, and Edgar stepped out onto the terrace. The mother and son regarded him silently for a few moments as he draped tinsel onto the potted fir.

'Shouldn't he have a coat on, Mother?'

'It's not that cold out. Let him be.'

The parents had not been in New York in over twenty years. Visits had always been the other way around. For Christmas Hermione and Dr. Bennet would fly to Morocco, where Edgar and Consuelo lived in a modest villa nestled in the Anti-Atlas. A retired high school math instructor, Edgar could afford a maid for his wife in Africa. In the States, while he had been teaching, this had been out of the question. Consuelo, though she had grown up with servants in Puerto Rico, had done her own washing and ironing in Queens. Indeed, Edgar – who had been disinherited by his Beacon Hill mother for marrying a Catholic – could not even give his wife, who had been disinherited for marrying a Unitarian, her own home at first. They had lived in a boardinghouse that their son now remembered as a veritable paradise, though he had nearly died there in Far Rockaway, six years old, of scarlet fever.

'Mother, what are you doing?'

'Take it.'

The ten-dollar bill fluttered over the silver teapot that separated them.

'I don't want you quarreling with your friends, Carlos. Use this for the postage.'

'Don't be silly, Mom.'

He plucked the bill from the gnarled fingers that belied the smooth, regal face. Back into her vinyl purse it went – not without a pang. When he thought of all the lovely leather handbags Hermione had bought for his mother in Agadir, it seemed almost an insult that still she would carry around this dimestore bargain. But his mother could never forgive Hermione for being so wealthy. She thought it had somehow compromised her son, even though he had explained over and over again how they lived on his earnings alone. Yes, Hermione had given away an enormous amount in charity and gifts to her family. But as far as their own living expenses went, Dr. Bennet had paid every cent. Why did she think he had given up his job teaching physics at Queens College? He would have rather taught. But it was impossible to live on such a salary among Hermione's friends. Furthermore, his mother knew perfectly well about the prenuptial agreement he had insisted on before marrying Hermione. In it he had made her family consent to keep their finances strictly separate. In case of divorce, he would not be given a cent. And if he outlived her, he refused to let one dime from her trust drop into his coffers. As a widower, Dr. Bennet was indeed forced to be frugal. He had saved so little from his days as a real estate agent for Hermione's father. If it weren't for his Social Security, he wouldn't be able to pay the rent on the apartment.

'No, I'm not going to call Joe,' he said when this suggestion was made. 'Why should I? He's the one who walked out.'

'He must have had some reason, son.'

'Yes, he's nuts – that's the reason.'

'Are you sure you didn't say something that might have offended him – inadvertently, of course?'

Too ashamed to admit that a volunteer had been in the apartment, Dr. Bennet had been forced to give an extremely condensed version of Joe Pollock's departure. Now he regretted having brought the subject up at all. It was too absurd, the idea that Joe Pollock had been pitying him.

'Mother, let's drop it. We've got far more important things to discuss.'

And so, while Edgar trimmed the fir outside, the conversation drifted back to where it had begun. Dr. Bennet wanted to know why his parents would not at least consider moving back to New York. There was an apartment opening up in his building – a co-op, actually, that they could buy quite reasonably. Wouldn't it be wonderful if they could be so close again?

Consuelo regarded him with a tenderness that reminded him of Far Rockaway, of those days he could stay home from school because of the fever. 'Of course, Carlitos. Why do you think we came all this way? You know how your father hates to travel.'

'You mean you will consider it?'

'We have an idea, son.'

Gently, the delicate cup she had sipped from descended, and gently, it toppled over, having landed on the edge of the saucer. The remains of the tea that pooled like oil on the dusky teak were ignored.

'Marion's son is getting married, you know.' Marion was Consuelo's maid's brother, a scholar who was an authority on the relationship between John Quincy Adams and Czar Alexander I. Marion lived rent-free on the grounds of the villa in a small hut, from which monographs were issued for the university presses of former French colonies.

'You could move in with Marion now that César's room will be free,' she went on. 'And Marion will be so lonely without César. You would be doing him such a favor.'

'Mother, I'm not sure I can live without electricity.'

'Your father and I have done it for twenty years.'

'I know, but . . .'

'And Carlos, my roses. You will be in the midst of my roses. I don't know how you can stand not seeing them. For two years now you have not come – and my Queen Genevieves have finally come into their own. They are simply too lovely, my dears.'

Her head bowed. For a brief moment she was so still, so shockingly peaceful that he feared she might have passed away. But then she raised her head.

'Mother, you know very well I've never liked Marion. He is a leech.'

'So?'

The painted lips, carmine, somehow balanced her pale luminous face. He stared in wonder, as at a daub of color that only a master could have gotten away with, a true genius.

'Aren't we all leeches, Carlos? My roses, don't they suck the life from the soil?'

'Mother.'

'You still don't know?'

'Don't know what?'

She fingered the cross that depended from the wide, immaculate sailor collar that made her navy dress seem almost a habit. 'You wrote, didn't you, son? You told me you had lost everything after the accident, all hope, any reason to live.'

Two years it had been since Hermione had slipped on some ice in Harlem and been struck by a semiparaplegic motorist. His parents had not been able to come to the funeral because Marion had to appear in court for drunk and disorderly charges. Some French tourists he had been guiding around the souk had falsely brought the charges because he had scolded them for their anti-Semitic remarks.

'But you didn't lose everything, did you, Carlos?'

'Don't, please . . .'

'You still are so vain, so moral. Let it go, son. Come live in my garden.'

Outside, Edgar reached up to top the fir with a dimestore star. From this distance, through the glass that reflected a drift of light, he seemed to defy any category of father or husband. Some aura of youth made his faint, self-deprecatory smile as sweet as the Queen Genevieves.

'Mother, please don't talk nonsense.'

Chapter Thirteen

Mr. Norris was gazing out the window, seeing nothing – not the Rambo look-alike selling T-shirts in the revolving souvenir emporium, nor the cirrostratus over Weehawken – when Bruce Powers tapped on the door. This was new, the tapping. Before, he would have just strode in.

'Busy?'

'What's up, Bruce?'

'Just wanted to thank you for the chow last night. It was good seeing Pearl Fay again.'

Mr. Norris smiled pleasantly. Pearl Fay was not speaking to him today because of Vanessa's toes. She said she could have understood if it had been Bruce's toes. But Vanessa's? Why keep that a secret from her all these years? Of course, Mr. Norris made his protests, explaining over and over about the yellow jacket and reminding her, in case it had slipped her mind, that he was a homosexual.

Still hovering in the doorway of his former office, Bruce (who was certainly not going to get an engraved invitation to come in, when he knew darn well he was welcome any time) went on, 'You and Pearl Fay doing anything tomorrow night?'

'As a matter of fact, I've got an ushers' meeting.'

'Oh – who's getting married?'

'No one.'

'Oh. Well, anyway, I was hoping I could pay you guys back, a little chow, you know.'

'That's not necessary, Bruce.'

'What about tonight?'

'Tonight?'

'Call Pearl Fay and tell her to—'

'No, no, we can't.' The arms waved in Nixonian denial. 'Pearl Fay's got this thing, a mothers' thing.'

A frown made the rugged face in the doorway seem even more handsome. 'You guys have a kid?'

'Bruce, the mothers of the girls in her synchronized swim team, they have meetings about costumes and raffles and stuff like that. She's the coach.'

'Oh. Well, some other time, huh?'

'Yeah, sure.'

Like over my dead body, Mr. Norris added to himself after Bruce finally left. Was it possible that that man – who came completely assembled with a wife and four sons – was getting any ideas about Pearl Fay? The thought had never occurred to Mr. Norris until after dinner last night, when Bruce offered to help Pearl Fay with the dishes. And she had accepted, exiling Mr. Norris to the den, where he was told to watch TV, the Mrs. USA Pageant, which she said she was sure he would enjoy – whatever that was supposed to mean.

'Norris, the ink for the toilet plunger boxes,' his new secretary said, striding manfully into the office. 'Give the artist hell. It's a .635 viscosity, so namby-pamby.'

'OK, I will.'

'Gotta be a .6352 at least. And no way, that tie.'

Trying hard to be more cutting edge, Mr. Norris had bought

the tie at a SoHo boutique that charged him half a month's salary practically. Perplexed, he removed the tie and put on the secretary's, which was narrow, black, and vinyl.

Not one to be bullied, even by a CEO, Mr. Norris had not hired a gay man to replace Penny. Instead, he had chosen a gay woman. Petite and lovely as the girl next door, Dusty eschewed manners and bras in a way that complemented her boss's more uptight, corseted approach to life. Of course, he had been warned by Human Resources that he could not come right out during an interview and ask if the interviewee liked women. But Dusty was forthcoming enough in her own way. With her cowboy boots firmly planted on his desk during their first – and only – interview, she regaled him with stories about her lover, Clarisse, who owned a wig shop in Rahway, New Jersey.

Loosening the tie he had tucked neatly under his collar, she said, 'Let it hang, babe.'

'You sure this looks all right?'

'Relax, Norris. Anything would be an improvement.'

It was so charming, the tough talk coming out in such lilting, dulcet tones. Despite her fierce nose ring, he felt protective of her and once or twice had given her soft bristling buzzcut a pat. Such a brave young woman, to stand up boldly to society, hiding nothing. This indeed was the vanguard of things to come. And he couldn't help feeling a little flattered, as well, that this vanguard had given him those cute whacks on the wrist when he had patted her head.

'By the way, Dusty – wait a sec.'

'What? I'm in a hurry.'

'Mrs. Pierce in accounting has a ticket she can't use, a big benefit for Lambda. She wants you to call.'

'You got to be kidding.'

'No. It's supposed to be a huge party, hundred dollars a plate. She'll give it to you for nothing.'

'Like, what does she think I am, Norris? Some sort of dyke? Forget it.'

'But . . . I mean, I thought . . .'

Her hazel eyes filled with tears. 'You, too, Norris? You think . . .' She closed the door for privacy. Then in a choked voice she managed to say, after one or two false starts, 'You of all people, I thought you were beyond such prejudice, man.'

'But I—'

'Just because I date a Cuban refugee who happens to be a transvestite anti-Communist, does that make me queer?'

'Clarisse is . . . ?'

'She's more man than any of these ass-kissing suits parading around this office, better believe. Her curveball's been clocked at eighty-nine miles an hour. Furthermore, if there's one thing Clarisse can't stand, it's these pampered rich white fags whining about their rights. They think they've got it hard – try being straight like she is and get arrested in broad daylight in Havana for being a *maricón*. I mean, Norris, how would you like it if some pig just assumed you were queer?'

'Well, actually, I wouldn't—'

'Yeah, right. Don't give me that bullshit. You'd die if anyone called you that. And if that Pierce thinks she can get away with calling me a dyke . . .'

'No, no, come back, Dusty. She didn't call you anything.'

He trailed her into the hall, where he was intercepted by Bruce Powers.

'Say, Norris, I have a bone to pick with you.'

'Not now, Bruce.'

But the ex-boss physically blocked his way. 'I just got off the phone with Pearl Fay. She said she doesn't know what the hell you're talking about, a mothers' meeting.'

'Bruce, please, I can't talk now.'

'She'd love to go out tonight.'

'Pearl Fay? Well, good for her – but I forbid it.'

There was no way of getting around Bruce Powers, physically. So Mr. Norris decided to confront the problem head-on. He was going to mince no words.

'You *forbid* it?'

'My gosh, Bruce, haven't you any sense of plain decency? You think Vanessa isn't going to find out about this when she gets back from Chicago?'

'She's back.'

'That's even worse. I won't have it, sneaking around.'

'Hey, Norris, what's with you? Vanessa is the one who wants to have you guys over. She wants to thank you for looking after me while she was away.'

They had drifted toward the Xerox machine, over which a crack reminiscent of Belorussia loomed.

'Bruce, that's very nice and all, but, you know, I don't think it's the greatest idea.'

'Oh, I see. You're too good for us now.'

'No, no, it's not that.'

In the pit of his stomach Mr. Norris could feel the hurt behind his ex-boss's sarcasm, the real pain fueling his resentment. He could not bear to give this man any more reason to distrust himself. Maybe Bruce wasn't cooking up any scheme, after all. Maybe he was simply trying to be a friend, to forgive and forget.

'OK, you win.' Mr. Norris held up both hands in surrender. 'We'll come.'

'Gee, thanks, Your Highness. I'm so honored.'

'Now, Bruce—'

'Look, don't patronize me, Norris. If you don't want to come, then be man enough to say so.'

Though this jab made him simmer, Mr. Norris still wanted to do the right thing, to behave like a gentleman. And yet he also wanted to be honest, to blurt out that he really didn't want to have dinner with them. Why couldn't everyone just leave him alone?

'You might as well know, buddy, Pearl Fay has already accepted. And she said she'd be happier if you didn't come – only I'm not supposed to tell you that.'

This made it clear now where his duty lay. 'I said I'd come, Bruce. Thank you. I'm very happy to come.'

Chapter Fourteen

While the men squeezed into a cab, whose door wouldn't open all the way, the debate faltered. On the sidewalk Mr. Norris had declared that first thing tomorrow morning he was going to sit Dusty down and tell her the facts of life. And if she couldn't handle the news that her boss was gay, well, she was free to find herself another job. Bruce, though, had advised him to let well enough alone. There was no need to mix up personal affairs with business. But if she kept on making homophobic remarks, Mr. Norris objected, it was an intolerable situation. He deeply resented her attitude. Bruce told his boss to lighten up. Didn't the girl have a right to free speech like everyone else? Who was he, Mr. Norris, to play thought police?

'You don't understand,' Mr. Norris resumed once they were under way. The cab had inserted itself into the busiest lane on Eighth Avenue. 'Vigoris told me to hire a gay.'

'A what?'

Mr. Norris could not bring himself to say it any louder. The driver, a native of one of those countries that might chop off your hand for onanism, was eyeing him in the rearview mirror.

'A fag?' Bruce supplied.

'Bruce.'

'Well, that's what she calls them – or used to.'

'Vigoris? Come on.'

'All the time, buddy – at least, until I got shafted. Hey, look – is that Llewelyn?'

A middle-aged man in suit and tie passed them on rollerblades.

'How awful,' Mr. Norris said. 'He shouldn't be hitching a ride like that.'

The man, who resembled Bob Llewelyn in NyLo's accounting department, was clinging to the rear of a city bus with one hand, his briefcase in the other.

'It's cool, Norris.'

'Cool? Do you realize how dangerous that is?'

'The moral patrol strikes again.'

'He's got a wife and two children and a brand-new house in Central Islip. No, that can't be Bob. I refuse to believe he would jeopardize—'

'Right here, driver.'

Still puzzling over the rollerblader, Mr. Norris alighted after a brief squabble about the fare. Bruce would not let him contribute a cent and would probably insist on paying for his ticket to Garden City. It was a long way to go for dinner, really an imposition, but Mr. Norris was trying his best to be a good sport. Strange, though – they were nowhere near Penn Station, he suddenly realized.

'Penn Station?'

'Yes, Bruce. Isn't that how you get to Long Island?'

'I thought I told you. Vanessa called from work. She's not going to be able to get away until nine, at least. So she insisted I take you guys out myself.'

'But—'

'Don't worry about Pearl Fay. She's going to meet us at the restaurant. Barbetta's is right down the block.'

'Couldn't we try something a little more reasonable?'

'I told you – my treat.'

'But that place costs an arm and a leg. I can't let you pay for us.'

'Look, Norris, let's don't get carried away with this boss thing. We're out of the office now.'

'But I'd be happy with something simple, honest. I don't like fancy meals.'

They were standing beneath a neon sign advertising 'Live Girls,' so close to their posh office building that they could have easily walked and saved the cab fare. Why, at a time like this, when he was just demoted, was Bruce intent on throwing away his hard-earned money?

'There's a Wendy's I like, Bruce. It's not too far and—'

An ear-piercing whistle caused a passing steed to shy. Smiling wanly at the policeman mounted upon the noble bay, Mr. Norris muttered, 'Stop that, Bruce. What the heck do you think you're doing?'

The officer's stony gaze, though, was directed at Mr. Norris, who heard his ex-boss saying something about Kim Novak and then whistle again.

'Huh? Where?'

But it was only Mrs. Norris crossing the wide avenue against the light. Admittedly, her white hair did seem glamorous from a distance, like bottled platinum. And there was something imperious about her flared purple coat with its ermine collar. Indeed, a Mayflower moving van actually ground to a halt for her without a single blast of its horn.

'Do you realize you were nearly run over?' He gave her his hand as she stepped onto the curb.

'Too bad they missed. My feet are just killing me.'

She leaned over and untied a strap on a spike heel.

'Pearl Fay, don't—'

'All the way from Lexington Avenue I walked. The cab wouldn't take me any farther. That's nice, isn't it? I paid her every last cent I had in my purse and—'

'Hold on. Don't tell me you took a cab from Yonkers?'

Massaging her heel, she groaned. 'What do you expect? I missed the train because I hardly had a second to change. I was coaching right up until six.'

'The bus, Pearl Fay. Haven't you ever heard of the bus?'

'Right. Twice I've been goosed on that express and – Bruce Powers, do you mind? Stop staring at my big ugly feet.'

Mr. Norris blushed. 'Please put that shoe back on.'

'What are you doing lurking outside a porn shop anyway, Lloyd?'

'He was running low on videos,' Bruce said. 'Had to get himself a fresh supply.'

Mr. Norris sighed. 'Come on. Wendy's isn't too far.'

'Wendy's? I spend seventy bucks on a cab so I can eat at Wendy's?'

'Don't listen to him,' Bruce said.

The bay's rump twitched as they strolled by. Mr. Norris was silent until the next corner. Then he declared that he wasn't going to spend a fortune in a fancy place, not after that seventy bucks.

'Bruce is paying. He said.'

'It's not right, Pearl Fay.'

'Fine,' Bruce said, taking Mrs. Norris's arm. 'You go eat at your Wendy's, and we'll go get something decent.'

Of course, there was no choice now. Mr. Norris had to accompany them, for decency's sake. But he certainly was not going to let Bruce Powers pay. That was out of the question.

Dawne Schmidlapp was waiting up for them when they got home to Yonkers. As threatened, she had moved in that Friday. For the time being, she was sleeping upstairs in the sewing room. As soon as Mr. Norris got back his own apartment in Manhattan, Dawne would claim the den for herself.

'I feel so awful, Mr. Norris, like I'm sort of in the way or something.'

'Please, call me Lloyd.'

'Pearl Fay told me you'd be gone by Friday. I never would've dreamed of moving in while you were still— Oh, Mr. Norris, would you mind holding on to that end?'

Dawne was measuring the window in the den for new curtains while Mrs. Norris was upstairs blowing up the raft in the sewing room. Dawne slept on the raft, which was a relic of the above-ground pool Mrs. Norris had bought for her husband's thirty-fourth birthday. The pool turned out to be more trouble than it was worth. Mr. Norris hated scooping leaves out of it, so Mrs. Norris had given it to her gynecologist, who needed an anniversary gift for his wife.

'Twenty-eight and a quarter.'

'Dawne, you know it's not going to be so easy for me to move back to Manhattan. There's someone living in my apartment now.'

'You sublet it?'

'In a way, except that she's not paying any rent.'

'You mean, like a girlfriend, Mr. Norris?'

'No, no, nothing like that at all.'

Now here was yet another person he would have to tell that he was gay. Why couldn't Pearl Fay have done that for him? Mr. Norris sighed.

'You can trust me. I won't say anything to Pearl Fay.'

'Dawne, she's a colleague, someone I work with, a young woman in Human Resources.'

'How nice.'

'It's not very nice at all, actually. Tudi is going through an extremely stressful time and needs a helping hand. She's had to leave her own apartment because her roommate – she's in advertising, the roommate – well, she's started moonlighting as an escort.'

'An escort?'

'You know, someone who . . .'

A hand went to Dawne's mouth. 'Oh, my goodness gracious.'

'It's been a terrible shock to Tudi.'

'Who's Tudi?'

'My colleague. She's a secretary in Human Resources, a temp actually. Anyway, she can't afford to pay me anything because her roommate is making her pay half the rent for her own apartment even though she's not living there.'

'That's so mean. I can't stand people who are mean, can you?'

'Not only that—'

'Would you mind sticking your thumb there? Thanks. You're a dream. Let's see, thirty-one and an eighth.'

'And that's not all, Dawne. Tudi just told me today that her cat has cancer. She needs an operation and—'

'Stop!'

'What's the matter?'

Her hands covering her ears, Dawne said, 'I'm like totally serious, stop. I can't stand hearing anything sad about animals. I'm not sure, but I think I'm about to cry.'

She stood there a moment in her Con Ed overalls, the ones she wore to read meters. With her work helmet on, she could be mistaken for a svelte and shockingly handsome man. (Veal and bananas had done wonders for her figure.) The helmet was off now, and her graying hair looked as frizzy as a mid-Victorian beard.

'I think I'm OK now,' she finally announced. 'But you better tell me something nice just to make sure. I don't want to have any bad dreams.'

Anxious for bed, Mr. Norris was removing his freshly ironed pajamas from the entertainment cabinet that housed the television, radio, video machine, gourmet popcorner, underwear, and socks.

'Come on, please, pretty please.'

'I'm sorry, Dawne. I just can't think of anything nice now.'

'Tell me about dinner. You must have had a really nice time tonight.'

'Delightful.'

Bruce had threatened to yank his balls off if he, Mr. Norris, didn't let him pay. And the bill was a nightmare. Two bottles of merlot Bruce had ordered, along with cognac afterward – not a drop of which touched Mr. Norris's own lips. On the way back to Yonkers, Mrs. Norris had heaved up her filetto di sogliola tartufo in the vestibule of the train. And then she had explained to the Metro-North conductor that she was pregnant. Ha ha. A delightful joke. A delightful evening.

'I'm so glad Pearl Fay had a chance to enjoy herself. She works so hard.'

'Works?'

'Oh, Mr. Norris, you have no idea what she goes through with us. Some of the girls on the team are such snobs. There's this one that hates the name, the Mermaidens, you know. She says it's sexist and just talks back to Pearl Fay. No respect.'

He yawned.

Barefoot, Dawne padded over to the sofa, which couldn't be unfolded yet because of the swatches laid out on the cushions. 'You know you hurt her feelings pretty bad when you refused to help out with the mothers' committee.'

'I'm not a mother, Dawne.'

'She told me how you've been looking all over for a place to volunteer and when she suggested the mothers' committee – well, I don't know if you were very nice to not even consider it. Of course, I shouldn't say anything. I feel like I'm butting in. Am I being too pushy? What I mean is, maybe you could have tried it, gone to a meeting just once.'

'I know nothing about sewing sequins.'

'Neither does my mama. But she joined. And my husband, he was a member.'

'Was? What happened? He quit, I bet.'

She contemplated a striped pattern. 'No, he passed.'

'Passed what? Oh – you mean he sort of . . . passed away? I'm sorry.'

'Right on my fiftieth birthday, I'll never forget. It was such a coincidence.'

Mr. Norris pondered this. 'I thought you were forty-six.'

'Who said that?'

'Pearl Fay.'

'Well, bless her heart. She's always lying about my age. I'm fifty-one and a half.' She looked up from the swatches. 'Where you off to?'

'I'm hungry.'

For dinner Mr. Norris had had an appetizer, period. Mushrooms, the cheapest thing on the menu.

'Look in the fridge, darling. There's a crumb cake I baked for breakfast. Pearl Fay will be tickled pink. She loves my crumb cakes.'

Ten minutes later he returned to the den with a curiously guilt-free conscience. He had eaten the entire crumb cake, which was indeed delicious. Heavenly. There would be nothing at all for Mrs. Norris in the morning.

'Good night, Mr. Norris.'

'Lloyd, please.'

'All right, darling. Anything you say.'

'Wait – aren't you going to put the curtains back up?'

'The old ones? Pearl Fay told me to throw them out. She hates them.'

'But I can't sleep with no . . . no . . .'

'No what?'

'Did you hear that?'

'What?'

'I thought I heard Pearl Fay scream or something. I better make sure she's OK.'

'Oh, she's fine.'

'Please, let me by.'

'Really, I wouldn't worry, darling.'

Another cry seemed to come from the bedroom directly above the den. And then some thumps, rhythmic thumps.

'Darling, no, please – believe me, she's fine.'

Thoroughly alarmed, Mr. Norris danced from side to side, but Dawne didn't budge from the doorway.

'Darling, it's Herbert. He's up there with her.'

'What!'

'Sit down, let me explain. I'm the one who called him.'

'You?'

'That's it, sit.'

'But don't you know . . . I mean . . .'

'Darling, I only found out this morning after you left for work. She told me about trying to kill herself with your vitamin C's. I was so upset I called Mama, and she wasn't in. Her boyfriend got on the line and he's a Rotarian, you know.'

'Dawne, please, get to the point.'

'It is the point. Herbert's a Rotarian, too. Don had his office number—'

'Dawne?'

'Don is my mama's boyfriend. He gave me Herbert's number, and so I called him up right there in the middle of work and told him how Pearl Fay just couldn't live without him. Excuse me.'

She plucked a swatch from the sofa and wiped her eyes.

'I said to Herbert, I hope I'm not being intrusive, but Pearl Fay almost died because of you.'

'But she didn't almost die.'

'And I told him how depressed she is, how she can barely function.'

'But she's functioning.'

'He admitted to me that he was dying, too, that his marriage was like this big fat mistake and he couldn't live without her. So I said to him, "Darling, you get yourself over here tonight, and I'll fix you the best Welsh rabbit you ever ate." That's what we did, too. We had dinner here after Pearl Fay left tonight. Funny thing was, he was sort of under the weather when he arrived – tippling, you know. Of course, you can understand, Mr. Norris, how nervous he must be. Pearl Fay, when he switched to that church in White Plains, well, she said she hated him more than anyone else in the whole world, and he was so scared of seeing her, he drank up all my Chartreuse. So I sent him upstairs for a little catnap and told him not to worry. See, I knew that once she saw him in the flesh, all that anger would just melt away – like cellulite. Am I right? Anger's just a front. You only get mad at people you love, that's one thing I learned from my own marriage. My Moony, he never once got mad at me. He was always so sweet and considerate.'

'I can't stand that thumping.'

'Relax, darling. You'll get used to it.'

'Please, out of my way, Dawne.'

He had sprung up from the sofa, but the doorway was blocked by her wistful smile. 'Oh, I just knew everything was going to work out for them. When two people are in love, there's no force in the world that's going to keep them apart.'

Chapter Fifteen

Dr. Bennet was removing the last of the tinsel from the fir when the glass door slid open. An almost tender breeze, so mild for January, stirred the calendar in his father's hand.

'You don't want this, son, do you?'

Dr. Bennet blushed violently. 'That's Joe Pollock's, not mine.'

His father hovered, neither inside nor out. From the terrace Dr. Bennet could see no wrinkles on the ninety-year-old face that was regarding, so impassively, Miss November.

'I found it under your pillow.'

'Dad, what were you doing under my pillow?'

'I was making your bed.'

'Don't make my bed.'

'When you live alone, son, you should always make your bed first thing in the morning.' As he said this, Edgar ripped Miss November to shreds, calmly. And Miss November was Dr. Bennet's favorite, a redhead with just the lightest dusting of freckles over the sumptuous bosom.

'Come inside. Lunch is ready.'

'In a minute, Dad.'

Shreds of the *Penthouse* calendar littered the asphalt flooring of the terrace. Some had drifted to the stone parapet, where they ascended in a contrary breeze. Dr. Bennet tidied up as best he could. He did not want any nudity landing on a neighboring terrace. How thoughtless his father could be.

Consuelo was having lunch at Columbia's faculty club with Marion, who had escorted the Bennets to New York in order to meet in person a history professor with whom he had been in correspondence about Henry Adams's misperception of his grandfather. Edgar and Consuelo's plan, so far, had gone nowhere. Dr. Bennet would not even consider a visit to the Anti-Atlas, much less moving there. He wished his parents would come to their senses and return to New York, where he could look after them properly. He wouldn't even mind having them move in with him, as long as Marion wasn't included in the deal. But Edgar and Consuelo loved Morocco and would not part with Marion. Indeed, they would not even take their son up on his hospitality during their Christmas visit. He had said they were welcome to stay with him – they meaning just the two of them. But Edgar and Consuelo chose to remain with Marion in a Village hotel that featured a shared bathroom at the end of the hall and stains on the carpet.

'I hope you enjoy Kansas-fried chicken,' Edgar said when his son finally sat down at the kitchen table.

'Kansas-fried?'

'Have you never seen the establishment on Broadway, Carlos? It's around 179th Street, I believe.'

Dr. Bennet munched a wing. Hermione had always been horrified by the cheap, greasy food his parents had eaten all their lives. Even in Morocco, hamburgers were their staple, along with french fries.

'There's a bulletproof plastic shield where one orders,' Edgar said, loading butter onto a biscuit. 'You speak through little holes to the clerk. Then when your poultry comes, it's like a bank – there's a carousel that swings it around so that the clerk remains safe.'

'Speaking of safe, I don't know why Mother insisted on having lunch with Marion and his professor. It's not a good neighborhood Dad – Columbia. You shouldn't have allowed her to go.'

'Well now, son, I didn't want her wandering off to Chet's on her own. Marion volunteered to accompany her after they ate at the faculty club with—'

'Smaller bites, please.'

One cheek bulging with an entire biscuit, the other with a load of fried skin, Edgar defended himself, eyes bright and eager as a chipmunk's: 'I always take small bites. It's your mother who—'

'And what do you mean by Chet's?' Dr. Bennet asked as he regarded his tumbler, into which crumbs had exploded from his father's mouth.

'Who said anything about Chet's?'

'You did.'

'Impossible. Your mother forbid me to mention his name to you today. She wants it to be a surprise when he shows up for tea this afternoon – just the two of you.'

'What!'

'Your mother thinks it's terrible that you won't speak to Chet. After all, he was Hermione's dearest friend.'

'Dad, I expressly told her last night to leave well enough alone. It's none of her business.'

'Exactly what I told her, too. I said we shouldn't go meddling in Carlos's affairs. And after you refused to give her Chet's phone number, I told her she had no right to look through Hermione's things in that box under your bed. That's where she found Chet's address, on an old thank-you note.'

'This is the limit! Do you think I'm going to let that fat queer into this apartment?'

Edgar shook his head sadly. 'Such language, son.'

'I'm sorry, but that man was a terrible influence on Hermione. Do you think she would have thrown away a fortune on all this useless furniture we have, those stupid paintings, if it weren't for . . .'

'Steady.' Edgar reached over and tried to pound his son on the back. Jerking away, Dr. Bennet went right on coughing. Some chicken had gone down the wrong pipe.

'Here,' Edgar urged, holding up his son's glass of water.

His face nearly mauve, Dr. Bennet overcame his repulsion at the sight of the crumbs scattered like the proverbial bread upon the waters. He drank – and immediately felt better.

Chapter Sixteen

No sign betrayed its name to outsiders. Though most of the club's members belonged as well to the Colony or Knickerbocker, these women found it hard to take such parvenu Upper East Side establishments seriously. The Leeuwarden itself was located on the very spot where the first private residence in Manhattan once stood, i.e., the first belonging to someone with a pedigree, not in trade. Since this spot was not easy to find, lost today in a maze of vendors who peddled bok choy and mud skippers on the sidewalk, it was not uncommon for certain elderly matrons to arrive out of sorts, having quarreled with their drivers as they backed down one-way alleys or somehow ended up on the Brooklyn Bridge.

With its venerable cracks, its pocked, peeling coat of gray, the Leeuwarden was often mistaken for a flophouse. No member, though, dared suggest any improvements to the facade. The vice regent of the privy council was known to be able to sniff out fresh paint from a mile away. It was an insufferably vulgar scent, almost as odious as the toilet water Edith Wharton's grandmother had sprinkled herself with when she had tried in vain to become a member of the Leeuwarden. (One does not ask to join; one is asked.)

Needless to say, not only was the phone unlisted, there was actually no apparatus at all for sending or receiving calls on the Leeuwarden's premises. (A member who was caught using a cell phone in a locked stall still has her purse searched at the door.) As for advertising the address with a street number attached to the jamb, well, you might as well expect to see one of those Trump women allowed inside. Which was why Mr. Norris was some minutes late. He had wandered up and down the narrow street hoping for guidance from some numbers. Three times he had passed the listing five-story frame house, unable to believe it could be a women's club. But then, by the process of deduction – it was the only place not selling eels or bird's nests or Buddhas – he finally ventured in.

Mrs. Kundaa was waiting for him in the lobby next to a bust of the Emperor Hadrian's mother-in-law. He apologized for being a little tardy. She nodded, but said nothing as she escorted him up a back stairway to the fifth floor.

The room she ushered him into made him feel tall, a man's man. Not only did the lintel graze his scalp as he entered, but a pewter chandelier depending from the ceiling swayed as it collided with his forehead. Though it was barely half past twelve, the room had a crepuscular feel to it, adrift in shadows. The lamp Mrs. Kundaa switched on cast a mellow light, but did not dispel them entirely.

'You must be wondering why I asked you here, Lloyd.'

'I'm glad you did,' he said bravely. At last, they would have it out. No matter what the outcome, it would be a relief. He could not bear the tension in the office any longer.

'I know that you must resent me, Mrs. Kundaa.'

'Resent you?'

'Because of Bruce, all that.'

With a wave of the knitting needle she had drawn from her braided gray bun, she dismissed such pettiness. 'To be quite frank, Lloyd, I was a little miffed at first. You were weak to let him push you around like that. But after all, he did say he would fire you if you didn't do his bidding. I guess we were able to teach that baboon a good lesson. And I hope you've learned one as well. Stand on your own two feet, man. Don't let people push you around. And – What's that?'

'I said, he's maybe not a baboon.'

'There you go again, defending the indefensible.'

'I don't like being his boss. It just doesn't sit right, Mrs. Kundaa. I wish there were a way things could go back to normal.'

'Bruce needs to be put in his place, and you, sir, need to start learning how to be a man.'

'I resent that.'

She looked up from the tea cozy she was knitting. 'Good, that's a start.'

'Bruce has four sons to provide for, and I just can't bear to see him—'

'Enough.' Her knitting needle rapped the lamp, which was designed originally for whale oil. 'The last thing I want to talk about is office politics. I'm sick to death of it. You have no idea what I go through, day in day out. Even Earleen is a trial. She's got this bee in her bonnet now about how she simply must become a member of this silly old henhouse.'

'The Leeuwarden?'

'Somehow she found out that unless you belong, you just don't rate. You're nobody, practically a joke.'

'I never heard of it before.'

'Of course. There's only a handful of women in the entire city that even realize they're being excluded. That Whitney woman, she's been in agony for years. Me, I don't see what all the fuss is about. The place is a wreck. The food beyond description.'

'Why did you join?'

'I didn't. I inherited my membership from a great-aunt who's directly descended from the original inhabitants of this island.'

'You're Dutch?'

'Heavens, no. We're talking about the aboriginal stock from

which the Algonquins, Esquimaux, and all that branched off. They were Tartars, straight from the Caucasus via the Bering Strait, when it wasn't water.'

Mr. Norris pondered this. Though she might behave like one, Mrs. Kundaa did not look at all like a cossack. Just plain normal suburbia, with perhaps a hint of trailer park.

'I have no shame at all in saying there isn't a drop of so-called blue blood in these veins – no English, no Dutch,' she went on. 'Aside from the Caucasian strain, my family can be traced no further than Lake Success, Indiana, where my father, Mr. Elvis T. Lucy, tried to sell galoshes made out of creosote. Of course, if I could, I'd resign my membership here. I detest these snobs – all of them parvenus, *Mayflower* riffraff.'

'Why can't you?'

'Why can't I what – resign? You may as well ask why I don't change the color of my skin. It's something you're born with, irrevocable. Once a member, always a member.' She sighed. 'Earleen doesn't realize what she'd be getting into. Of course, the chances are slim for her. There's such competition this year. But Earleen's determined to make it. She claims she has pedigree – much better than that Whitney woman's – Mary Jo? Mary Lou? What is that woman's name?'

Mr. Norris shrugged. 'Ms. Vigoris is from an old family?'

'Claims she's related to Sophocles, on her mother's side. I tried that out on the privy council. But it didn't go over very well. They seem to think he was an invert.'

'What's wrong with that?'

'Nothing, as far as I'm concerned. This place could use a good shaking up. I didn't even hide the fact that Earleen's a member of the Yale Club.'

'Is that bad?'

'Just not done, Lloyd. Anyway, enough of Earleen. I came here to get away from any office politics. It's actually a very personal matter I wish to speak to you about, Lloyd. I hope I may confide in you.'

He shifted uneasily on the sofa; a stray horsehair pricked him. 'Mrs. Kundaa, I'm not sure it's a good idea for people who work together to get too personal.'

'Oh, that's a splendid attitude. After all I've done for you . . .'

The lamplight flickered as if the electricity were severely rationed in the most meager doses.

'And after you come crying for help to me, sir, for being an invert yourself.'

'I never—'

'You dare deny this?'

'I wasn't crying for help. I was simply trying to – And I'm not an invert.'

She peered over her drooping bifocals at him. 'You know, I always suspected that myself, that you weren't really that way.'

'No, no, no – I mean that word, "invert," it's not appropriate. I prefer—'

'Here we are again, talking about you. And look, just look at these hands.'

She had dropped her knitting and thrust her shapely hands out, practically in his face.

'See, they're trembling. I'm a wreck, and all you can talk about is me, me, me!'

He tried his best to look compassionate, but really, the hands weren't trembling, not as far as he could see in the musty twilight.

'You don't know how much I'm yearning, just yearning beyond anything you can imagine, Lloyd.'

Discreetly, he moved an inch or two away.

'I'd give anything now for a cigarette. But I simply mustn't have one. Don't let me have one, Lloyd.'

'OK.'

'Don't let me reach in my handbag for one.'

'Uh, is this what you're yearning for, Mrs. Kundaa, a cigarette?'

'I promised Walter I'd give them up for good. And he's letting me have one more chance.'

'Walter?'

'My boyfriend. He caught me smoking a couple of weeks ago and broke up with me. But he's giving me another chance.'

'Oh.'

'"Oh" – is that all you can say?'

'I think it's wonderful that you're giving up smoking, but you know, it's getting sort of late. Are we going to eat? I'm about to faint.'

Her needles clicked. 'We're waiting for Walter.'

'We are?'

'He's going to join us. I've always wanted you two to know each other.'

Mr. Norris just sat there.

'I think you might be a good influence on him,' she went on, frowning at a mistake she had made. She unraveled a stitch or two. 'Despite everything, S. Lloyd, you have character. I will never change my opinion about that.'

'How long do you think he'll be?'

'Oh, if you must.'

The cozy was tossed aside. She rooted in her handbag, and out came a sandwich wrapped in waxed paper.

'We're eating here?' He regarded the tuna fish on black bread. No mayonnaise. No butter. 'Isn't this a bedroom or something?' A narrow wooden bed, the size of a casket, seemed to adorn the other end of the room. And jutting from a wall was a sink.

'We'll have more privacy here. You don't want to go down to the dining room, Lloyd, trust me. It's tripe today and treacle surprise.'

He took a bite. Having had no breakfast at all that morning, he would have appreciated one of Mrs. Kundaa's ten-thousand-calorie heroes. But of course, this would be the day she chose to become health-conscious. Fiddling with an electric toothbrush that had been lying on the horsehair, he asked if there was any ketchup.

'Catsup?' a woman at the door said. He had not noticed her and wondered how long she had been standing there.

'The chamberlain,' Mrs. Kundaa muttered, retrieving her cozy.

Never had a woman looked more the part – even if he wasn't quite sure what 'chamberlain' could possibly mean, as far as a women's club was concerned. Her cool *haute école* beauty, highlighted by jodhpurs, reminded Mr. Norris of the star of the movie about birds going bananas and attacking people in Marin County. In fact, for all he knew, it could be the very woman herself. Only she wouldn't look so young, would she?

'What is the meaning of this, Countess?' the chamberlain demanded.

'Am I forbidden to knit?' She plied the needles coolly.

'I mean him.'

Mr. Norris switched off the vibrating toothbrush. He was wondering if he had heard right. *Countess!* Impossible.

'And *him*.'

The other him, somewhat blending into the chiaroscuro behind the chamberlain, gave a little wave.

Mrs. Kundaa's broad, plebian face contracted. She was not amused. 'How can you be so stupid, Walter? I told you to sneak up the back stairs.'

With an admonition that she had five minutes to escort these gentlemen off the premises, the chamberlain retired, the taps of her boots clicking crisply over the seventeenth-century planks.

'Men aren't allowed?' Mr. Norris asked after he had been introduced to Walter, an unprepossessing specimen who was both a little shorter and a little younger than his girlfriend – maybe in his late fifties, early sixties.

'Of course not,' Walter said. 'But my darling is determined to integrate the Leeuwarden. It's her own private Little Rock.'

'Eat your tuna, Walter. I got the kind you like – in water, no dolphins.'

Mr. Norris put down his sandwich. 'I don't think we should be doing this. I'm going.'

'Would John Wayne run away, S. Lloyd?'

'Look, I just don't need any more trouble in my life now,

thank you very much. And by the way, did she call you "Countess"?'

'My merry little widow is so modest. She hates her title, doesn't she?'

'It's all nonsense,' Mrs. Kundaa said. 'What does a Vatican City title mean anyway? It didn't prevent my poor Serge from working himself to death at the DMV. And what's this?' she added, as Walter deposited a brown bag on her lap. She peered inside. 'An eel? Why are you giving me an eel, Walter?'

'I'm not. Just put it somewhere for me, my love. I don't want it leaking on my suit. It was just dry-cleaned.'

As Mrs. Kundaa set the eel beside a chamber pot, she said, 'I wouldn't try to escape on my own, S. Lloyd. You'll need me if you don't wish to be detained by the footladies downstairs. Now come be brave and finish your sandwich. Walter, that's *his* sandwich.'

'He said he was going.'

'Give it back to him.'

'That's all right,' Mr. Norris put in. 'He can have it.'

Chapter Seventeen

'Is that you, darling?'

Mr. Norris didn't bother to reply as he took off the boot-like shoes Dusty had picked out for him. The electric mud scraper was still not working.

'How was your day?' she shouted from the living room.

He wished she wouldn't raise her voice like that. It was very wearing on the nerves.

'What did you say, darling?'

'Dawne, please, I'm coming.'

The sink was filled with dirty dishes, but nothing was bubbling away on the stove. And the oven wasn't on. What in the world were they going to eat? Of course, he didn't blame her for not having fixed him breakfast. She had left at 5:30 in the morning to go read meters. But after only a bite of tuna for lunch, he could not wait forever for supper.

'Dawne, do you realize it's after seven and – Oh, I'm sorry.'

In the living room Dawne was squatting on the floor beside an extremely rotund man, a stranger. Though he sported dreadlocks, he did not seem Jamaican. More like a Finn.

'That's all right, darling. We're just about through.'

A half hour later, though, they were still there. By the time the man left, Mr. Norris was quite keyed up – and not only from hunger. Just what in heaven's name was going on – all that colored chalk, the little blackboard?

'Did Pearl Fay say you could invite just anybody in like that?'

'Like what? Are you saying he weighs too much, Lloyd?'

'Don't be ridiculous.'

'If you must know, he happens to be one of my students.'

'Exactly what I was afraid of.'

Dawne taught a course in air-conditioning repair at a minimum-security facility cattycorner to the Yonkers RacePark Mall.

'If you think Pearl Fay is going to allow you to start bringing felons home, well, I'm just going to have to put her foot down.'

'Elton is not a felon.' With a sponge, she wiped the blackboard clean. 'He happens to be one of the sweetest men I know. He's a guard at the facility. And he volunteers up on the hill.'

'What hill?'

'The Home for the Aged Blind. He reads.'

'Reads?'

'Reads aloud to them. They're halfway through *Men Are From Venus*.'

Subdued by a twinge of conscience, he wandered into the kitchen. As soon as he got back his own apartment in Manhattan, he would find a good agency and start helping people. Strange how his resentment had festered against those two old men. He knew, of course, that he shouldn't have taken it personally, that they were nothing to him at all. But still, it hurt. It made him wary of ever trying to help anyone again.

'What are you doing, Lloyd?'

Dawne had come into the kitchen with her blackboard, which she simply leaned against the ironing board, which she hadn't bothered to put away.

'What are you doing?'

If there was one thing he hated, it was needless questions. There he was at the sink with a scourer in his hand, suds up to his elbow.

'You don't have to do those, darling.'

'Pearl Fay never lets a dirty dish sit in her sink.'

'Well, Pearl Fay isn't here now, is she? We can finally breathe.'

Thanks to Dawne, Pearl Fay had decided to join Herbert at a convention for lawnmower-parts dealers in McComb, Mississippi. It would be killing two birds with one stone, Pearl Fay figured, since McComb was only a few miles from Tula Springs across the state line. She would be able to visit her mother, as well – something she had been feeling guilty about, not seeing enough of her mother. Mr. Norris found this reprehensible, using her own mama as a beard. He thought she was through sneaking around. He thought her new policy was truth and honesty above all else. So heartfelt were his objections that at one point it looked as if he had won Pearl Fay over. She said she would call Herbert and tell him that unless he left his wife and filed for divorce, she would never see him again. But then she and Dawne had stayed up all night repairing headgear for the Mermaidens, and the very next morning Dawne had booked a flight for her to McComb via Memphis, Jackson, and Meridian. Weighed down by guilt, almost as if he were the one committing adultery, Mr. Norris nevertheless found one small consolation. At least he would not have to worry about anything untoward developing between Bruce Powers and Pearl Fay. There would be one less headache at work.

'Those are the ugliest shoes I ever saw on a man,' Dawne said.

The elderly gentleman delivering pizzas looked stricken. Feeling sorry for him, Mr. Norris added a couple of dollars to his tip before closing the front door.

'That was a terrible thing to say. Did you see that poor man's face?'

'I was talking about *your* shoes, darling. You don't think he thought I meant . . .'

She flung open the door and cried out, 'Yours are wonderful! I adore your shoes, darling.'

But the delivery man was already backing the minivan down the drive. Next door, the old Italian pouring salt into the ice-cream machine on his rickety back porch glanced down at his brogans and shrugged.

'Oh, I feel just awful, Lloyd.'

'You should. And by the way, these shoes cost two hundred and thirty dollars.'

'That's a sin.'

'Could you move that mridanga, please? I don't know why I have to have your mridanga on my kitchen table.'

'You sound just like Pearl Fay.'

He set the pizza down beside the drum. Starving, he hoped Dawne had been telling the truth when she said she wouldn't want anything for supper, nothing at all.

'A real sin, darling,' she said, helping herself to a slice loaded with turkey pepperoni and lactose-free cheese. 'They look like something a fag would wear.'

The mozzarella stuck in his throat. His eyes watered. She pounded him on the back.

'Thanks,' he said, as she brought him a glass of water.

'You OK?'

'As a matter of fact, no. I find your language extremely offensive.'

'"Darling" doesn't mean anything. I call everyone "darling."'

He waved his slice impatiently. 'Hasn't Pearl Fay told you anything at all about me? For your information, I just happen to *be* a fag.'

She smiled sweetly. 'Bless your heart.'

'Don't bless my heart, Dawne. I am.'

'You're not either.'

'I most certainly am. And if this fact bothers you, well, you're more than welcome to move right out of this house.'

Still standing, she patted his head. 'You're cute, you know? But you're no fag.'

'Would you please stop using that word?'

'Lambie pie, don't you know what "fag" means? It has nothing to do with your sexuality. I know a lot of straight men who are fags.'

'Oh, come on.'

'It just means you're all about style, like you got to be stylish all the time. Believe me, Lloyd, you've got an awful long way to go for that.'

Something touched his rear end. Looking around, he saw she was resting a foot on his chair. Though the Dickey crew sock was thick, the foot itself seemed surprisingly delicate.

'Do you mind, Dawne?'

'Huh?'

'Your foot.'

'It itches.' She picked her blue Con Ed helmet off the counter and scraped her sole with that.

'So, I'm not a fag?'

'Definitely not, sweetie. And please, don't take such big bites. My Moony used to eat like that, practically inhaled the food. And look what happened to him.'

'Would you maybe like to turn that thing off?'

She had directed the built-in light on her helmet at his slice.

'You're more like a closet queen,' she said, obliging. 'That's what I told Pearl Fay.'

'But I'm not in the closet.'

'Makes no difference. It's your basic personality type. You'll always have women fluttering around, making a fuss over you. And you'll enjoy all those rumors about sucking toes and stuff. Pearl Fay, you know—'

'I can't stand—'

'She was pretty upset about that picnic for a while. The idea that you might ever have fooled around with another woman, it makes her wild. You never have, have you?'

'Stop goosing me, please.'

Dawne laughed, a lovely, silvery laugh that sounded both lady-like and free. 'See, you love it, being teased about women. That's how your type clings to its manhood. You want to have your cake and eat it.'

'I resent that, Dawne. It's not fair at all. Would a closet queen tell his secretary that he was gay, the secretary that everyone warned him not to tell because she was so homophobic?'

To hear himself dismissed by this woman – handsome as she might appear with the helmet on – was too galling after what he had accomplished that morning. He had finally stood up to Dusty and told her the facts of life. Oddly enough, though, Dusty had simply shrugged and said, 'So? What do you want me to do about it?' Of course, Dusty had just broken up with her boyfriend from the wig shop in Rahway. It was straight cross-dressers she was prejudiced against now. She said she would never trust another one as long as she lived.

'Lloyd,' Dawne said, taking another slice, yet still standing (she never actually sat down at a table to eat), 'you can tell all the people your little heart likes, it's not going to make any difference. You're still your basic closet queen. Oh, lamb, don't look so hurt. There's nothing the least bit wrong with being a closet queen. Some of my best friends are, I swear. Please don't make me feel bad for saying all this. I'm just trying to help. When I tease you about girls, well, I do that to my friends, and they just love it. Once you accept who you are, nothing anyone says can hurt you.'

Though he hadn't finished even a single slice, he pushed the pizza away. He had lost his appetite. 'Speaking of types, what about your parading around in those overalls? Did you see the way that delivery man looked at you? He must have thought you were a . . . One of those, you know . . .'

'A dyke?'

He winced. 'I was going to say les – You know, someone who—'

'You don't like that word, do you?' She glared. 'Dyke.'

'I would never use that term on any woman – it's degrading. My secretary happens to have a crewcut and nose ring, and I don't call her that. Of course, she doesn't have to go around looking the way she does. Is it my fault that I thought she might like women? So it turns out she hates gays and . . .'

'And dykes! Of course, you *would* have a secretary like that!'

With a sob Dawne yanked another slice from the box and bolted from the kitchen.

He caught up with her in Pearl Fay's bedroom, where she now occupied the other twin bed, at least for the duration of the parts convention in McComb.

'Dawne, you don't understand. I wasn't calling you that. I know you're extremely feminine and really pretty and just because you dress funny—'

'You male pig! I *am* a dyke! And I'm proud of it, too.'

He just stood there.

'I always suspected you hated me, Lloyd. I thought it was because maybe you thought I was intrusive when I was trying so hard to blend in with everyone here. But now I know the real reason. You can't stand dykes. You can't even say the word, like it's something too disgusting.'

'Look, I don't care what you are, Dawne. Really. And I'm sorry if I – But would you please stop crying. And look, you're getting cheese on the sham.'

'Leave me alone! You're just like my mama's male pig boyfriend!'

'I like all kinds of women, every kind.'

'Then why did you tell me to get out of this house when it isn't even yours and I'm paying rent and you're not!'

'That was when I thought you were straight. You really do seem straight to me, I can't help it.'

'Go ahead, kick a man when he's down.'

'Dawne, please, I'm sorry, but—'

'I wish I was dead! I really do!'

'The sham, Dawne, please be careful.'

Chapter Eighteen

The buzzer sounded, but Joe Pollock stayed right where he was. One of the pieces of dyed macaroni that festooned the wall of his Eleventh Street apartment had fallen off – and he was determined to glue it back on exactly in place. Ever since he had been promoted to sergeant some forty-five years ago, Joe Pollock had made a tradition of decorating whatever room he happened to find himself in at Christmas – whether it was Cologne or Manila or Mobile – with a flag made entirely of red, white, and blue macaroni. Above his nonworking fireplace hung a gilt-framed, laminated article from the December 12, 1959, issue of *Stars and Stripes*. In it Sgt. Pollock explained how each year he used a fresh batch of macaroni for his Yankee Noodle. And how much trouble it had been to revamp his Noodle because of Hawaii and Alaska.

The Noodle used to come down promptly on January 2. But in the past few years, Joe Pollock had begun to wonder why it couldn't stay up a little longer. Was there any law that said Christmas decorations had to be down so soon? The doggone thing took more and more out of him, weeks of painstaking dyeing that began in early November. And it was getting harder and harder to make the noodles stick. Every morning he'd wake up to a new bald spot. So why not give folks more time to appreciate all the work that went into it? As a matter of fact, he had a potential student coming by that very afternoon, a dame who played the alto recorder. Surely she would be impressed. The Noodle covered an entire wall and made the living room, which looked out on an airshaft, one of the most upbeat places a person could ever hope to take lessons in.

'Hold your horses!' he called out.

The blue macaroni finally back in place, he looked at his watch. 1:35. If it was her, she was an hour early – not a good sign. Too eager. He didn't like dames who were too eager.

Out on the landing after buzzing the downstairs door, Joe caught a glimpse of brown trousers. No, this definitely wouldn't do. He wasn't going to teach any dame in trousers, thank you very much.

'Pollock!'

And such a mannish voice.

'Go away!'

'UPS!'

'What?'

'Delivery!'

A minute later the UPS man had trudged upstairs with both boxes, one in each hand. Joe Pollock signed the computerized tablet.

'You look like you could handle yourself in the ring,' Joe said, adding 'Sergeant' to his signature.

A few white hairs on the UPS man's chest bristled over the open top button of his shirt. 'What's that?'

'Ever do any boxing?'

'Have a nice day, sir.'

Joe Pollock slammed the door shut. So he finally got his clothes back from the Doc. Sure, the guy had been holding them hostage, trying to lure Joe back to Washington Heights. But Joe Pollock was no sucker. He wasn't going to take the bait. The Doc had to learn his lesson. No one feels sorry for Joe Pollock. Absolutely no one.

As he ripped open a carton to make an inventory of his silk shirts, he noticed the return address. Dr. Edgar Bennet. Was the Doc going a little gaga? Surely he could remember his own name. You drink all that tea, though, and there's no telling how it affects the old noggin.

'So what do you think of a man who never learns how to defend himself?' Joe Pollock asked his new student. She was seated with her back to the Yankee Noodle. Looking straight at it, she had told him, she wouldn't have been able to play a note. She would be admiring it too much.

'All my life,' he went on, 'I've considered it my duty to teach my boys how to defend themselves.'

'How nice. How many sons do you have, Joe?'

'I'm talking about my band, the men in my band.'

'Oh, of course. How silly of me. Roger did say you never were married.'

Roger was this woman's brother-in-law. Joe had bumped into him at a free afternoon concert at Juilliard. During the Vietnam War, Roger and Joe had both conducted bands in Manila. Now Roger was teaching theory at the school there in Lincoln Center. When he heard Joe complain about not being able to find a single student to teach in all of New York, Roger had suggested his sister-in-law. Joe was dubious at first. He had had such bad luck that he didn't even bother to ask Roger how much she weighed. He just figured it would be another dud. But when he opened the door for her, it had been a pleasant surprise. She was a little old – mid-fifties, he'd say – but comely. And her lacquered ginger-red hair looked so neat. Not a strand was out of place.

'Monteverdi,' he said, examining the music she had brought. 'Let's hear a scale first.'

From her ample lap she picked up the recorder. It was a good scale, beautifully executed. But then as she descended from B^b, he noticed the ring. Married. It was the very first question he should have asked Roger. How could he have been so dumb?

'You know, you can tell a lot from a scale, Midge.'

'Madge.'

'Every single band I conducted – eleven in all – the first thing I made them do was play me a scale. Funny how the men who could take care of themselves, they always could play me an honest scale. Good with their fists.'

'How interesting.'

'Yes, ma'am. It was the weaklings I had trouble with, the ones who got picked on. I had a bassoon once, couldn't get nowhere with him. His scales were awful. Then I taught him a little about the manly art – bolstered his confidence. You got to go the extra mile for some folks. It's part of your duty, you know.'

'I hope this doesn't mean we're going to fight, Joe.'

'What? No, ma'am, you play a mean scale. And that bassoon, he learned how to play one himself. I figure that, including the bassoon, plus the clarinet and that piccolo in Fort Dix, I must have saved a good baker's dozen men from becoming fairies. Not a bad record, I'd say.'

'You can't be serious, Joe.'

'You calling me a liar? If anything, that's a conservative figure.' He stubbed out his cigarette. 'What gets me, you think I get any gratitude? Not a one of them realizes what I did for them. Not a single one. They've all gone on to live normal lives, every last one of them married. And they haven't a clue. Not a clue who saved them.'

'Joe, really, I'm sure your intentions were very well meant, but don't you think if they really were gay, they would have been better off—'

'In the brig? Court-martialed? Their wrists slit?'

'Really, Joe.'

'You think I haven't seen all that with my own eyes?'

'Well, I . . . Times have changed. I'm sure servicemen today . . . Oh, Joe, what are you doing?'

'I can't teach you nothing,' he said, unscrewing the recorder. He placed the two parts gently in her case, but did not close it. Something was missing. He had such a strong sense that something was still missing. And then looking at her, the ginger hair dyed so expertly, he remembered the ivory belly dancer. It was still in Washington Heights.

'Joe, please, I'm sorry. I didn't mean to offend you.'

'Let's hear it then.'

'What?'

'The Monteverdi, take a whack at it.'

Chapter Nineteen

On Saturday afternoon Mr. Norris was watching television in the den while Dawne was upstairs studying in the sewing room. For the past three years she had been a part-time student at CUNY, working toward a master's degree in counseling. The paper due on Monday – a three-hundred-word essay on Michel Foucault – meant that Mr. Norris was not to disturb her for any reason at all – not even a fire. She'd just as soon die, anyway.

Mr. Sunnyside was just about to be crowned Mr. Queens, heavyweight division, when the door to the den shot open, banging against the wall.

'Didn't you hear the doorbell? You make me come all the way downstairs, and it's for you.'

'Who is it, Dawne?'

'How should I know?'

'Thank you, I'm coming.' He smiled pleasantly to help her see that he did not hate her, that he was not a male pig. With a sigh she went back upstairs.

First he had to find a breath mint. Champagne, of course, was not supposed to smell. But he wanted to be sure that the mimosas he had been sipping were not detectable. Any odor would give a false impression that he drank during the day on Saturdays. And nothing could be further from the truth. The only reason he had made an exception on this particular Saturday was because of the lawnmower convention in McComb. And because he wanted to be extra pleasant for Dawne's sake.

No mints. But there was some mouthwash in the entertainment cabinet. He gargled while tucking in his shirt and then spit out the free WinTerFressh (NyLo had designed its label) into a pot of wilting petunias.

The man on the front stoop looked vaguely familiar. Well-nourished, with a bland, all-knowing look, he was most likely someone from Queen of Heaven. Could it be the new priest, the one he had confessed to behind a screen last Saturday? Father McBride was on vacation, and Mr. Norris had not wanted the new priest to get a bad impression of him so early on. So he had knelt behind a screen rather than sit in a chair for the more modern face-to-face reconciliation.

'Your fly.'

'Huh?' Mr. Norris looked down. 'Won't you come in?' he said, zipping up.

'You're having your meter read?' the man asked, one gray wiry eyebrow cocked.

Mr. Norris kicked aside the Con Ed overalls that Dawne had left lying on the floor near the stairs. 'No, Father, this is just, you know, our boarder's, the lady who answered the door.'

'I see – the lady in the negligée.'

Of course, Dawne would have to study this afternoon in one of Pearl Fay's frilliest Victoria's Secrets, with nothing on underneath. It was so childish of her to try to get back at him that way. As if he really cared what she wore.

'That wasn't really her negligée. It's my wife's. See, she's a lesbian, doesn't like men at all.'

'So that makes it OK, I guess. Your wife's a lesbian, and one has one's needs.'

'Oh, no, no, the one upstairs, she's . . . I don't have any needs, really. And actually, I don't have a wife, either.'

It was so hard to think straight with the television blaring. The crowd roared as Ms. Kew Gardens, clad only in the skimpiest thong imaginable, showed off her triceps.

'Loathsome,' the man muttered as Mr. Norris hastily shut the door to the den.

'It was actually men I was watching, Father. I hate it when they switch around like that.'

'What's with this "father" business, Norris? Anyway, I was on my way upstate to pick up the Countess and thought you might like to tag along. She's a houseguest of that dreadful bore, Lady Schuyler-Tuft, and I must rescue her posthaste.'

Of course – it was Mrs. Kundaa's boyfriend. But Mr. Norris felt little relief. He'd almost rather it were a priest snooping around than someone connected with the office – and with Mrs. Kundaa, of all people.

'I'm sorry, but I'm—'

'There's a Henry Moore on the grounds and several Saint-Gaudens. People actually pay to see Schuyler-Tuft's little cottage. And yet for you, my child, admission is free. The Countess insists you come.'

'I'd love to some other time, but, see, I'm so busy this after-noon.'

'Yes, I can see.'

'Tell her I'm really sorry and explain . . .'

'Oh, I'll explain all right.'

'Wait, I . . .'

But without even bothering to say goodbye, the man had walked out the door in a slightly prissy, huffy way that discouraged Mr. Norris from pursuing him any farther. Besides, it had started to rain. Who wanted to look at Henry Moore in the rain?

The BMW pulled expertly out of the drive into the street.

*   *   *

'Who was that?'

Mr. Norris looked up from *Phèdre*, which he was reading during commercials. 'No one.'

'What do you mean, "no one"? Pearl Fay will want to know. I told her I'd keep tabs on you and I'm about to give her a call.'

'If you must know, it was Mrs. Kundaa's boyfriend. I've forgotten his name.'

'Who's Mrs. Condom?'

'Kundaa. Pearl Fay knows.'

'Maybe I'd like to know myself – or is that being too pushy?'

'Actually, it is being a little pushy.'

'Like a dyke, huh?'

'No, it has nothing to do with being a lesbian. It's just that I'd like to have some privacy in my life – just an ounce or two.'

Her eyes welling with tears, Dawne turned from the doorway and hurried upstairs.

After Mass on Sunday, Mr. Norris decided to overcome his scruples about doing any work on a day of rest. It would be a sin he was sure Father McBride would understand when he got back from the Galápagos. Indeed, Mr. Norris wondered if it might even seem silly, confessing that he had done Dawne's laundry on Sunday – and ironed. More than anything, Mr. Norris wanted peace in his life. He did not want Dawne resenting him. Why couldn't she see that he was basically, deep down, a nice guy? As he labored in the basement, spraying starch on the overalls to get rid of the double crease, he looked forward to going straight to bed as soon as he was through. Those mimosas had been a terrible idea yesterday. Never again. He was so drained he could barely see straight.

'What did you go and do that for?' Dawne said from the twin bed he had once occupied, before the divorce.

He hung the overalls he had brought upstairs on the canopy post of Pearl Fay's bed. Then he went all the way back down to the basement for the plastic laundry basket, filled with Dawne's towels and linens, everything neatly folded. When she saw this, she put down her Foucault.

'Come here.'

'I used a softener – I hope you don't mind.'

'Come here.'

He took a step or two nearer the bed, close enough for her to reach out and yank him by the belt. The hug was awkward. He had to balance on one arm. And it was quick. She gave him a little shove before he could return the hug.

'Peace, darling?'

'Peace.'

'Where you going?'

'To bed.'

'But what about those people?'

'What people?'

'Didn't I tell you? While you were at church, Walter called.'

'Walter?'

'That man who came over to see you yesterday. He said they were going to drop by or something on their way back to the city.'

'They? No, it's out of the question. You'll just have to call them back and tell them I'm totally, completely indisposed.'

Foucault was back in her hands, and she was highlighting with a Marks-a-Lot. 'Huh?'

'You'll have to—'

'I don't have the number. And besides, it would be rude.' Her shapely legs pedaled the air, then scissored with the pointed toes of a synchronized routine. 'You're not going to make me be rude, say what you want.'

'It's very inconsiderate of you, Dawne. You should have checked with me first. I'm dying, literally dying, and now I'm supposed to entertain Mrs. Kundaa and her boyfriend?'

'Go take a nap. You'll feel better.'

'How can I? The house is a mess. We're going to have to clean, you know.'

'Mm.'

'What time are they coming?'

'Mm.'

'Dawne?'

'Heavens to Betsy, do you want me to flunk out? Please, lamb, I've got to concentrate. They said around six or sevenish, OK? Now I'm begging you, let me get this paper done.'

The slender columns of the split-level seemed to warp as the headlights of the BMW swept over them. It was tenish – 10:22, to be precise. Dawne was already in bed. Mr. Norris, still dying, had nonetheless managed to make himself and the house presentable. Enormous doses of caffeine – coffee alternating with tea – had helped, even if it did make his colon a bit queasy. As soon as Mrs. Kundaa and her boyfriend left, he would dose himself with paregoric. Without this medicine to look forward to, he could never endure such a visit.

Mrs. Kundaa was swaddled in a floral mohair shawl that Walter's great-great-grandfather, she explained, had bought in Mysore during the Mutiny to protect the finish on his fortepiano. As Walter unwrapped her, he pointed out the hand-stitched decorative border, which Mr. Norris dutifully admired. Then he took the André Pink Champagne Mrs. Kundaa thrust upon him and said yes, he would do the honors.

'But it's not chilled,' Walter protested.

'All right, we'll have it after dinner. Go chill it,' she said to Mr. Norris.

He blinked. 'Dinner?'

Mrs. Kundaa turned on Walter. 'I told you we should have stopped at that Denny's.'

Walter drew himself up. 'But I was told there was a T-bone going to waste, and if we didn't eat it, she was going to throw it out.'

'No one said anything to me about dinner,' Mr. Norris declared. While cleaning, he had come across the leftover T-bone on top of the breadbox. Eating the steak had helped neaten up the kitchen.

'That woman who came to read your meter,' Walter said, 'she told me when I called this morning not to worry about dinner. My Special K could eat the steak, and I could have a—'

'Why you listen to a meter reader, Walter,' Mrs. Kundaa said, 'I'll never know. You must forgive my fiancé, Lloyd. He's getting Pearl Fay mixed up with some repairman who answered your door yesterday. You see why I have never approved of ladies going into the rougher trades. It leads to no good.'

'Actually, Mrs. Kundaa, Mrs. Schmidlapp does work for Con Ed and—'

'And here we go again,' Mrs. Kundaa sang out in her thrilling contralto. 'Me, me, me! I just mentioned the biggest event of my entire life – not including Serge's funeral, of course – and you blithely skate right over it. You are impossible, S. Lloyd.'

They had drifted into the parlor, where Walter was pulling out alphabetized CDs from the spinning wheel.

'Big event, Mrs. Kundaa? Walter, please don't—'

'What do you think the André's for? Soon,' she declared, brushing some crumbs from her black dress, 'it will be Mrs. Edgecombe.'

'Oh.' Mr. Norris frowned. 'Have I met him, this Edgecombe?'

'Oh, Lloyd dear, you are a card. Didn't I tell you he was a card, Walter? Anyway, it was only a few hours ago, in Lady S-T's orangery, that I accepted Walter's proposal.'

'*My* proposal?'

'Hush, Walter. There's no need to bore Lloyd with such details.' Taking Mr. Norris's free hand, she pulled him down beside her on the settee. 'Walter's still a bit concerned about his genes. His mother and father are second cousins, you see, and he couldn't stand the thought of passing on anything iffy. That's why we've waited so long. We've been dating ever since Walter got back from Vietnam.'

'It wasn't just that,' Walter observed. 'It was your smoking. I said I'd never marry a smoker.'

'Oh, yes, there was that, too. And of course, it goes without saying, there was Serge. I've been in mourning so long, and Walter's been so patient. Not once has he been impetuous, not a single liberty taken with me. And they say men are at the mercy of their hormones.'

Mr. Norris blinked.

'I'll never forgive that woman for spreading that vicious rumor that Walter once spent the night in my apartment.'

'Your landlady?'

'She paid for it, though. It cost her a pretty penny.' Mrs. Kundaa's smile was grim. 'In any case, we have surmounted every obstacle, Walter and I. Except one. Can you guess what that is, S. Lloyd?'

Mr. Norris shook his head.

'We are in need of a best man. Do you happen to know of anyone who might be available?' She gave Mr. Norris's hand a painful squeeze. 'Someone with a sterling character and a heart of gold?'

'No, I don't.'

'Don't be coy, dear. You know very well whom I'm referring to.'

'Why me? What have I ever done to deserve . . .'

'Nothing at all except to comport yourself with dignity and couth. I was just saying to Walter on our way here to Yonkers that I consider you the last bastion of decorum in this disgraceful age we live in.'

'But, Mrs. Kundaa, I'm really not that decorous at all.'

'Do you hear that, Walter? Only a true gentleman would dare admit such a thing. And, Walter, I must insist you take off my shawl.'

'I'm cold.'

'Turn up the thermostat then. And do something with this bottle. Put it on ice.'

Mr. Norris let Walter take the champagne into the kitchen. Meanwhile his head swirled with excuses, trying to sort the plausible from the implausible. He simply could not be the best man at the wedding Mrs. Kundaa had started to plan aloud from the settee, their hands still linked. It would take place at Rothermeer, Lady S-T's estate, when the cherry and dogwood were in first bloom. There would be no minister, of course. A judge from the traffic court would do, someone her dear Serge used to play Parcheesi with. She supposed she would have to have the girls from the Leeuwarden. But the footladies would be invited as well. And the janitress. No bridesmaids, of course. That, she said with an emphatic squeeze, was a silly tradition, absolutely demeaning to all concerned.

'A best man is sort of silly, too,' Mr. Norris ventured.

'Nonsense. You can't throw the baby out with the bathwater.'

'But I hardly know Walter. If he doesn't say who he is, I forget.'

'What does that matter? You've known me forever, and soon Walter will be like a brother to you, one of your dearest friends.'

'But I don't like him.'

'No one likes Walter at first. Believe me, I should know. But he grows on you. Beneath all that horrid snobbery, that bossy way he has of ordering everyone around like recruits, as if he were still in that moronic navy – well, what do you expect me to do, S. Lloyd? I'm sixty-something. I can't wait forever for the perfect man, can I?'

Though she had freed his hand, the look in her eyes prompted him to exclaim, 'No, no, you can't. Walter actually isn't so bad. I know it must be hard to find men around your age – not that you're that old. You don't look sixty-something at all.'

'I know most people think I'm only forty-nine. They tell me that all the time. But that still makes me a year older than Walter.'

'He's only forty-eight?'

'Hush, if he heard you say that . . .' She was rummaging about in her handbag. 'It's been another one of those obstacles we've had to surmount, his age. He claims I'm robbing the cradle.'

He shifted an inch or two away from her. 'Has he ever been married before?'

'You're joking, of course. Do you think I would touch another woman's leavings? That's what's made it so hard for me, dear. I refuse to even *look* at a divorced man.'

'Does narrow the field a bit.'

'You're telling me.'

'But – Mrs. Kundaa!' He plucked the cigarette from her lips. She had lit it without his even noticing. It was the smell, the smoke, that had alerted him.

'Oh, Lloyd dear, thank you, thank you. I didn't even realize what I was doing.'

'We better open this window. Move over a little so I can—'

'I just went on automatic pilot.'

'Quick, spray something.'

'I beg your pardon?'

'You must have some perfume or something. Hurry.'

She peered inside her alligator handbag. 'Keys, toothpicks, Phillips head, unmentionable, pepper gas – ah, Walter's hairspray.'

Fortunately, the Hermès was scented. Mr. Norris took the bottle and sprayed her liberally – then himself and the settee cushions for good measure.

'It's awful,' she said between coughs. 'I can't stand that odor.'

'Let's go, then. The kitchen.'

Walter was seated at the cherry dinette table while Dawne rooted through the refrigerator.

'Lloyd darling, how could you not feed this poor man? He's starving, absolutely starving.'

The light from the vegetable bin made the purloined Victoria's Secret she had on a bit too transparent.

'Go back to bed,' Mr. Norris said. And then to the room at large: 'She has to get up at five.'

'How can I sleep with all your racket, darling?' The refrigerator slammed shut. 'I just know there was a T-bone somewhere.'

'My Walter doesn't eat meat,' Mrs. Kundaa said, yanking the

mohair shawl from his shoulders. 'If he did, though, he might not be so cold all the time.'

'That's exactly what I just told him,' Dawne said. 'He's got to change his diet.'

'I believe I can determine what's best for my fiancé to consume, Miss.'

'Mrs.,' Mr. Norris corrected. 'The widow Schmidlapp.'

'What?'

'I told you, Mrs. K,' Walter said. 'You wouldn't believe there was a meter reader living here.'

'Darling, really,' Dawne said to Mr. Norris, 'be a good boy and find that steak. My conscience won't let me sleep until this man is fed. When you ask someone to dinner, it's kind of rude not to feed them anything, don't you think?'

She goosed him into action with a raised bare foot.

'Stop that!' Mr. Norris said, stumbling forward into Mrs. Kundaa's generous bosom. As he freed himself from her impulsive embrace, Walter wagged a finger.

'Naughty, naughty.'

'I believe I've had just about enough of Yonkers,' Mrs. Kundaa said. Her face was as crimson as the gossamer threads of the negligée that had alighted upon Mr. Norris's shoulder.

'You smell so good, darling,' Dawne said, sniffing his neck.

'Get away from me, please. Now look, she's going. Mrs. Kundaa, wait! Don't forget Walter! Walter, get up. How can you just sit there? Go explain about Mrs. Schmidlapp. Tell her she doesn't mean anything. She's nothing at all.'

'Right, Walter,' Dawne said, slamming a can of tuna onto the counter. 'I don't mean a thing in this house. I'm just the resident dyke, that's all, maid, cook, and scrubwoman. So what'll it be, whole wheat or rye!'

'See what happens when you play rough?' Walter said as headlights flared in the drive. 'Someone always gets hurt.'

'Run, Walter,' Mr. Norris said, shoving him toward the kitchen door. 'She's leaving!'

'Let her go. See what I care.'

Barreling out into the drive, Mr. Norris waved both arms vigorously. But the BMW bumped over the curb and, after sideswiping the neighbors' rhododendrons, continued down the street at a rate just slow enough for Mr. Norris to give chase for a block or two. He was hoping this might induce a heart attack. But instead, he just kept on living.

Chapter Twenty

At six on the dot Mr. Norris descended from the fiftieth floor to the marble lobby. He was still brooding about the message on his voice mail from Mrs. Norris. Be sure to clear out all the jasmine from the gutter on the roof before it blooms again in the spring, she reminded him, and oh, by the way, she and her mama were going to take a little side trip to New Orleans to sample a new hybrid of black and blue popcorn. Since Dawne had yet to provide him with a meal in Yonkers and he was too exhausted by work to cook for himself, Mr. Norris decided to get a bite to eat in the city before loading himself aboard the express bus.

NyLo's Eighth Avenue address was on the very frontier of propriety. Though the building, headquarters to a law firm that had recently donated a million dollars to the Needy Swimsuit Model Fund, was even taller and classier than its neighbor, the Worldwide Plaza, it was also directly across the street from lap dancers. Standing on the corner, unable to determine if he had the energy to walk all the way to Wendy's, which would be more economical than a restaurant, Mr. Norris happened to

catch a glimpse of the Beak emerging from the lap dancers'
establishment.

So that was that, the mystery solved. Not only was the Beak
straight, but he was a lowlife, as well. Oddly enough, this seemed
to perk Mr. Norris up. No longer would that tanned, chiseled
face trouble him on the elevator. No longer would he have to
glance furtively at the deep creases alongside that patrician nose.
No longer would those rugged veined hands clutching the furled
umbrella, bespoke, no doubt, from a London shop so exclusive
that it refused to serve the Royal Family, the umbrella he always
seemed to carry, rain or shine, no longer would the strength in
those hands, accustomed, no doubt, to the rigging and tackle of
a trim yacht . . .

Mr. Norris suddenly realized the man was walking straight
toward him, across Eighth Avenue. And he, Mr. Norris, was
just standing there, obstructing pedestrian traffic. Making an
about-face, he retreated back into the marble lobby. The last
thing he wanted was for that creep to think that he had been
gaping at him. Or worse, trailing him. A loathsome man, probably
cheating on his wife, and yet so blinded by his swollen ego that he
could actually believe that decent folks would care to notice his
existence at all.

Now what did that homewrecker mean by heading right for the
revolving doors? This was outrageous. He was actually coming
inside the building, and it was time for everyone to go home!

A lush stand of bamboo, newly imported for the three-story
atrium at the south end of the lobby, provided a suitable place
for Mr. Norris to take umbrage. The Beak, unaware, strolled right
past him.

'Yoo hoo, Mr. Norris!'

He winced as his name seemed to ricochet off the steely Calder
mobile that loomed above. Peering out from the foliage, he saw
what was threatening to become a familiar face. Seated at one
of the grillwork tables provided for the general public, Walter
Edgecombe beckoned.

'What are you doing lurking in the bamboo?'

'Hello, Walter. I was just on my way to Wendy's.'

'Dear me, is that the young lady you have stashed away in your apartment?'

'That's Tudi. And who told you I had someone stashed away?'

'Who do you think, dear?'

'Mrs. Kundaa knows very well that I'm just doing it to help the poor girl. Tudi's roommate is . . .'

Mr. Norris had promised Tudi not to tell anyone about her awkward circumstances. Indeed, he couldn't blame this poor temp in Human Resources for not wanting people in the office to know that her roommate was a call girl.

'Relax, Mr. Norris. I'm sure Tudi and Wendy are all dykes, too. Now do Uncle Walter a favor and bring him a martini. Make sure it's ShopRite gin and a twist, straight up.'

'Where am I supposed to find a martini?'

With a wag of his little finger, Walter indicated a bar that Mr. Norris, in all his days at NyLo, had never noticed before. His unvarying route to and from the elevator bank did not include a view of the wagonette with its red-striped awning at the far end of the lobby.

'I'll watch our places here. I figure I have just enough time to get loaded before I go up and rescue my mohair from the Dragon Lady.'

'Really, Walter, I can't—'

'Hurry along.'

In the interest of office diplomacy, Mr. Norris headed for the bar. Even though Walter and Mrs. Kundaa were no longer an item – they had broken off their engagement after that unfortunate visit to Yonkers on Sunday – it would be wise to keep Walter as an ally. Walter had no difficulty understanding Dawne's very minor role as a boarder and promised to explain to his ex-fiancée just how Sapphic the widow Schmidlapp was. Mr. Norris, of course, was uneasy about certain rumors that had begun to circulate in the office about him, that he was not as completely gay as he claimed, that he was something of a sly operator. Penny, his former secretary, had never quite recovered from those harsh words about her derrière. The more Mr. Norris apologized, the more fearful she seemed. As for Dusty, she continued to smirk every time he alluded to his minority status. 'Bruce Powers is known in the industry as the biggest ballbuster around,' Dusty had recently informed Mr. Norris. 'So don't play that helpless little minority act around me, Norris. You broke that pig. I don't know how, but you did. And if you pat me one more time on the head, I'm going to have you up for sexual harassment.'

'Do you think maybe you could put ShopRite gin in it? And a twist instead of this olive here?'

'Look, Mac,' the bartender said, 'I don't need to hear this *after* I make the drink.'

'But I said, I mean I thought I said . . . Never mind. Thank you. Gee, I didn't realize you sold sandwiches and stuff here, too. They look so good. I should—'

'Next.'

Laden with the martini, a glass of 1% fat milk, and a bag of nonfat pork rinds, Mr. Norris returned to find that the place Walter had been holding for him had been usurped.

'Thank you, Miss. Just set it down here. That's good. Now where are you off to? Sit.'

'There's no chair,' Mr. Norris pleaded.

Walter leaned back and appropriated one from a neighboring table. 'There. Set that little fanny down, Miss Norris.'

Mr. Norris sat.

'This is the guy I was just telling you about, Monke, the one who was stalking me.'

'How do you do?' the Beak said, giving Mr. Norris his hand.

'I was not stalking . . . I was just . . .' The rough, callused palm sent a thrilling charge, enough voltage to stand the bride of Frankenstein's hair on end.

'He was lurking in the bamboo right over there,' Walter went on. 'It's been years since I've been stalked. My diet must be working.'

'You look familiar,' the Beak said, still grasping the paralyzed hand. 'St. Patrick's?'

'Every day,' Walter supplied. 'He's NyLo's resident saint.'

'Well, folks, got to run. I'm really late for a meeting.'

As the Beak headed for the elevators, Walter moaned. 'What a hunk. Mr. Chadford Monke-Peelston the fourth.'

'He's too short. And he's not that good-looking.'

'You blind, Miss?'

'Walter, would you please stop calling me that?' The milk helped relieve his parched mouth. 'I find it degrading and offensive.'

'The man is a dream, the perfect husband for you, *Ms.* Norris. Ah, how quaint. She blushes.'

'He's too dark. And that beak of his . . .'

Walter set down his plastic stem glass. 'Hold it right there, Norris. Most of my friends are Jewish, my dearest friends, so don't start in with any of your Louisiana good ole boy talk. I won't stand for it.'

'What are you talking about? I just said he was too tanned. And he's not even Jewish.'

'No, but his wife is. She's on the board of the Anti-Defamation League. And he's got a Jewish stepgrandmother.'

Mr. Norris tossed off the rest of his 1%. 'So why are you telling me he'd make such a good husband?'

'You object to the grandmother?'

'Walter, please, enough nonsense. He's married. You shouldn't tease about married people. And besides, how do you know him, anyway?'

'I was waiting for Mrs. K here a week or two ago, having a drink, and he came over and started chatting with me.'

'Hold on. You mean to say you're just sitting here, and he comes over and starts talking to you?'

'He had a petition. They've been trying for months now to drive the X-rated places out of the neighborhood. So I signed.'

'And then he just happens to mention he has a Jewish stepgrandmother and a wife on the board of whatever? Really, Walter . . .'

'You're beginning to look a little green, my pretty. Someday Uncle Walter will teach you how to make friends, too. Anyway, he happened to walk by a minute ago, and I asked him how the petition was going, and he said the lap dancers across the street just tore it up, so it's back to the drawing board and – and why am I telling you all this? It's none of your business.'

'Walter, you tell the man I've been stalking you, you call me "Miss" in front of him . . .'

'I thought you wanted everyone to know your deep, dark secret.'

'My deep, dark secret has nothing to do with him – or you either.'

'Dear Mr. Norris, just because I told you the other night in bed that you weren't my type, that doesn't mean that everyone finds you so plain and unattractive. Surely there will be someone out there for you.'

'Don't say "in bed," Walter, please.'

'But we were. We went to bed together.'

'Walter, you appropriated my fold-out sofa on Sunday. I wouldn't call that "going to bed together."'

'But I was the one who wanted to take the bus back home. You made me spend the night.'

'Look, you were in no condition to get on any bus. And I hope when you go up for your shawl, Walter, you'll apologize to Mrs. Kundaa for all those terrible things you said to her.'

'What terrible things?'

'Don't you remember? When she came back to get you, you said some truly dreadful things that I wish I hadn't heard. I realize it must have been all that champagne you guzzled, but still, I can't blame her for driving off again without you. It was inexcusable behavior, especially when I warned you not to drink so much.'

'You're one to talk.'

'For your information, I didn't touch a drop. Not a drop. You drank the entire bottle yourself and then broke open a bottle of my wife's Glenlivet.'

Mr. Norris did have some paregoric, though. Without this tincture of opium, a rather healthy dose, he never could have endured Dawne's refusal to let a man – i.e., Walter – sleep next door to her in the sewing room upstairs. She said she had learned her lesson the month before when her mama's boyfriend wandered into her bedroom with nothing on and blamed it on Alzheimer's. So Dawne had tossed the raft downstairs and told Mr. Norris to blow it up. The trouble was, neither Mr. Norris nor Walter was in any condition to blow anything up properly. It leaked, too, the raft. So who could blame Mr. Norris for creeping onto the sofa bed once Walter began to snore? He kept as close to the edge as possible, giving himself no room at all, practically on the verge of falling off – but did all this consideration prevent Walter from suddenly sitting up and declaring, 'Don't touch me! I don't want you touching me, sir. You're not my type at all'? Desperate for sleep, Mr. Norris had told Walter not to worry, if he were the last man on earth he wouldn't touch him. So would he please shut the heck up and go back to sleep.

When Walter returned from the wagonette, the olive had been transformed into a delicate spiral of lemon zest. And the Bombay into ShopRite.

'And furthermore, he didn't charge me. Let that be a lesson to you, Norris. Learn to speak up for what you want.'

'But I tried. He just wouldn't listen.'

'You're too intimidated by looks.'

The bartender, an Italian, was indeed stunning. As Mr. Norris chatted with Walter, he did his best not to glance at the man.

'Well, are you just going to let it sit there?'

Mr. Norris regarded the martini Walter had brought him. He had asked for another milk.

'I really should be going.'

'Run along, then. You'll miss *Petticoat Junction*.'

'I don't watch TV.'

'Dawne says that's all you do. And you wonder why you can't find a boyfriend.'

'Advice from an expert.'

'Ah, we're getting catty, are we?'

Mr. Norris took a sip. It was amazing how little he knew about this man he had slept with. And how little he wanted to know, especially after Mrs. Kundaa had refused to let Walter break off the engagement. No, she herself had already broken it off, she proclaimed after returning to Yonkers on Sunday night. She knew all along that it was a terrible mistake to have anything whatsoever to do with a navy man.

'It's too strong, Walter. I can't. I better get going.'

'Ken!'

'Pardon?'

'It just came to me – you and Ken.'

'Who's Ken?'

'Well, if you think that guy you keep on staring at is something, wait till you see Ken.'

Mr. Norris sank back into the iron chair. 'He looks like that bartender?'

'Only not so gray and washed out.'

'Washed out? I've never seen such a build.'

'Ken's much younger – only forty-five. You don't mind a younger man, do you?'

'Walter, I'm forty-three.'

'No, come on.'

Mr. Norris suddenly remembered that he had just turned forty-four the week before. Yet he hadn't lied. He really had forgotten, mainly because there had been no celebration, no cake. Mrs. Norris, who usually made such a fuss over birthdays, hadn't even E-mailed him. Dawne he hadn't told. The only one who had done anything at all was Tudi, who had bought him a drink at T.G.I. Friday's after work – and the bartender had brought out a side of buffalo wings with a candle stuck in it.

'Is he Italian?'

'Ken? No, he's nothing – from Iowa.'

'But he's handsome?'

'Very picky, too. He hardly ever dates.'

'What does he do?'

'He's an auteur.'

'A writer?'

'Dear child, he makes films. Pauline Kael says he's the next Bergman.'

'You're kidding. I love Bergman. I saw *Persona* three times when I was thirteen or fourteen.'

'Impossible. The movie was condemned by your pope, wasn't it?'

'By the Legion of Decency. So?'

'Don't you believe in being decent? Have you no respect for the wisdom of your Church? Imagine what the Legion would say about a date with Ken. Maybe I better not tell him about you.'

'Walter.'

'No, I'm serious. Why should Ken get involved with someone who thinks he can go to Mass every day and then try to pick up Italian bartenders? Personally, I find the whole thing rather revolting. Either you have integrity or you don't.'

'Integrity? You're talking to me about integrity?'

'What's that supposed to mean?'

'Well, Walter, one minute you're getting married, the next you're ... whatever.' From the look Walter was giving him, Mr. Norris figured he had waded in deep enough. Just imagine the havoc this man could wreak if he ever reconciled with Mrs. Kundaa. It was bad enough when the two of them were ex-boyfriend and -girlfriend. 'What I'm trying to say, Walter – the Vatican, see, that's not what it's all about. They don't define what it means to be Catholic, not for me. Let them make their stupid pronouncements about being gay, fine. In the meantime, half their clergy are gay. Those old men in the Vatican, well, I actually feel sorry for them – just imagine having to take four hundred years to forgive Galileo. And besides, I don't stop being an American every time the president or Congress does something I don't approve of, something I think is horribly immoral even. Look at Vietnam. I was going to be a C.O. because of that.' But then he had gotten married, of course.

'A C.O.?'

Mr. Norris took another sip, a gulp, actually. 'Right. I had studied up on one of the Church fathers who talked about just wars and—'

Walter's iron chair screeched over the pale marble. 'There's a limit, Norris. I could maybe overlook your anti-Semitism, deplorable as it may be – and your craven, hypocritical church-going. But I will not sit down with a man who shirked his duty to his country. When I think of what I and my men endured so you could sit back with your lily-white hands and congratulate yourself on how pure and moral you are – well, it's enough to make one ill. You are a disgrace, sir. Good evening.'

And with that, Walter headed for the elevators.

Chapter Twenty-One

Mr. Norris met Ken for coffee that Friday, only two days after Walter had walked off in a huff and left his martini to be finished by Mr. Norris, who didn't like to see things go to waste. If he had any backbone, Mr. Norris perhaps would have told Ken, when Ken had phoned him in Yonkers to ask if he'd like to get together, that he, Mr. Norris, declined to meet him on the grounds that he was not a disgrace and had no respect for anyone who dared call him a disgrace. But the voice on the other end of the line was so manly, so appealing, and visions of a Conan-like Ingmar Bergman danced in his head. This helped Mr. Norris reason more clearly. After all, why should Ken be penalized for Walter's obnoxious behavior? Furthermore, if Walter had really and truly thought he was a disgrace, would he have given Ken the number in Yonkers? Obviously, Walter hadn't been entirely serious at the time, or he had changed his mind later about what it meant to be a C.O.

Why Ken had chosen a Japanese restaurant for coffee Mr. Norris was not sure. Neither was he happy about the time Ken had chosen, 3:45. Mr. Norris hated leaving the office so early, but Ken was not available at any other hour. So Mr. Norris took the train all the way down to Tribeca after being tempted to tell Dusty that it was a business appointment. Instead, he had told the truth. He had a date, the romantic kind. With a man.

'Is something the matter?' Ken asked, as the waiter set a thimbleful of green tea in front of Mr. Norris.

But it wasn't the tea – although Ken should have known they wouldn't have coffee here. Rather, it was Ken himself. How could Walter have said he was better looking than the Italian bartender? There was no comparison at all. Mr. Norris was violently disappointed. He had spent hours the night before wandering through Barney's, Saks, and Bergdorf Goodman looking for the perfect shirt and trousers. And then, after a hurried lunch at his desk that afternoon, he had shaved in the executive washroom and slapped himself with the men's cologne that Mrs. Norris had once told him was foolproof.

'I'm fine.'

'We could go somewhere else if you really must have coffee. It's just that this place is so quiet. I like being the only customers.'

Mr. Norris shrugged.

'What's your name again?'

'Norris.'

'Boyd Norris?'

'Lloyd.'

'Funny, the minute you walked in, I had the feeling we'd met before.'

'Maybe in another life.' As a matter of fact, Ken did seem familiar. 'Just joking,' he added dully.

'Good. I hate all that New Age crap. Or any other sort of crap. You don't believe in any crap, do you?'

'Not in crap, no.'

Outside on the deserted sidewalk a pigeon slouched around like a belligerent drunk. Both men watched it for a moment, hoping to be entertained. As the bird got more and more boring, Mr. Norris considered starting an argument about religion. The only trouble was, it might go on too long. The sooner he could leave, the better.

Ken cleared his throat. 'How is it you know Walter?'

'I don't really know him at all. He's just the friend, the ex-friend, of someone I work with.'

'There's a lot of ex-friends.'

'The ex-fiancée.'

'You work with Kundaa?' He scratched his gray crewcut. 'How can you stand that joint? It's a friggin' nightmare.'

'NyLo? You've been there?'

'Walter asked me to fill in for K ration once when she was in court with her dry cleaner. Never again, man. All day long one fat pig after another ordered me around like I was some sort of maid. They got to have half and half, no cream, a teaspoon of brown sugar, take it back, it's not really brown, it's too sweet. Scum, they're all scum at that joint, rich, filthy bastards.'

It was Lewis, *Mr.* Lewis, minus the blond goatee. And a little sore on his earlobe now where once there had been a gold ring.

'Actually, they're not all scum there,' Mr. Norris said. 'Some are just your average decent, hardworking taxpayers.'

'Don't make me laugh. There was one guy you wouldn't believe. He actually got down on his hands and knees in the CEO's office, groveling. Made me want to puke – and when he left, the boss lady told me he'd been trying to cop a look up her—'

'Well, anyway,' Mr. Norris said loudly, 'I thought you were a filmmaker.' *Oh, God*, he prayed, *please don't let him recognize me.* 'Didn't Pauline Kael say you were the next Bergman?'

Mr. Lewis winced. 'Thanks, pal.'

'But that's a huge compliment, isn't it? I mean, Bergman is my all-time favorite.'

Mr. Lewis's face became even more sour.

'Well, he is.'

'I make cartoons, Boyd, animated cartoons.'

'Oh.'

'She told a friend of mine they were about as lively as *Hour of the Wolf*.'

'Well, anyway . . .' Mr. Norris craned his neck, looking in vain for a waiter. 'Anyway, at least, you know, uh, it's sort of good they broke up. I'm glad they're not getting married, aren't you? I mean, I think I'm glad.'

'Who? Oh, them. Don't be so sure, pal.'

'But they said, both of them, I heard with my own ears.'

'Same thing happened when her old man croaked. Walter was all set to make an ass of himself and marry her.'

'When was this?'

'Must be twenty years ago. I put the kibosh on that, better believe. High time Mrs. K knew the truth about her dear Walter. So I told her he wasn't quite as prim and proper as she might like. Of course, I got my ass hauled into court for it.'

'She sued you?'

Mr. Lewis smiled. 'And lost. Oh, brother, did she ever lose. You should've seen that string of witnesses I was able to come up with, including myself. If I didn't feel so sorry for her, I would've countersued. And Lord knows, I could've used the dough. But I just couldn't.'

'Maybe it would've taught her a good lesson.'

'She's been taught already, believe me.'

Mr. Norris rubbed his foot, which had gone to sleep. They were sitting shoeless on cushions. 'Doesn't seem like it to me. Every time I see her, I feel I'm on the verge of being sued.'

'Yeah, know what you mean. Poor woman, she's still trying to make up for what happened to her, way back. Never got any justice.'

'What? Back when?'

'Over in 'Nam. She was an army nurse, right?'

'She was?'

'Got herself stoned one night during Tet. Bombs going off everywhere, can't blame the old girl for getting high. Next thing she knows, a French lieutenant jumps her. She gets plowed, then goes running out in the street for help and gets zapped. Shrapnel. Out cold, would've bled to death if our pal hadn't come along.'

'Walter?'

'He tore off his shirt, stopped the bleeding, then carried her to a shelter. That's how they met.'

'My God. It's so . . . Come on, did Walter tell you this? You know how he—'

'I was there myself, pal. Right when it happened.'

On the plate between them was a flesh-colored blossom. Mr. Lewis peeled off a petal, a strip of ginger.

'What's worse,' he went on, chewing, 'she was brought up on charges of dereliction of duty. No one except Walter would believe she had actually been raped. The French lieutenant was a stud, had his pick of the litter. He said she'd been hallucinating from the hash she'd been sucking up, sort of a wish fulfillment since she was no Raquel Welch. So after she was reprimanded, she had herself a nervous breakdown and was shipped back to the States.'

'My God.'

There were two pigeons now. Mr. Norris gaped at them as if they were a species long thought extinct.

'So, Boyd, do me a favor, will you?'

'Huh?'

'You're not going to be another of his one-night stands, are you?'

'Whose? I don't know what you're talking about.'

'Come off it, pal. Walter told me how you tried to put a move on him, crept into bed and all. By the way, it really did his ego good. He needs this so bad now. He's really down on himself.'

'I'm sorry he is. But I'm afraid I can't be much help in that department. And besides, he doesn't like me at all. He despises me.'

'Don't let that fool you. The more he insults you, the more he cares. Just look at him and Kundaa.'

'Fine. But I don't like him. I really don't. And I really resent the fact that he told you I crept into bed with him. That's a total misrepresentation.'

'Why don't you give him a chance, Boyd?'

'Lloyd. And what do you mean, give him a chance? A chance for what?'

'Do you think he would've called me and asked me to meet you if he didn't really like you?'

'So?'

'So, he's smart enough to know he needs all the help he can get. Which is why I'm not across the street right now licking envelopes and sucking up to a bunch of assholes. Let them fire me, good. This is the kind of friend I am. I'd do anything for that little bastard. He's tough as shit, that bitch, a real survivor. Thirty years I've known him and I've never met anyone comes close. You make half an effort with him, man, and he'll make you a happy—'

'Hold on. This is impossible. You think I want to be with someone who calls me a disgrace and keeps on getting engaged to an eighty-year-old woman? You got to be kidding.'

A smile made Mr. Lewis look as serene and mysterious as a room opening up to a farther room in a Vermeer.

'I see. So you know, Lloyd – sorry, Boyd.'

'Know what?'

'Don't play dumb. Who told you? Was it Mrs. K?'

Mr. Norris did not want to hear what was coming. It really wasn't fair at all. He had so much to worry about as it was.

'Look, man, I'm not talking about a huge commitment, moving in with him or anything.'

'Ken, I'm sorry, I've really got to get back to the office.'

'Just hang in there with him. Be a friend. Don't fade away now. I mean, for all Kundaa's faults, you got to hand it to the old bat. She stuck by him. That whole engagement thing you know, she just wanted to take care of him, protect him. His family hurt him so bad. They're loaded, Walter's folks, money coming out the wazoo. But when they found out about his Act Up stuff, that was it. Cut him off completely, even went to court to tie up whatever funds they could. Won't speak to him. Luckily, he's got a few bucks stashed away they can't get at. But they've done everything else they can to make sure he's miserable.'

'Oh, God, no . . .'

'You sure you're OK, pal? You've looked sort of funny ever since you came in here. Maybe you ought to go lie down somewhere. I'll get the check.'

Mr. Norris reached for his wallet. 'No, I'll . . .'

'Where the hell is that waiter? Hey, you know, I think I got it.'

'Got what?'

'Where we met.'

'There he is,' Mr. Norris said, hauling his numbed limbs from beneath the table. He wasn't sure he could walk. 'You go on. My treat.'

'Queer Nation. I used to see you at Queer Nation, didn't I? Why'd you stop coming?'

Mr. Norris shrugged. 'Check, please,' he said to the waiter.

'We need all the bodies we can get to protest the St. Patrick's Day parade this year. You'll come to the cathedral, right?'

'I'll be there, yes. Let's see, the tip, mm . . .'

Chapter Twenty-Two

They hesitated on the stairs leading down. Consuelo gave Marion's hand a reassuring squeeze. There was nothing to worry about. The subway would be safe. Millions of ladies and gentlemen would not ride it every day if it weren't safe, now, would they? But Marion still wanted to pay for a cab – with his own money. She told him to put those traveler's checks back in his pocket. Use them for something really nice, maybe one of those brownies he had been longing for. And besides, the subway would be quicker. They didn't want to be out after dark, did they?

She urged him down into the lower depths, and from there to an even lower platform, where each footstep echoed dully. Swarthy and tough as a Bedouin, Marion glowered fiercely as they waited for the C. Twenty years ago he had fought hand-to-hand against the Polisario guerrillas in the Spanish Sahara, defending the right of the Moroccans to colonize this land. And yet now the poor man shivered like a whippet. Consuelo stroked his leathery hand. Only once before had she seen him this unnerved, and that was when Carlos's wife had unleashed her fury on him for not supporting the Polisario Front. Her lovely blue eyes flashing, Hermione had called Marion a racist, a colonialist oppressor while he just stood there mute, transfixed by her beauty. So unwisely, Consuelo had tried to make peace between them. She explained how Marion had changed his name from 'Charles' because of his hatred of de Gaulle. Didn't Hermione also hate de Gaulle? Yes, of course – but Hermione hated de Gaulle for making war on the Algerians while Marion hated him for making peace with the Algerians and betraying France.

Why was it that Consuelo was not surprised at all when, two years ago, shocked by the news of Hermione's death, Marion had confessed to her. After that terrible argument about de Gaulle, Hermione had found him, Marion, in the rose garden. They had lost their heads again, only this time without words. Marion didn't think he would ever live down the shame of betraying Dr. Bennet. Consuelo reminded Marion that he was forgiven, already. She herself would never say a word to her son about this. It will be Marion himself – years later, amid the roses, lost, mourning Consuelo – who will confess to Dr. Bennet. The spell of his own grief broken by this awful revelation, Dr. Bennet will finally know what his mother had always known, that he himself was forgiven – and could now forgive.

Consuelo hopes to remind Marion of this forgiveness by the gentle pressure of her hand. But he pulls his free now. He tells her he will never forget. But you must forget, Consuelo says. No, he will never forget the insolence of Professor Ingrid at lunch that day. How dare she tell him that John Quincy Adams had no right to take Florida away from Spain? Did the professor not understand the real essence of the Monroe Doctrine, that it was not racist, that Adams was helping the people of Florida to . . . He is silenced as the train thunders by. And then, just when it seems the C might keep going, it stops for them. It opens its doors for them – and for Madge, who squeezes past Marion so she can claim the last seat.

Madge cannot stand because of the pain in her legs. They don't know what it is, no one does. She has been tested by all the experts from Boston to Geneva. Her own doctor thinks there is nothing physiologically wrong with her. She talks to a psychiatrist about how her mother used to force her to eat beets. She takes a regimen of pills from a homeopathist, including extract of beets. An acupuncturist needles her ears once a week. There is also a 900 line that connects her to a nun in Biloxi who has a record of miraculous cures. And she has taken up the alto recorder again. Roger, her brother-in-law, recommended this. He saw a clip on MSNBC about the medicinal effects of classical music.

While skimming a paragraph on Julia sets in *Communications in Mathematical Physics*, Madge begins to wonder if she was in pain during the lesson. She cannot remember any. She was so perplexed by the Yankee Doodle that she forgot about her legs. And then it turned out the crazy old man really knew about phrasing. She had never known Monteverdi could sound so poignant. The old man made her realize that she had been going about it all wrong. He made it so easy, so natural. From an exercise, almost a duty, it was transformed into pure song. She cannot wait to thank Roger. She had wanted to study with someone at Mannes, but Roger had begged her to give the old man a try first. The poor guy has no one at all, Roger said. He's dying of loneliness. Roger told her about their days in Manila, how Sergeant Pollock, desperate for company, used to pick up the tab for everyone at the bars. He never would let anyone else pay. Roger said the sergeant made a pass at him once when they were both drunk. The next day Roger pretended he couldn't remember a thing that had happened. Neither could the sergeant. He said he'd never had such a hangover. And then Sgt. Pollock sort of drifted away, didn't socialize with him anymore. Got transferred to Köln, Roger thought. Or was it Guam?

The train lurches. Madge fears she might cry out with the pain, which has returned with a vengeance. She tries not to see the beautiful old woman clutching the pole at the other end of the car. Why does no one give her a seat? Someone should give her a seat.

Consuelo can smell her Queen Genevieves, yes, even here beside the stranger's soiled raincoat and Marion's horrendous cologne. He uses Ralph Lauren instead of taking a shower. The gentleman in the soiled raincoat, one foot bare, the other in an unlaced Nike, turns and asks for a loan of forty-five cents. He will pay it back, he swears.

Carlos has warned her. It is against the law to give on the subway. Once you are underground, you can't give.

But this, of course, is a loan. She puts the exact change in the raw, chapped hand. Then squeezes it shut. Of course, it is not the Queen Genevieves, she realizes. The smell is wilder, ranker, even more nostalgic, a ferocious salt-sweet beauty that makes her heart leap.

Oh, please, please, someone give her a seat.

Chapter Twenty-Three

'Walter, you sit where Dawne's sitting. Dawne, get up, sugar, and take your glass.'

Mrs. Norris was back. Her heart was heavy. She was more in love than ever, but Herbert still couldn't do it. He would not leave his wife. It would be setting such a bad example for his children, both of whom happened to be in the midst of wretched marriages that he had warned them about. There he was at the Grande Frump Casino and Hotel in the French Quarter, trying to recover from the stress of the parts convention in McComb, when the younger daughter puts in an emergency call at four in the morning to tell poor Herbert that she just discovered lipstick on her husband's crew socks, puce lipstick, a shade she never wore. Then right in the middle of the Super Bowl the other daughter, a pregnant Rhode Island state trooper, worries for an hour on the phone about her husband's shopaholism. What was she supposed to do with a man who buys three dozen cans of Miracle Tire Restorer at Kmart? What with all this and Mrs. Norris's mother sampling gourmet popcorn across the hall, was it any wonder that poor, dear Herbert hadn't been able to function at all in New Orleans? He was a wreck.

'Why do I have to move, Pearl Fay? I don't see what difference it makes where we sit.'

'Dawne, please try to cooperate. My nerves . . .'

With a theatrical sigh reminiscent of her choreography for *The Rite of Spring* – the Mermaidens sighed in unison just before executing a reverse triple corkscrew – Dawne switched places. 'I can't eat this pork anyway, so why do I have to be here? I should be studying for my test on Sandra Bullock.'

'People who are brought up right always dine together in the evening. They don't squirrel away crumb cakes in their schoolbags, and they take their helmets off at the table.'

'Why can't she eat pork?' Walter inquired as he removed Dawne's helmet for Mrs. Norris.

'I can't stand crayfish,' Dawne explained.

'Crayfish?'

'There's crayfish in Pearl Fay's pork stuffing.'

'Stop it, stop it!' In agony, Mrs. Norris clapped her hands over her ears. 'I've told you a hundred times, Dawne Schmidlapp, it's *craw*fish. Why do you torture me with that horrible Yankee accent?'

'Why do *you* put them in your stuffing?'

Mrs. Norris hated to lose her composure in front of company. She apologized to Walter in a kinder, gentler tone of voice and then, turning to Dawne, who persisted with her whys, said, 'We call it dressing, dear, not stuffing. And if you simply must know, it looks like you've been putting away more than veal and bananas while I've been visiting my mama.'

'Pleasingly plump,' Walter said. 'Just the way I like them.'

For a moment it looked as if Dawne might retaliate with a wounding aspersion on Walter's own embonpoint. But thankfully, the woman had sense enough to hold her tongue. Mrs. Norris, of course, was in no condition to be entertaining company. She was on the verge of another breakdown, brought on largely by her mother's obsession with the new organist at her Baptist church. They had hired a man to replace the *Playgirl* woman, an elderly man. Her mama kept on going on and on about the poor organist, how his wife never gave him a proper home-cooked meal, how he once wore a blue sock with a brown sock to the Wednesday evening service, how it was common knowledge that years ago when the organist and his wife were living in Opelousas, the wife had been caught red-handed with their piano tuner. Her mama thought the organist must be some kind of saint, even if he wasn't Catholic, since he not only forgave the piano tuner – the tuner was blind, after all, and didn't realize how homely the woman was – but he also forgave his wife, who had no excuse to speak of, who was really nothing but a hussy, a common tart. Every morning when Mrs. Norris and her mama had their complimentary continental breakfast at the Frump, Mrs. Holsum would use that word at least three or four times – 'red-handed' – even though she knew perfectly well how that word grated on her daughter's nerves. And then poor Herbert, who was pretending to be one of the pastors at the Southern Baptist Unity Fellowship Conference being held at the casino, kept on forgetting to sound Southern in front of Mrs. Holsum. 'New Or-leenz' he would say instead of 'N'orluns.' And worst of all, 'crayfish.'

'Don't you think we should wait for Mr. Norris?' Walter asked.

'My loin has waited as long as it can.' Mrs. Norris spooned some dressing onto his plate. 'I'm not going to let it dry up trying to keep it warm.'

It was Mr. Norris's idea to invite Walter over for a nice dinner one evening. He had explained to Mrs. Norris that he wasn't romantically interested in the man – nothing like that at all. But he did feel that he would like to do whatever he could for Walter as a friend. Mr. Norris told her how Walter had saved Mrs. Kundaa's life during the Vietnam War. And then how Walter's family had disowned him when they found out he was in Act Up and was sick and everything. Weary as she was of life, Mrs. Norris did not need any further persuading. Walter gave her a new reason to live, as she cleaned the house from top to bottom for his visit. (Disgraceful what a mess Dawne and Mr. Norris had made while she was away.) And besides, Dawne had filled her in on a lot that Mr. Norris had left out – such as how Mr. Norris had busted up Walter's engagement. On the very same day that Mrs. Kundaa had announced her formal engagement, Mr. Norris had stepped right in and put a stop to it, actually slept with Walter that very night. Both Dawne and Mrs. Norris were hugely impressed with Mr. Norris's swashbuckling bravado, abducting Walter from that dirty old woman's arms at the last possible moment. So romantic did it seem that they had both shed a few tears as they repaired the sequins on Mrs. Dvorak's daughter's bathing costume.

Of course, when Walter showed up for dinner this evening, Mrs. Norris couldn't help being a little disappointed. For one thing, he looked nothing like Fabio, which was how she had been picturing him all along in her mind's eye, a pale Fabio, wan, hesitant. No, Walter was about as far from Fabio as you could get. And wasn't the least bit wan, either. He looked as sturdy and compact as one of Herbert's riding lawnmowers.

'I don't mean to be intrusive,' Dawne said as she passed Walter his plate, generously loaded down by Mrs. Norris, 'but your family must be the most horrible, mean people in the whole world.'

'Dawne,' Mrs. Norris cautioned.

'What? I'm just saying that until Lloyd told me about Walter's family, I thought *I* had the meanest family in the world. My mama's boyfriend used to make fun of lizzies – that's what he calls them – used to make fun of them right behind my back. I had to keep facing him all the time if I didn't want my feelings hurt. But to throw you out and cut you off without a cent just because you're sick . . .'

'I beg your pardon?'

'Dawne, please. Try a biscuit, Walter. They're made from scratch, none of that Bisquick stuff. Then you can pour this cane syrup over them.'

'Who said I was sick?'

'It's OK, Walter.' Dawne reached through the centerpiece of hydrangeas, grapes, and bananas and squeezed his hand. 'Lloyd told us, darling. We want you to feel right at home here. From now on we're going to be your family.'

'But I'm not sick at all. I've never felt better in my life.'

'Pearl Fay, didn't Lloyd tell us how his family cut him off when they found out about Act Up?'

'So I gave Act Up a check for twenty grand – does that mean I'm sick?'

'Oh, Walter, I must apologize for Dawne. And for Lloyd. I can't imagine how they can say such things. Dawne, you may be excused. Go study for your test.'

'No, no, let her stay, Mrs. Norris. It's not her fault. I don't mind.'

'Darling, I'm so sorry, really, but I swear, cross my heart' – Dawne crossed her heart – 'that's what Lloyd told me. Oh, Pearl Fay, isn't it wonderful! His family isn't mean after all. And Walter, you're not going to pass!'

'Dawne, please don't wipe your eyes on my good tablecloth.'

'Indeed, Mrs. Schmidlapp, spare those tears. First of all, I don't know how excited I am about not passing away. And secondly, my family *is* mean, the meanest in the world, as you say. That part Mr. Norris got right. You see, when my uncle found out about my contribution to Act Up, he started proceedings so he could stop payment on the check.'

'Proceedings?' Mrs. Norris said.

'To have me declared a minor again, legally speaking. He wanted to take over my finances, be appointed my guardian, so I wouldn't be able to make any more contributions to Lambda and GMHC.'

'How awful,' Dawne said.

'My uncle never forgave me for dragging the Edgecombe name through the mud when I marched with the Gay Veterans in the Gay Pride Parade. I was interviewed on Channel Two, they picked me. But the judge reprimanded my uncle in court, gave him a good dressing-down for his prejudice.'

'Right on!'

'Dawne, please, let Walter continue.'

'Then two cousins of mine testified about how I had disrupted Mass at St. Patrick's a few years ago. But the judge, she said – Toss me another one of those biscuits, Dawne.'

Another was tossed.

'I'm actually on a strict diet, you know. But if I'm invited out, I always sample a little of everything in order not to be rude. Anyway, the judge said I had a constitutional right to free speech. It was all clear sailing from then on, right past two sisters, a stepfather, an aunt, and four uncles who testified against me. But then Mrs. K took the stand.'

'Your fiancée testified against you? How mean! I hate her!'

'Actually, she testified *for* me. I begged her not to, but she showed up anyway. It was a disaster, of course. She told the judge about our first engagement and how it was broken off by vicious rumors and how on our subsequent dates no one could have behaved more like a gentleman. Then she told the judge that the real reason my family hated me was because she had blackballed all the women – my mother, my aunt, a second cousin, and a niece or two. Where's that syrup?'

'Blackballed?' Mrs. Norris passed him the Limoges gravy boat.

'There's this silly club my aunt's been dying to get into for years. Mrs. K never forgave my aunt for saying she'd rather see me dead than married to her. So Mrs. K blackballed her and every other female in my family who tried to get in. Unfortunately, that included the judge herself.'

'The judge was a relation?'

'Yes, Mrs. Norris, she was. A second cousin. And when she found out that Mrs. K was the one who had kept her out of the Leeuwarden – such a silly place, the most ghastly tripe – though to be fair, I once sampled some headcheese there that wasn't bad at all. Now on Tuesdays they have waterzootje and sweetbreads—'

'Walter, you don't mean to say . . .'

He shrugged. 'Sadly, we were declared legally underage.'

'But that's so unfair, darling! It's a travesty of justice.' With some violence Dawne wrenched a banana from the centerpiece, then apologized to Mrs. Norris, who told her, why stop there, why not go ahead and eat the hydrangeas, too.

'I'm sorry, Walter,' Mrs. Norris said, ashamed that company should hear her raise her voice yet again. 'My nerves, I've been under considerable strain . . . Anyway, Dawne's right. It isn't fair at all. I think you've been the victim of a gross miscarriage of justice.'

'Well, who said life was fair, girls?'

'But can't you appeal? Surely, having a family member as the judge, that can't be right.'

'Actually, I was all set to appeal, even though the judge said that being married to a second cousin doesn't make her my second cousin, especially since the second cousin was the son of a stepuncle once removed. In any case, I thought I had a case and that Mrs. K could prove she had blackballed the judge and that was why I had lost. But then . . .'

'Then what?'

'Then I broke off the engagement with Mrs. K. She's not going to lift a finger for me now.'

'Maybe you could get engaged again,' Dawne said. 'Just for a while, see, until all this is settled.'

'Dawne, really. Walter, you must excuse her. She says things without really thinking first.'

'I do so think first, Pearl Fay. Like maybe I try to think why he gets engaged to the wrong sex all the time. I'm sorry if this sounds intrusive, Walter, but really, you can't blame me for wondering, can you?'

With a shrug Walter continued sampling the crawfish dressing. 'Actually, I can't help wondering myself sometimes. But you must remember, of course, that the first time we were engaged was back in the Dark Ages. People didn't think too clearly then. And I must confess that I did like the old bat – in a way. But mainly, I felt sorry for her. She had suffered quite dreadfully from her general discharge from the army. Complete nervous breakdown and all that. Hospitalized at Payne Whitney. And while she was there, her husband committed suicide. He was a manic-depressive, the Count, used to dreadfully abuse her. That's why she enlisted in the first place, went to Vietnam to escape him. So you see how noble I felt, asking this poor woman to marry me. And the fact that my aunt was positively incensed didn't hurt a bit.'

'Oh, darling, you're such a nice man. I knew the minute I saw you you were one of the nicest people in the world. But still, do you think you should've gotten engaged to her again, you know, the second time? Once was not enough?'

'Indeed, Mrs. S, once was more than enough. But she caught me at a weak moment when she proposed last Sunday in the orangery. I had just lost my majority, been publicly branded as jailbait, so to speak. And I hadn't gotten the result of my HIV test back yet. I was petrified, absolutely certain I was going to turn out positive. As far as I was concerned, my life was at an end. I had nothing to live for. So why not make at least one person's dreams come true before I drifted off to the Happy Hunting Grounds? The poor dear wanted me so badly, you know. She even gave up smoking for me.'

'You're a saint, darling, a positive saint.'

'Negative, my dear. Just got the results a couple of days ago. And did I mention my little sailboat? That was another thing. On the day Mrs. K proposed, I'd just found out my guardian had it hauled away, sold right from under my nose. I was planning to live on it, too, up in Maine. I figured since my allowance wasn't enough to cover all these mortgages I've been juggling in the city and out on Fire Island and Saratoga . . .'

'You poor thing, forced to live in a little sailboat, all squashed up.'

'Yes, maybe it's just as well it's gone. Wasn't really much use to me anyway, not for the past two, three years. It's just been sitting there gathering barnacles. My crew, you see, they're suing me for back pay.'

'Pearl Fay, he's talking about a yacht. We're sitting here with a man who – Oh, Walter, this is so exciting!'

'Terribly exciting, isn't it, not having a yacht. I can't tell you how thrilling it is when friends don't return your calls. For my fortieth birthday I took twenty of my dearest friends on a cruise to the Bahamas. Did one of them call to wish me a happy forty-eighth? I put myself in so much debt for them that Con Ed turned off my electricity. And on that little cruise to the Bahamas, a gentleman from a collection agency got aboard, said he was a friend of a friend, and then once we were out at sea, threatened to break my leg. He was dreadfully good-looking, so handsome that he's made me phobic to all attractive men. Apollophobia it's called. I can only date bland or ugly men now.'

'Oh, so that's why you fell for Lloyd?'

'Is it that obvious, Mrs. Schmidlapp? I thought I had disguised my fondness for him.'

'You went to bed with him, Walter.'

'But I had on a rather severe chastity belt, my dear. I was too concerned about my health. And besides, even if I had made a move on him, he would have rejected me.'

Mrs. Norris's silver fork hovered before her tender lips, bruised by repeated attempts to bring Herbert to life at the Grande Frump – all in vain, of course. 'You don't mean to tell me that you and Lloyd didn't do anything, nothing at all?'

'No, ma'am, we didn't.'

'You mean he wasn't lying to me?'

'Sadly, no. I've given up on him altogether and introduced him to a friend of mine, the one decent friend remaining to me.'

'Why did you call me "ma'am" just now?'

'I did?'

'You said, "No, ma'am." Well, never mind. In any case, Walter, I'm telling you right here and now that I'm not going to hear any more of your defeatist talk. So a corrupt and horrible judge took away all your money. Well, she can't take away your self-esteem. No one can do that but yourself. And furthermore, you could almost thank that judge for showing you who your true friends are. Did you really want to spend the rest of your life surrounded by freeloaders?'

'Some of them were actually quite charming and talented. And I could pretend they really did like me for myself.'

'But now you can't pretend anymore. Now it's time to wake up and smell the coffee, baby. You've got one of the truest, most wonderful persons on God's green earth to be your friend.'

'Thank you, darling.'

'Not you, Dawne. I'm talking about S. Lloyd Norris.'

'There's just one tiny problem with that, Mrs. N. He doesn't like me.'

'There you go again with that defeatist talk. How do you know he doesn't like you?'

'He said so. I'm not his type at all. He likes big musclemen.'

'Well, it's high time he grew up and stopped being so superficial.'

'That's right, Pearl Fay,' Dawne said. 'If you can do it, I don't know why he can't. Herbert is nothing to look at, if you ask me.'

'No one asked you.'

'Who's Herbert?'

'Never mind that, Walter. We're talking about Lloyd. If he wasn't interested in you, do you think he would have asked you over here to dinner tonight?'

Walter shrugged.

'Do you realize, Walter, you're the only man he's ever invited over? I've been begging him to go out and find someone, but he's never come up with anyone but you.'

'Really?'

'Yes, really. Believe me, Walter, I know that man inside out. When he starts denying something, well, you can be sure he's got something to deny. For your information, sir, he actually told me point-blank that he wasn't interested in you romantically. And he kept on repeating it.'

'Really?'

'He said you weren't his type at all.'

'Funny, that's exactly what I told him.'

Mrs. Norris slapped her hand down on the embroidered linen cloth. 'I rest my case.'

'Oh, I'm getting chills all up and down my spine,' Dawne said. 'I don't know, Mrs. Norris. I'm still not convinced.'

'What more do you want? An engraved invitation?'

'Was he ever in Queer Nation?'

'What?'

'Mr. Norris told Ken – that's my friend, my best friend – he told Ken he was in Queer Nation.'

'Don't make me laugh, darling.'

'This Ken must be mistaken, Walter. Lloyd would never say such a thing. He was probably just pulling your leg, Ken was.'

'No, he's not that kind of guy. We were in Vietnam together, and he's totally serious, never bullshits – pardon my French. He said Mr. Norris was going to protest the St. Patrick's Day parade in front of the cathedral in March. They had tea together the other day, and Ken called me afterward and—'

'It's all nonsense. Dawne, hon, please don't heat your merlot with that candle. You might break the glass and look, wax on my good cloth, for heaven's sake. It's an heirloom, Walter. My mama's family hid it from the Yankees when they plundered Tula Springs, and now she's dripping wax all over it.'

Dawne reinserted the beeswax into the candelabrum. 'You know, maybe Lloyd *is* going to protest, darling. I think I might have been a good influence on him while you were away.'

'Impossible.'

Walter poured cane syrup over his dressing, which sat atop a biscuit. 'There's a simple explanation, ladies. Mr. Norris is after my friend. Don't you see, Ken's in Queer Nation himself. And he's going to the protest at St. Patrick's.'

'Walter, I refuse to believe that someone as moral and upright as Lloyd Norris would be two-timing you with your own best friend.'

'Tudi says the same thing – how moral and upright he is.'

'Who's Tudi?'

'A temp in Human Resources, very comely young thing – a model.'

'Yeah,' Dawne put in, 'the girl not paying any rent in that apartment he won't move back into. I don't see why she gets to have a whole apartment to herself rent-free and I'm forced to sleep on a raft and pay rent and not even get to enjoy the curtains I put up in the den myself. He's the one who gets to enjoy them. It's not fair.'

'Wait, Walter, back up. Model? What does that mean, "model"?'

'She's trying to break into modeling. In the meantime, she temps at NyLo. And by the way, Dawne, she tries to make up for the rent as best she can. Just the other day she took him out to dinner. His birthday, I believe. Everyone at NyLo is talking about how nice it was of Tudi to remember. When I went to get my shawl back from Mrs. K, that's all that was on her mind.'

'Oh my God, his birthday . . .' It was the first time Mrs. Norris had ever forgotten his birthday, even after they were divorced. Why couldn't she have at least phoned him from the Grande Frump? This made her so mad – at herself, of course. Not him. He had a right to let someone take him out to dinner on his birthday. But why a female somebody? And why a model female somebody? Who didn't pay any rent, not a cent . . .

Chapter Twenty-Four

'Just why is that model of yours not paying any rent?'

'What model? I don't have any model.'

Mr. Norris had arrived home in time for a lukewarm slice of pork – or rather, half a slice. He was trying to remember if, after his hasty visit to the bathroom under the stairs, he had washed his hands. And wondering if he did, indeed, know someone who was a model. But surely a man handsome enough to be a model would be easy to remember.

'Oh, I remember now. It all came back to me.' This was Dawne speaking, not Mr. Norris. 'See, Pearl Fay, she's an escort, so she can't afford—'

'Dawne, please, she's not an escort.' Mr. Norris had been so discreet, telling no one at the office about Tudi's problem with her roommate. But now he remembered that he had told Dawne when she had first moved in. Why, oh why, couldn't he have kept his big mouth shut!

'But you said, Lloyd . . .'

'Her roommate is an escort, and quite frankly, it's none of our business one way or the other. I promised Tudi I wouldn't tell a soul.'

'Severinus Lloyd Norris, do you mean to tell me you're keeping a hooker rent-free in your apartment? A *female* hooker?'

'She's not a hooker, Pearl Fay. I resent that deeply. She happens to be one of the sweetest, most innocent young girls I ever met. Now I don't want to discuss this another second, do you hear?' He coughed. 'The reason the poor girl had to move out of her apartment is because she has moral integrity and refuses to share a space with someone she didn't know that well to begin with, someone she only met through a roommate referral service. I happen to be protecting Tudi's honor and dignity and self-respect. I mean, Walter, how would you feel if someone you lived with suddenly started bringing men home who left money on the dresser? Never mind, don't answer that. By the way, Pearl Fay, is there no more pork? I'm starving.'

'Guilty,' Walter said. 'Blame me. I couldn't stop. Besides, I didn't think you'd show up.'

'I'm really sorry, Walter. I had to give a speech tonight, you know. I hope Pearl Fay explained why I was so late.'

Mr. Norris had delivered an address to the Trust Benefits Committee of the Amalgamated Labeling Artists Union. He had worked on it for weeks. Three people had shown up.

'Why do I smell gin on your breath?'

'How can you smell gin on my breath from way over there, Pearl Fay?'

'That's what I'd like to know.'

After the speech, Mr. Norris had fortified himself for the dinner with a martini in the atrium. And this time the Italian bartender had actually smiled at him. Which had encouraged Mr. Norris to purchase another martini.

'Here this poor girl is sleeping night after night on a raft with no curtains while some sweet, innocent tart is lounging around your apartment rent-free. Do you think that's fair, Lloyd?'

'She's not a tart.'

'Model, tart. What's the difference?'

'Who said she was a model?'

'Mrs. K told me your Tudi was in the Vicky's Rumor catalog once,' Walter said.

'She never said anything to me about modeling. Anyway, it just shows she's enterprising. Would you mind passing a biscuit, Walter?'

'All gone.'

'That's OK. Maybe there's some dressing left.'

'Guilty again.'

'Well, I should cut down anyway. It's really OK, Walter. And you know, I shouldn't be eating pork and all this stuff. I've been meaning to become a vegetarian now for years. Pearl Fay, didn't I tell you Walter can only eat vegetables and tuna without dolphins? What kind of meal is this, anyway?'

'I thought a change for one evening might do him good.'

'You can't do that, Pearl Fay. It could have serious consequences. I really must apologize for her, Walter. She sometimes takes matters into her own hands.'

Mr. Norris was still trying to forgive Mrs. Norris for her latest escapade. Imagine the gall of booking a room for her mother and herself right across from Herbert's. And then to pretend that she really didn't have all that much fun. Why couldn't she just admit that she loved every minute of it? Lord knows, if he ever had the chance to spend half his life rolling around in bed with someone he loved, he'd at least admit it was fun – even if it was a terrible sin.

'Darling, you don't have to worry that pretty little head over Walter. He's not sick at all. Why do you go around telling everyone he's sick?'

'I never—'

'It was rather un-Christian to spread such a rumor, Mr. Norris.'

'But, Walter, you mean you're not . . . ?'

'He's completely, totally negative, Severinus Lloyd. You should be ashamed. And then you reel in here late, three sheets to the wind, and tell everyone you're in Queer Nation while stashing call girls away in your apartment – what's got into you? I've never seen such behavior in all my born days!'

'Calm down, Mrs. Norris. Let's not be too harsh. I'm sure Mr. Norris has some perfectly good explanation for these rather curious phenomena.'

'It was Ken, he told me. Just the other day, I swear. Let's call him right now, you'll see.'

Mr. Norris yanked a cell phone out of his vest pocket. As a general rule of thumb, Mr. Norris could be said to hate cell phones. He often made fun of people talking on them as they walked along the sidewalk – at least, in his own head he did. And he deplored aloud the accidents that they were said to cause while people drove. But the Italian bartender happened to sell them as a sideline. And it was true what Luigi, the bartender, had said. What if Pearl Fay had another emergency with vitamin C and had to reach him right away, and he wasn't in the office but was sitting in the atrium having a martini, on the house? That's right, go ahead, have another, buddy. On me.

'Put that thing down,' Mrs. Norris said as he tried to figure out how to switch it on. 'And what in heaven's name are you doing with a phone in your pocket? Aren't two extensions in this house enough for you? Or are you intent on throwing away every bit of your salary so there's not a cent for my old age?'

'Darling, are you really going to march in the St. Patrick's Day parade? I'm so proud of you.'

'Why would I march in the St. Patrick's Day parade, Dawne?'

'I mean not march in it.'

'No, I'm not marching in it.'

'Oh, that's wonderful! Don't be mean to him, Pearl Fay. He's not marching.'

Mr. Norris did not want to go to T.G.I. Friday's, but Tudi said she knew the waiters there and felt bad going anywhere else. He ordered a turkey bacon-cheeseburger, no appetizer. She was not quite so frugal. In fact, she said she always ordered the most expensive things on the menu so they'd get a bigger tip. They were struggling talk-show hosts, two of them. The other was a struggling makeover artist. And on Wednesdays there was a struggling novelist who had won some award or other way back in the seventies. Tudi thought it was maybe like the Pulitzer or the Tony.

'Last night? Oh, I gave a little dinner party.'

'How nice, Mr. Norris. Whom did you invite to it?'

'No one, really. Now about the apartment, Tudi—'

'Did you prepare petits fours? I always think they add such a nice touch.'

'Mm. Anyway, I really have to move back in soon. Right away.'

'But it's so small. I can barely fit in myself.'

'No, I don't mean we'd *both* live there.'

'Hi, Joey! Look, there's Joey. Wave.'

Mr. Norris did not wave. He had no idea who the man was who had just walked in.

'Tudi, I don't mean to be pushy or anything, but' – Oh Lord, he was beginning to sound like Dawne. He really did have to get out of Yonkers— 'but the fact is, I think we need to set a date, a definite date.'

'You mean those rumors are true?'

'What rumors?'

'That you're not really gay. I always stand up for you, Mr. Norris. I tell them how you never ever once made a pass at me or come to get anything at the apartment except for that one time when I was in the shower and you needed that tie—'

'Tudi, I'm—'

'Or was it a tie? It was something like a tie – maybe spaghetti. Anyway, there's Alan. Ignore him. I'm not speaking to him.'

'When I say date, I mean a specific time that you will vacate the apartment.'

'You mean move out? But where am I supposed to go?'

'Tudi, I'm not sure that should be my problem. I hear, by the way, that you've been getting some modeling jobs.'

'Who told you that? I'd like to know. Because it's a lie. I had one single go-see for a catalog and I didn't even get the job.'

'Please don't . . . Here.'

He handed her his handkerchief. She dabbed at her eyes and then blew her nose.

'I suppose I should just give up trying to be moral, Mr. Norris. I suppose I should just move right back in with Lana and close my eyes to all that goes on.'

'No, no, I don't mean that. But there must be somewhere else you can go.'

'Paying two rents isn't that easy for a temp, you know. I can't even afford Avenue A. But I suppose if you want to evict me, there's nothing I can do.'

'Don't use that word, Tudi. It makes me sound like—'

'Hello, Alan.'

Mr. Norris looked up and saw a dashing, square-jawed man in a leather jacket glaring down at him.

'So who's the creep?'

'He's not a creep, Alan.'

'If I say he's a creep, he's a creep.'

Mr. Norris wrenched his hand free from Tudi's grip. He hadn't even realized she had been clinging to him.

'I told you I wasn't speaking to you, Alan. Kindly bug off, please.'

'I don't bug off till the creep bugs off.'

'The creep isn't going to bug off.'

'Yes, the creep is,' Mr. Norris said.

'Sit down.'

Mr. Norris was shoved back into his chair.

'You know who I think you are, creep?'

'Not really.'

'I think you're the dirty old man giving my girl a free ride in your apartment. Why don't you make her pay rent, huh? That's what I'd like to know.'

'He's nice, that's why, Alan.'

'Nice. I'll give him nice.'

Tudi screamed as the table toppled over. Mr. Norris reached down to help Alan, who had been leaning too hard on the wobbly little round table when it gave way, tumbling him to the floor.

'You OK?' Mr. Norris said, as his hands clasped the rock-hard biceps. *Oh, please, God, let him fall in love with me, please,* Mr. Norris prayed.

On his feet, Alan was surrounded by three waiters, who began to hustle him toward the door.

'Hey, it's fine, you guys,' Mr. Norris said. 'He didn't do anything. Alan, here, if there's anything wrong . . .' He slipped him his card just before the unfortunate boyfriend was propelled onto the street.

Marion stumbled over the naked spokes of an umbrella, ravaged by the wind. He had been glancing over his shoulder, worrying aloud about the man who was following them. Consuelo told him never mind about the man, and look where he was going.

Four more steps and they were aboveground once again. The wind stung tears into Consuelo's eyes. Marion shielded his own with his hand. Spires jutted like thorns, fiercer than any she had ever felt. The noise deafened any scent. And yet the crueler the fortresses, the more precious the treasure. She looked up. He was upon her, the man in the subway. One bare foot pressed against the concrete. Raw welts amid the dirt.

Her eyes met his, bold and frank. Two coins dropped into her hand. Fifty cents.

And then he was gone, melting into the crowd that revolved into the Virgin Superstore.

'He gave you money? But this is impossible. You cannot have beggars giving you money, Consuelo.'

'He wants to give, Marion. Let him give.'

'Where are we? I think we got off at the wrong stop. This does not appear to be a residential neighborhood.'

'We'll ask in here.'

'No, Consuelo. It says "Live Girls."'

'They can tell me, can't they?'

'Come, take my arm. We will walk briskly.'

'Ask the constable, Marion.'

'No, no, it's not necessary. Come.'

'Oh, what a beauty.'

'No, Consuelo. Please don't touch the horse. He might bite.'

Mr. Norris glanced at his watch. He wished to goodness she would hurry. He had to get all the way down to Tribeca by six if he was going to meet Ken on time. The nerve of that guy to make him think Walter was sick. A face-to-face confrontation was in order. Mr. Norris was not going to be put off by any of Ken's feeble excuses – e.g., his boss wouldn't let him talk on the phone at work, he had to buy a new microwave. The man certainly had time for a cup of tea.

In the shop Mrs. Norris raised her arms above her head and then brought them down in a butterfly stroke behind the heinie that was known to stop traffic. She had come into the city to stock up on a special kind of elastic her girls needed for their bathing costumes. Apparently, this elastic – Sel-U-Lite or something like that – could be found only in a certain little shop in the garment district, a neighborhood she was afraid to walk around in on her own. So she had met Mr. Norris at his office, where she had introduced herself to Dusty. Eavesdropping, Mr. Norris had heard them discussing Dusty's latest boyfriend in the women's room – a personal trainer who had been turned down six times by Chippendale's. But he was still trying. After her nose was powdered, Mrs. Norris insisted on visiting Human Resources on forty-nine. Mr. Norris asked why this was necessary. She said if he wasn't man enough to get his own apartment back, then she would take a crack at it herself. Fortunately, Tudi was not in the temp pool. Her supervisor said she had never returned from her luncheon. There had been a terrible brawl in the restaurant, but Tudi had been too upset to go into any details on the phone. All the supervisor could gather was that her boyfriend had been knocked down and stomped on, roughed up bad. She was at home taking care of him now, if Mr. Norris wanted to call her. Mr. Norris said that would not be necessary.

'Come in here, Lloyd.'

'What?'

'You heard me.'

Mr. Norris did not want to go into the elastic shop. *Solo al mayor*, a sign warned. *Wholesale Only*. He was not wholesale. Neither was she. Besides, it was so depressing. There was absolutely nothing to see. Cards of elastic lined the walls. That was it. He couldn't begin to imagine how the Korean hovering around her could possibly make a living off this. There weren't even that many cards. Maybe just a couple of hundred.

'Which do you like better?'

He regarded the two strands of elastic she thrust in front of his nose.

'Pearl Fay, they're the same.'

'They're not the same. One is ivory. The other is pearl. I would go with the pearl, for obvious reasons, but I don't think it wears as well as the ivory. Mr. Tung, do you mind if he uses your facilities?'

'You wholesale, too, gentleman?'

'It's OK,' Mr. Norris said. 'I'm fine.'

'But you just told me outside you had to go,' Mrs. Norris said.

'We have excellent facilities,' Mr. Tung said, plucking a card from the wall. 'See, finest quality.'

'No, no, Mr. Tung. He means little boys' room. Make wee-wee.'

'Ah. This way, gentleman.'

'No, really, I'm fine.'

He escaped back to the sidewalk, where he was forced to wait a good five minutes in the freezing cold. Five that seemed an hour.

He could not believe his watch. Every time he looked at it, he wondered if the battery might be running down.

'You were very rude, Lloyd. You can't just walk away from people when they're trying to do you a favor.'

'I'm not going to use someone's bathroom under false pretenses. I'm not a wholesaler. And neither are you. So where is it?'

'Where is what?'

'The elastic. Didn't you buy any?'

'No. I'm going to come back later with Dawne. It's too important a decision for me to make by myself.'

'You're going all the way back to Yonkers and then—'

'Don't be silly. Dawne's meeting me at Gramercy Park. She's reading meters there today. We're going to have dinner – you can take us out.'

'Sorry, I'm busy this evening.'

'OK. My treat, Diamond Jim.'

'Look, I had a big lunch and . . .' Mr. Norris wished he hadn't mentioned lunch. Not a good subject to bring up. How lucky that he hadn't told her he had gone to Friday's with Tudi. It would have made things so awkward on the forty-ninth floor. Not that he had anything to hide. He was perfectly innocent.

'Why are you looking like that, Lloyd?'

'Like what?'

'Where did you have lunch today?'

'Where did I have lunch?'

'Honestly, if you're not that hungry, then just have a salad. Dawne knows a nice little bistro with a garden.'

'Great, it's snowing and you and Dawne—'

'Don't be a wiseacre. It's an enclosed garden, a hothouse that's famous for its orchids.'

'I'd rather not eat in a hothouse, Pearl Fay.'

'Suit yourself. You don't mind taking me down there, though? I can't just stand around the park all alone waiting for her. It wouldn't look right. Not in the dark.'

'I can't.'

'Why not?'

'I've got to meet someone downtown.'

'Who?'

'Tribeca. I have to get all the way down to Tribeca.'

'Flag that cab for me, hon. We'll share it downtown. It's the least you can do.'

Chapter Twenty-Five

Mr. Norris's ears ached from the cold, perhaps more than normal ears would, those that didn't protrude so boldly into space. As for Mrs. Norris's, hers were protected by a lynx hat. Snow had accumulated on the fur in a Dr. Zhivago-esque way as ex-husband and ex-wife shivered in front of the locked iron gates of Gramercy Park, the north side.

'Are you sure you said the north side?'

'Don't ask me that again, Lloyd.'

'Why didn't you just tell her to meet you in the hotel across the street? You could've been nice and warm and safe in the lobby.'

'How was I supposed to know there was a hotel across the street? I'm not a Svengali.'

In the cab to the park, Mr. Norris had phoned Ken on his cell phone. He had told him he was going to be a few minutes late. Ken suggested they put off the tea until some other time. But Mr. Norris was firm. He said he would be there by six-thirty.

'Pearl Fay, I'm sorry but I can't wait another second. I've got to go.'

'You had your chance at Mr. Tung's.'

'I mean, go meet Ken.'

'He can wait an extra minute or two. It's not going to kill him.'

'Why don't you go across to the hotel and wait?'

'I can't see through walls, that's why. Oh, never mind, Lloyd. If you must go, go. I'll be mugged and picked up for streetwalking, but you go to your little rendezvous. You ask me, it's disgusting.'

A pert blond in a J. P. Morgan sweatshirt jogged past them again, his fifth or sixth lap around the park. On the third lap, Mr. Norris had been smitten. He ached to hold the banker in his arms.

'Disgusting? What's disgusting?'

'You sneaking out with Ken.'

'Sneaking? You heard me on the phone. I'm not hiding anything. There's nothing to hide.'

'That's even worse. Anyone with a sense of decency would be ashamed, would at least try to sneak away. Don't you realize that Ken is Walter's dearest friend? Walter offered to take him on a cruise to the Virgin Islands once, just the two of them, and Ken refused. In fact, he never once set foot on Walter's yacht.'

'That's a friend?'

'Yes, that's a friend. He knew the yacht was ruining Walter and he told him so. They were in Vietnam together—'

'Yes, I know.' If the banker slipped on the ice, then Mr. Norris could run to his side and . . .

'So they only tell each other the truth, no matter how much it hurts. Severinus?'

'What?'

'Listen to me. This is important. Walter fell in love with Ken back in Vietnam. But Ken couldn't handle it. And now here you are horning in, trying to ruin Walter's last chance at happiness.'

'How many times do I have to tell you – I'm not interested in Ken!'

'Right, just like you're not interested in Walter. Why can't you be satisfied, Lloyd? What's wrong with Walter? He would be such a good husband for you.'

'Of course, he's just what I've been yearning for, someone who hates Catholics and calls me a disgrace.'

'Sure, once you find out he's not rich, you drop him like a hot potato and go chasing after his best friend.'

'It has nothing to do with money. And I'm not after his best friend, understand? I just want to clear up this mess about Walter, what Ken told me about him, how he was sick when he wasn't. It offends me deeply, Pearl Fay. I don't go around spreading rumors or lying. I want Walter to understand that. I want you to understand that. Ken's not going to get away with it, that's all. I mean to make him admit—'

'Is that her? I think that's her. What in heaven's name is she doing over there? Come.'

Oh God, Mr. Norris prayed as they crossed the street, *please make him slip now. Not so he hurts himself, but just—*

'Lloyd!'

A zebra-striped Land Rover blasted them with its horn.

'Don't yank me like that, Pearl Fay.'

'You almost got run over. Why don't you look where you're going?'

'I'm looking.'

Under the marquee of the Gramercy Park Hotel, Dawne was making a big show of consulting the jeweled watch on her wrist. 'I've been waiting almost an hour, darling. Where have you been?'

Mrs. Norris said she had got there as soon as she could, but wanted to compare and contrast some elastic first. 'Anyway, we looked all over for you. In fact, Lloyd almost got run over, checking out this eighty-year-old jogger.'

'He was not eighty.'

'Looking right over his shoulder as he crosses the street. How you ever got to be a vice president, Lloyd . . .'

'I'm sure he's a very good vice president,' Dawne said, patting one of his mittens.

'If he's going to get run over, the least he could do is get run over because of someone attractive.'

'He was attractive,' Mr. Norris said. 'And he was only forty or so.'

'Hon, if you weren't so vain and had your glasses on, you would've seen he was at least – And by the way, Dawne, have you been waiting all this time inside the hotel?'

'What do you expect? They have a nice bar here. I wasn't going to stand out in the snow like some sort of nitwit. Oh, that's such a swell hat, Lloyd. Where did you get it?'

'Give it back, please.'

She had taken his stocking cap, which he had bought at a newsstand that day, and tugged it over her gray hair. Apparently, Dawne was still mad at Mrs. Norris for wearing fur. They had argued about the lynx hat at breakfast that morning. To teach Mrs. Norris a lesson, Dawne declared she was going to start wearing a coat she had vowed never to wear again, a synthetic mink given to her by her late husband. A woman could be stylish, warm, and uncruel all at the same time – that was the message. And except for Mr. Norris's cap, she did indeed look stylish this evening. Besides Moony's anniversary present, she had on an actual dress. And heels, high heels that looked so much more respectable than Mrs. Norris's stilettos.

'Did you do something to your hair?' Mr. Norris asked when she finally handed the cap back.

'I tamed it for her,' Mrs. Norris said. 'Got some of that frizz out, then styled it so it hugs the—'

'I hate it,' Dawne said.

'It looks very nice,' Mr. Norris said. 'Oh, sorry,' he added as a doorman bumped into him with a valise.

A cab was unloading, and Mr. Norris said he would take it as soon as everyone got out.

'I'm not riding in that,' Dawne said. 'I want a traditional cab.'

'This is for me, Dawne. And what do you mean by "traditional"? Just because this isn't dirty and all banged up . . .'

It was one of the new yellow minivans with plenty of room in back. And so clean. Even the driver looked clean, his hair neatly parted.

'Let's wait for another, darling. I don't like that shape.'

'Fine, you can wait all night for the right shape. I'm taking this.'

'The perfect gentleman,' Mrs. Norris said.

'Look, I don't know why you two need a cab, anyway. Aren't you eating around here? I'm going all the way down to Tribeca.'

'Lloyd, darling, I thought you were going to buy us dinner, you know, to make up for the other night. Isn't that what you said, Pearl Fay?'

'He's got other plans, Dawne.'

'Make up for what? I haven't done anything.'

'No? You ruined Walter's dinner,' Mrs. Norris said. 'I spend three days cooking and cleaning for that friend of yours, and then you come barreling in, drunk as a skunk, telling the most awful fibs and making me feel like a perfect fool. And now, Dawne, now he wants to run off with Walter's lover.'

'That jogger?'

'No, Ken. They have a little tryst set up this evening.'

'That's so creepy and mean. Poor Walter.'

'Pearl Fay, I am not having a tryst. I've told you over and over—'

'Filth! Trash! Animal!' a woman screamed as she was handed out of the nontraditional cab by the doorman. From the depths of her Gucci bag she drew a can, aimed, and fired straight at Dawne, who collapsed into Mr. Norris's arms. While he struggled to stay on his feet, Mrs. Norris took off after the perpetrator.

'Dawne, are you all right?' Mr. Norris said from the sidewalk, where he had landed after stumbling backward over a suitcase. Dawne herself had somehow managed to stay upright.

'Oh, Lloyd, she's ruined my poor coat. Here, get up. People are looking.'

'It's not ruined,' he said, after taking the outstretched hand. 'Just a little stiff.'

'Really?'

'I got a look at the can, Dawne. It wasn't paint. Just some AquaNet.'

'Oh, how humiliating.'

'What's humiliating about AquaNet?'

'Would you be quiet? People can hear,' she whispered fiercely, while smiling graciously upon her audience. 'Let's get out of here. I can't stand another second. Go get Pearl Fay. Hurry.'

'A what?'

'A boarder. You know, someone who pays rent in your house and eats things.'

Mr. Norris was trying to explain Dawne Schmidlapp to Ken. The two women were in the unisex room of the Japanese restaurant rinsing the hairspray off Dawne's fake mink. Though Mr. Norris would have preferred to have met Ken alone, he was not a heartless man. Dawne had been quite shaken up by the incident. As had Mrs. Norris, who had broken down and wept in the cab they all shared. She was thinking what a close call it was, how her lynx could have been lacquered. In any case, by agreeing not to leave them alone for the rest of the evening, he would at least prove once and for all that he was not interested in Ken, not in the least.

'Listen, Ken, when they come back, would you do me a big favor and tell them exactly what you told me about Walter, how he was in Act Up and got sick and—'

'Never said he got sick, pal.'

'But I could swear you did. You were explaining why Mrs. Kundaa was going to take care of him and—'

'Yeah, 'cause of the trial, being declared a minor and all that.'

'That's what you meant? Why didn't you come right out and say so?'

'I thought you knew. You acted like you knew everything already.' Mr. Lewis took a sip of green tea. 'Reminds me. Walter says you weren't ever in Queer Nation. What do you mean by telling me—'

'Never mind. Here they come. I'll explain all that later. And I never really said . . . Did it come out?'

Dawne kicked off her pumps and settled down next to Mr. Norris. 'It's fine.'

'You should've pressed charges, hon.' Mrs. Norris unwound the spaghetti straps of her stilettos. 'I cornered the woman in the lobby, Ken, but Dawne here made me let her go.'

'How can I press charges when I agree with what she did? I think people *should* be sprayed if they wear mink. Like, hello, what do you think I make those monthly pledges for, anyway?'

'Dawne, honey lamb, you can't really think this was all about mink. No one in their right mind would mistake that nylon carpet you're wearing for mink.'

'What in the world are you talking about, Pearl Fay?' Mr. Norris said, adjusting his shoeless foot so it didn't touch hers – or was it Mr. Lewis's?

'I've been thinking the whole thing over. I mean, if this was really an anti-fur attack, she would have gone straight for my lynx. But you notice what she said. She didn't say anything about innocent minks. And she didn't use any red paint.'

'So?'

'I think this was a hate crime. The woman must've thought Dawne here was a lesbian.'

'Preposterous,' Mr. Norris said.

'Yeah,' Mr. Lewis said. 'Don't start getting straight folks mixed up in hate crimes. I mean, this lady doesn't even look gay, not the least bit.'

'I beg your pardon?' Dawne said. 'This is just great. I spend half my life walking around this city in overalls and no one says a thing. Then Pearl Fay talks me into looking like Grandma Moses and I get a woman spraying AquaNet at me and you, you tell me I don't look gay at all. For your information, sir, just because I've never been able to find a girlfriend, that doesn't mean I'm not gay and damn proud of it, too.'

'Sorry, sorry. No one said anything to me.'

'Yeah, well, no one should have to say.'

Mr. Lewis squirmed a little on his cushion. 'Actually, I'm beginning to see it now. You guys do look sort of gay, kind of.'

'Me! You calling *me* gay.'

'Now, Pearl Fay.' Mr. Norris reached over and patted her hand. 'He was just trying to be nice. Ken, this is my ex-wife, remember? She's the one who's not gay.'

'You didn't tell me that, pal. I'm sorry, Pearl Fay – he's right. I was just saying that to, you know . . .'

'So you don't think I look gay, not really, huh?' Dawne said.

'Hey, Dawne,' Mr. Norris said, 'he makes cartoons. Isn't that nice?'

Dawne just sat there.

'Remember how we used to go see Porky Pig at the Ritz, Pearl Fay?'

Mrs. Norris just sat there.

'What kind of cartoons do you do, Ken? Are there little animals in them and things?'

'No.'

'That's interesting. You know, I read about some new software, it can actually take a sketch and—'

'Don't give me that computer crap. Every frame I draw by hand, myself.'

'Boy.'

'Can't stand that frickin' computer animation. Plain garbage. No soul. You ask me, frickin' computers ruined this whole country, not just Disney.'

'Oh.' Mr. Norris cleared his throat. 'Shall we order some sake? A sea urchin or two?'

Chapter Twenty-Six

Tea is forbidden. Her homeopathist has outlawed it not just on medical grounds, but moral as well. He explained to Madge, right after her second lesson with Joe Pollock, how the British used tea as a weapon or something in the Opium Wars, when they were forcing the Chinese to buy opium. Madge can't quite keep it straight in her mind, but knows Hong Kong's release from British domination has something to do with it, too. So she can't help feeling guilty as she stands in line at intermission, even though she is going to specifically request that her tea be both non-English and non-Chinese.

Two minutes and thirty-three seconds she waits – and then gives up. The pain is too much. She won't be able to experiment to see if tea might help. She must sit. Now.

A bench ten yards away. But she can't make a beeline for it. Skirting a fragrant cluster of three men, she treads on the toe of a lady orbiting another cluster. Madge winces in sympathy, but there is no time for an apology. She must sit.

She has almost made it to the bench when two elderly matrons plop down on it. Madge almost screams. They have left no room for her with their handbags and stoles. On a subway this would make each of them liable to a fifty-dollar fine. But here at Avery Fisher, Madge has no recourse to the law. She must hope they will notice her standing there, her eyes wide with polite desperation.

But they don't look up. They are preoccupied with a pale brownie, unwrapped by sturdy hands bedizened with sapphires and rubies.

'Have a bite.'

'Me? I don't want it.'

'Sure you do.'

'Not with teeth marks on it.'

'Those aren't teeth marks.'

'They're your teeth marks. I can tell.'

'So I took a bite. Kill me.'

Murmuring an apology, Madge descends. A chinchilla tail is yanked free from her weight. She apologizes again as the women get up. They wonder aloud why the mayor doesn't lock up all the riffraff in this city and throw away the key. Though she doesn't agree with this sentiment, Madge smiles pleasantly. Then after they are gone she worries that this might have been an allusion to her.

She fishes out her mother-of-pearl compact. No, her lipstick isn't smudged. Her hair isn't mussed.

With champagne in plastic cups, a young woman and man take the place of the two matrons. Madge squeezes considerately toward the edge of the red velour bench, at an angle so she doesn't see their faces.

'I'm going outside.'

'We just sat down.'

'Just one little puff. I won't be a minute.'

'It's freezing out. Come on, tell me what you thought of the Prokofiev.'

'The what?'

'Elmo, sit. Try to carry on a little civilized conversation. Come on, sit.'

'OK, I'm sitting.'

'Did you like the Prokofiev?'

'The violin thing? Not so bad. I thought I'd hate it. You know, all scratchy and modern. But that ending, it really got to me.'

'Those trills, yes. It seems to me what heaven must be like, all that pain and yearning—'

'Pain?'

'The ache, you know, all our loneliness, it's still there, but somehow there's a new angle on it, you see it all differently, in a richer, fuller pattern that—'

'Doris, do I have the seven-ten tomorrow?'

'Bob is seven-ten. You've got four and noon.'

'Balls. And I've still got my homily to do. So maybe I can work in the violin thing somehow, how the scratchy and ugly parts, like . . . Was he Catholic? No, huh. What was the first piece? Mozart, right? He was Catholic.'

'Prokofiev thought Mozart was boring. He made fun of him in—'

'So?'

'Well, Mozart's like the pope of music. You could say how—'

'No, no, I need a good joke. Give me a couple good jokes. You think of them now, and when I get back . . . One puff, that's all. I promise.'

'What if not taking that one puff, Elmo, what if that's what saves your life.'

'I don't get it. That's a joke?'

'No, I—'

'Got to do better than that.'

As he leaves, Madge can't resist getting a glimpse of the girl's face. Yes, she is plain and normal – with some unfortunate acne scars. But the eyes, their radiance, makes the pity tugging at the older woman's heart a nuisance.

Chapter Twenty-Seven

'No calls, period, Dusty. Not even Pearl Fay. I've got to get this report done.'

'I'll tell everyone you're home sick.'

'No, don't lie. Just say – Oh, if a Mr. Lewis calls, put him through, understand?'

'But you just said—'

'Mr. Ken L-E-W-I-S. What are you looking at?'

'Your hair.'

'What about my hair?'

'Are you using hairspray to puff it out?'

'Don't be ridiculous.'

'You are.'

'I am not.'

'You are.'

'Go away. Leave me alone.'

'Did anyone call?' Mr. Norris said as he walked in the kitchen door.

'That's right. Put it right in front of the refrigerator.' Mrs. Norris snatched the briefcase he had set down and handed it back to him.

'Any messages?'

'Would you hush, Lloyd?'

'Don't tell me they're meditating again.'

Although Mr. Norris was extremely pro-prayer, even in schools, he really was not happy about strangers meditating in his living room – his ex-wife's. Two guards from the correctional facility were meeting with Dawne now for wordless instruction from the Inner Power.

'I'll talk if I want,' Mr. Norris said after he was hushed again. Normal mainstream prayer, even if it were Protestant, wouldn't have bothered Mr. Norris so much. But Dawne seemed to have gotten mixed up in something demanding absolute silence in the house. It had all started when Elton, her air-conditioning pupil, became worried about Dawne's working so hard and never going on any dates. So he had introduced her to two colleagues of his at the facility, Candy and Erma. They channeled the wisdom of Shirley MacLaine and Pat Robertson. As far as Mr. Norris was concerned, he just hoped one of them – either the polite Candy or the pretty Erma – would fall in love with Dawne quick and get her out of the house. He was tired of having to walk on eggs in his own home.

'I don't know why they have to pray here,' he went on as he trailed Mrs. Norris upstairs.

'Do you want her to find someone or not, Lloyd? Besides, it would be unconstitutional. I can't interfere with the religious rights of a tenant. The Housing Authority would hand me my ass on a platter.'

'Sit here?'

'Yes, right on top of the skirt I just ironed.'

'You sure no one called?'

'No, Ken didn't call.'

Mr. Norris blushed. 'Uh, let's see.' He coughed. 'Does this go in the salmon-pink bin or plain pink?'

Mr. Norris was helping her sort sequins in the sewing room. Normally, this was an activity reserved for the mothers' committee. But two of the mothers had come down with the Idaho flu. And Mr. Johnson, the committee's sergeant at arms, was in Piscataway buying an insecticide for the rust mites infesting his turnips. His company made an extract from Japanese turnips and rutabagas that was an ingredient in an all-natural cat food you could order from an E-mail address listed in the back of a bodybuilding magazine.

'Look, Lloyd, don't you ever try to put anything over on me again. It won't work. I know you like the back of my hand.'

He dropped a few sequins into the teal bin. 'OK, so I like him. Is that a crime?'

'Yes, after you say you don't like him and aren't interested in him at all and make such a fuss about how pure your motives are.'

'Well, I was telling the truth then, Pearl Fay. I really didn't like him at first – not until we all had dinner last week.'

'And he started insulting poor Dawne.'

'He wasn't insulting her. He was simply being factual. He said he didn't understand how anyone could believe in the literal truth spoken by both Pat Robertson and Shirley MacLaine.'

'And he told her to stop acting so childish. You don't talk to people that way, not people you don't know.'

Mr. Norris shrugged. Mr. Lewis's honesty was so refreshing. He hadn't the slightest worries about pleasing other people or ingratiating himself. A man with rock-solid integrity. And when Dawne had accidentally spilled sake on Mr. Lewis's denim workshirt, Mr. Norris couldn't believe how solid the pecs beneath were as he helped Mr. Lewis wipe it off.

'He's not a gentleman, Lloyd. No gentleman would ever tell a lady what he really thinks of her. And what he said about you? Doesn't that bother you at all?'

'What?'

'That you're a complete hypocrite, trying to be a Catholic and gay.'

'He's got a right to his opinion.'

'Are you going to stop going to church because of him?'

'No, of course not.'

Mr. Norris's plan was to convert Mr. Lewis, eventually. But there was no need to rush things along. One step at a time.

'And what about Walter? You know he has a crush on you.'

'I'm sorry, but I don't date minors.'

'You don't, huh? What about your little model?'

'Tudi happens to be twenty-seven years old. And for heaven's sake, why bring her up?'

With machinelike precision, Mrs. Norris deposited five similar-looking sequins into five different bins. 'Her boyfriend happened to call, that's why.'

'Alan?'

'Yes, Alan. We had a very interesting little chat. He's broken up with her, you know.'

'No, I didn't.'

'He can't stand the idea of her not paying any rent.'

'Well . . . Did he leave a number?'

'What?'

'Nothing.'

'I just hope you're satisfied, Mr. Norris. Add another notch to your belt. Here's yet another relationship you've busted up. And Alan sounds like such a nice young man.'

'He's not that young. He looks around forty.'

'I suppose that makes it all right, then.'

'No, I meant—'

'That's sage, Lloyd. Don't put it in the avocado bin.'

'Are you here this morning, Norris?'

'No, no calls. I still haven't finished this report, Dusty.'

'What about Mr. L-E-W-I-S?'

'Did he call?'

'No.'

'If he does, put him through. And also, if an Alan calls, I'll take it.'

'Alan who?'

Mr. Norris didn't know his last name. It was a little embarrassing.

'Hey, Norris, you don't mean Alan Supervia, do you, man?'

'Who's Alan Supervia?'

'Tudi's ex.'

'Go away, I'm busy.'

'The guy whose arm you nearly broke.'

'It was just a sprain. And it wasn't me.'

'Some brawl, huh? Six or seven guys, I heard, all mixing it up over that twerp. I just don't see what's so great about that airhead.'

'Tudi's not an airhead. Now go away. Leave me alone.'

Chapter Twenty-Eight

On Friday at six Mr. Norris hurried straight from work to his apartment over the nurses' uniform shop. Tudi had landed a job modeling antipersonnel vests for a Pentagon video. It was being taped in Atlantic City, which meant that his apartment was now free for the entire weekend. Until Sunday at five, at least.

Mr. Norris was tearing the price tag off the denim workshirt he had bought during his lunch hour – Ralph Lauren – when the buzzer rang. His hair! He still hadn't sprayed his hair!

'Kind of dark,' Mr. Lewis said when he walked in.

'Well, you can open these blinds during the day.'

Mr. Lewis peered between the slats. 'What's that?'

'An ice cream factory.'

'An ice cream factory?'

'Low fat.'

Mr. Lewis sniffed one of Tudi's sweet williams on the sill. 'I don't know. How much did you say?'

'Twenty-one hundred.'

'You got to be kidding, Norris.'

'That's what I pay. But you could have it for less.'

'How less?'

'Well, like you said at dinner, you told Dawne it'd take you maybe two, three months to finish your film—'

'Don? Who's Don?'

'The lady at the Japanese restaurant, the one who got sprayed.'

'Oh, right.'

'So if you need a place to stay for now, well, just give me whatever you can afford, like maybe what your other sublet is.'

'I can't afford the other sublet. That's why I'm moving.'

'Oh. Well, whatever . . .'

Mr. Lewis gingerly probed a green latex tulip that emitted a pulse of light. 'What the . . . ?'

'An air freshener, Tudi's. She'll take it with her.' Mr. Norris unplugged it from the socket. The smell was clashing with his Georgia O'Keeffe for Men, sixty-five dollars an ounce. 'And those posters' – he gestured toward the musicians on the wall, pierced and tattooed widows of metallic superstars – 'those aren't mine, either.'

'So when is she moving out?'

'She promised in two weeks.'

Mr. Lewis sidled past the mini-refrigerator and stuck his head inside the bedroom. 'My closet's bigger than this, pal.'

'It's the bed. That's what makes it seem so small. I shouldn't have bought a king-size bed.'

'How do you get dressed and all? There's no friggin' room.'

'Sure there is. You stand on the bed.'

'And look up at the mirror, huh?'

Mr. Norris blushed. Without asking him, Tudi had installed reflecting tiles on the ceiling. 'Those will be easy to take down. They're not mine, of course.'

'Could I keep the leopard bedspread? It's cool.'

'You'll have to ask Tudi. She might sell it to you.'

Taking a step back into the kitchen, Mr. Lewis accidentally turned on the trash compactor.

'See?' Mr. Norris said as a horrible screech filled the apartment. 'You won't have to take out the garbage every day.'

'Twenty-one hundred a month and they don't even give you a stove?'

'This microwave will do a turkey in twenty minutes.'

'Anybody would have to be out of his mind to rent this place. What is it, about three square feet?'

'Ezra Pound used to live here. Did you see the plaque outside?'

'Is that why you got it, Norris – because a Fascist lived here?'

'Actually, I didn't read the plaque until after I signed the lease. I just thought, you know, it'd be easy to clean. You can do all the vacuuming from the love seat, sitting down. And anyway, I didn't have any time to look around. Plus, I was in a state of shock, from the divorce and all.'

Mr. Lewis leaned over and blew out a candle on the table that folded down like a Murphy bed. 'Why's it so dark in here?' He switched on an overhead light. 'Your hair.'

'What?' Mr. Norris peered at himself in the microwave's window. A strand was sticking straight up, like Alfalfa's. And something was wrong with his Ralph Lauren. It was buttoned wrong – he had skipped one at the bottom.

'It looks bigger in the dark,' Mr. Norris explained as he squashed down the strand.

'Huh?'

'The apartment. I find if you keep the lights low . . .'

Mr. Lewis reached over and grabbed Mr. Norris's crotch. 'Just as I thought, pal.'

'No, you don't understand, I . . . I drank too much water.'

Mr. Lewis had backed off, surveying him with folded arms. 'Drank too much water? Look, pal, don't bullshit me. What kind of dope you take me for?'

'Ken, I . . .'

'You ask me over to look at this apartment that I can have for practically nothing, right?'

'No, I was going to ask for a lot, really.'

'And there's shrimp and caviar set out here on this table . . .'

'That was for me. I'm just trying to eat healthy.'

'And I bet you got wine chilling in that joke of a refrigerator.'

'No, no, don't open it. You'll let out all the . . .'

Mr. Lewis took out the bottle of chardonnay. The price tag was still on it. $39.95.

'You think I'm some piece of trade, Norris?'

Mr. Norris hung his head.

'You think you can buy me with this crap?'

'Look, I was just trying to help.'

'Help?'

'I really admire what you're trying to do, Ken. I know it can't be easy drawing an animated film by hand.'

'You bi's disgust me.'

'Bi? Who's bi?'

'Tudi's not enough for you?'

'Ken, believe me. I just like men, period. Tudi has nothing to do with me.'

'No?'

'I swear.'

'What about that dame who got sprayed? She sure seemed to like you, pal.'

'She's a lesbian, Ken. Didn't you hear her say that?'

'Sure I heard all right. But I saw, too. Those looks she gave you.'

Actually, Mr. Norris would rather not talk about Dawne at all. How could he possibly explain to Mr. Lewis the latest development, what had happened since she had got sprayed? Over their sea urchins, Dawne and Mr. Lewis had had a terrible argument about religion, which had only made Dawne more religious than ever. She had subsequently announced to Mr. and Mrs. Norris at breakfast this very morning that Candy and Erma had converted her. She was now an ex-gay. Mrs. Norris had been very accepting and embraced her Mermaiden and cried. But Mr. Norris had thrown down his napkin in disgust. How could a woman who had been married all of her adult life, who had never once slept with a woman, how could such a woman have the audacity to call herself an ex-gay? She never was a gay to begin with!

'In that drawer there,' Mr. Norris said.

Mr. Lewis pulled out a corkscrew and applied it to the bottle. 'I don't get you, Norris.'

'There's nothing to get. I just like you a lot, Ken. An awful lot. I admire you, your integrity, the way you—'

'Integrity? So you try to buy me? Man, let me tell you something. This is chickenfeed. If I wanted, I could have done much better than this.'

'Ken, please, I wasn't . . . It's about me, not you. I just needed a way to see you again.'

'So you made up all this crap about the apartment?'

'Well, actually, I mean . . .'

'Why didn't you just call and say you wanted to go out?'

'Because I didn't think, unless I had something, some reason, I didn't think you'd be interested.'

'So let me speak for myself, how about it? See, pal, you don't have to act like some sneaky, slimy old pervert.'

'I don't?'

'No.'

On the coffee table in the living room were the remains of the lobster bisque that Mr. Norris had heated up for supper in the microwave. Mr. Lewis had shed his workboots. Though he usually didn't drink more than a glass of wine, he said the chardonnay was so good they should open another bottle. Mr. Norris apologized. The other bottle was a merlot.

'What? Two people in this dump?' Mr. Lewis said as Mr. Norris poured the merlot. 'You aren't serious?'

'Why not?'

'Look, pal, no offense, but you'd drive me nuts.'

'I'm very neat.'

'Hands off.'

'Sorry. And I'm quiet. I don't listen to loud music.'

'Don't grovel.'

'Am I groveling?'

'You want to grovel, save it for your boss lady.'

Earlier, over caviar and shrimp, Mr. Norris had confessed. He had reminded Mr. Lewis of the man on his knees in Ms. Vigoris's office. Yes, it was he. But he had only done it to prevent Mr. Lewis from feeling degraded, so Mr. Lewis would not have to wipe up the coffee on the Norwegian rug, which he probably didn't realize was an original work of art, designed by the CEO of one of NyLo's biggest clients, an Arkansas foot-powder dynasty. Mr. Lewis said it would have been better, much better, if he had never confessed. There were some things in life he'd just rather not know. But Mr. Norris said it was weighing on his conscience. He had to.

'I could sleep out here. You could have the bedroom to yourself. I wouldn't be allowed in it.'

'Hands off.'

Mr. Norris continued massaging Mr. Lewis's wonderful deltoids, which ached, Mr. Lewis had said, from too much word processing. 'I'd be at work almost all the time, Ken. You'd have the place to yourself, really. I'd promise to come home late.'

'Look, Norris, forget it. I need my own space. Period.'

'I don't think you realize how much I . . . respect you.'

'Stop.'

Mr. Norris released his shoulders and moved aside. 'Ken, what I'm trying to say— I want to do the honorable thing, whatever it is men can do when they . . . I mean, if it weren't illegal, I'd ask you to marry me.'

Mr. Lewis just sat there on the floor, his head against the love seat. 'You're nuts, you know.'

'Why?'

'First of all, you don't know me. You just don't ask people you don't know to freakin' marry you.'

'But I do know you. There's something so good in you, so wonderful, wounded. I just know we're meant for each other.'

'Really? Then figure this one out. I think this whole marriage thing with men is a bunch of crap. It's not natural.'

'Ken.'

'Don't "Ken" me. It's sick, a sick imitation of a sick society. People aren't meant to be monogamous – not even women. Scares the shit out of me, the whole idea I'd have to wake up to the same old face for the rest of my life. My God, there ought to be some compensation for being gay. I mean, we suffer enough for it as it is. Why lay this monogamy crap on us, then? It's a guilt trip, pal. And I've had it with guilt.'

'But sometimes guilt is a useful—'

'Can it, Norris. I didn't come over here to talk.'

'Huh?'

Mr. Norris picked up the packet of mayonnaise Mr. Lewis had tossed onto the cushion. Did he want a hamburger?

'Hamburger? Are you blind, Norris?'

'I sat on my glasses this afternoon. The frames are all bonkers.' By now, Mr. Norris realized what he was holding in his hand. But for some reason, he couldn't really acknowledge it. 'Dusty said she could fix them and ended up breaking off the thingamajig, but anyway, they've got good hamburgers at this diner around the corner, or I could heat up another lobster bisque. I got two just in case you were really hungry, and there's more merlot, look. Do you like red or white better, I wasn't sure. That's why I got both.'

The hand continued to squeeze his crotch.

'Shut up, Norris.'

'Shut up?'

'You're big, you know.'

'I am?'

'Hasn't anyone ever told you, pal?'

'I just thought I was sort of normal.'

'No, sir, you're not normal at all. The first time I saw you, I had a hunch.'

'A hunch?'

'Yeah, I said to myself, "This guy's not normal."'

'Please move in, Ken.'

'Stifle.'

'You can pay half the rent. Or . . . Or we could find a bigger place, cheaper. We don't have to live in the Village.'

'Quiet, will you?'

'Ken, don't open that.'

'Got to.'

'No, don't.'

'Look, pal, I'm not going down on you without this—'

'No. Stop.'

'What the . . . ?'

Mr. Norris finished zipping up his stonewashed jeans. 'Can't we just hug for a while?'

'You for real?'

'Let's give ourselves time, Ken. Get to know each other . . .'

Mr. Lewis sat there a moment. Perhaps it was the merlot that made him look dazed, stupefied.

'You're the biggest ass I ever met,' Mr. Lewis said after he yanked on his workboots.

'Please, don't go.'

'Let me out of here.'

Mr. Norris turned the lock in the right direction and opened the door. 'Can I call you sometime? Please?'

'In your dreams, pal.'

Chapter Twenty-Nine

The leopard wasn't warm enough. Mr. Norris huddled beneath it, too weary to search for a proper blanket. From time to time he would doze off, thinking he was still awake. Hour after hour dragged on until suddenly he sat up, alert. Something was different. Thudding painfully, his heart told him he was no longer alone. And yes, through a crack in the bedroom door, he could see a dim light.

Hope surged through him as he threw off the coarse hide and crawled to the foot of the bed. 'Ken, is that you?'

Perhaps Mr. Lewis had returned, regretting his harsh words, his callous behavior. Like the prodigal son, he would be welcomed back with open arms. Mr. Norris would hold him close through the long night, soothing every doubt, not asking for any apologies, any promises – no questions at all . . . Except maybe one: How had he managed to get back inside the apartment? Mr. Norris was sure he had locked the door.

After hesitating a few moments, Mr. Norris took courage and threw open the door. But it was neither a burglar nor Mr. Lewis who spun around from the mini-refrigerator, a shrimp in one hand, a gun in the other.

'Don't shoot!' Mr. Norris's hands lifted in vague surrender. 'I didn't do anything, officer! I'm innocent.'

With the gun, the policeman raised the brim of his cap. Mr. Norris, horrified, recognized the face. What had once seemed so supremely handsome had now become the very countenance of the Judgment Seat. Why, oh why hadn't Tudi ever bothered to mention that her boyfriend – or ex-boyfriend – was one of New York City's Finest!

'Innocent of what, man?'

'We didn't do anything, honest.'

'We? I thought she was in Atlantic City.'

'Oh, Tudi – yes, of course. She is.'

The jumbo shrimp plopped into Mr. Supervia's mouth. 'She said you'd be using the place tonight. But, man, you scared the shit out of me, banging open the door like that. Take it easy, will you?'

'Yes, I will.'

The muscles of his square jaw bulged as the shrimp was pulverized – tail, feelers, and all. 'You seen any place mats around here with Mexico on them?'

'I don't think so.'

'They're mine, you know. I thought long as I was in the neighborhood, I'd drop by and pick them up. See, I was doing this gig on Patchin Place and – Gotta take a whiz.'

'Be my guest.'

As he headed for the bathroom, Mr. Supervia squirted a Chia with his gun. Mr. Norris regarded the droplets on the sheep's foliage with relief – and some puzzlement.

'Yo, man,' Mr. Supervia said from the bathroom, 'no hard feelings, huh? Like sorry about Friday's, roughing you up and all.'

'That's OK.'

'See,' he went on, back in the kitchen again, 'like I couldn't believe you were really a faggot. You don't seem like a homo, you know. Anyone ever told you that? And then there was all that rent stuff, not charging Tudi a cent. So I called up your old lady to get the real lowdown. Figured if anyone should know if a guy's a homo, it'd be his wife. And she says, yeah, no doubt about it. No bi shit. Just plain unadulterated queer. Shake?'

'No, Mr. Supervia, I won't shake with someone who calls me a faggot.' Besides, the man hadn't washed his hands. He had just relieved himself – with the door wide open – and walked out.

'You mean I was right about you, man? You're not—'

'No, no, those words. I object to your language.'

'So what do I say?'

'You've never heard of gay? Or maybe just plain human being?'

'OK, human bean – shake.'

Conquering his fear of herpes, Mr. Norris shook, a brief manly grip that made him wish he had put a robe on over his pajamas. He edged closer to the counter so that only his top half was showing, and tried to focus on women – Mrs. Kundaa, in particular – while the man went on talking.

'You know, Norris, I've been thinking. Maybe it's a mistake breaking up with, uh . . .'

'Tudi?'

'Yeah, I mean maybe she wasn't really fooling around on me all this time. Like she was telling me, too, how you been bugging her lately, trying to get her out of here. She said you'd been acting like a real twit lately.'

Mr. Norris tried to ignore the reflection of himself in Mr. Supervia's badge, which seemed rather large. 'I'm divorced, you know. Is it a crime for a divorced twit to want some peace and quiet in his own apartment?'

'So what do you think? Should I get back together with her again?'

Mr. Norris sighed. 'Isn't Tudi a little young for you?'

'What's that supposed to mean?'

'I don't want to sound intrusive or anything, but Tudi is only twenty-seven.'

'Yeah, so? How old do you think I am? You think a forty-five-year-old would have pecs like these?'

Without undoing a single brass button, Mr. Supervia managed to expose some well-defined cleavage.

'Still think I'm too old, Norris?'

'Hm . . .' The pecs rippled.

'You think those dames on Patchin Place would pay me two hundred bucks to deliver a jaywalking summons if I looked like your average forty-five? They all thought I was thirty.'

'Oh, it's Velcro,' Mr. Norris commented as the uniform was spliced back together again. 'Well, look. It's after two. I've really got to get some sleep. Good night, Mr. Supervia. And if you'd like to take some of those shrimp back home with you, feel free.'

In bed again, Mr. Norris did his best to fall asleep. But every time a phosphorescent digit advanced in the stomach of Tudi's Pocahontas clock, the click would register, loud as a cuckoo. On the Arts and Entertainment Channel the previous week, Mr. Norris had found himself watching a biography of Wayne Newton. Mr. Newton, it seemed, was a descendant of Pocahontas. Trying his best to be true to Mr. Lewis, Mr. Norris began to wonder now if perhaps Mr. Newton and Mrs. Kundaa might be related.

'Open up!'

Mr. Norris bolted upright. The pounding threatened to crack the veneer paneling on the door. Slipping into a robe, Mr. Norris called out, 'Just a minute, will you?'

'What's the big idea?' Mr. Supervia demanded once Mr. Norris managed to get the door open. 'You locked yourself in.'

Mr. Norris shrugged. 'So?'

'Just who do you think you are, anyway?'

'I'm afraid I don't understand, Mr. Supervia.'

'Listen, boy, any homo worth his salt don't lock his door when I'm around. Something's not kosher here, see? Like why didn't you stay up a little longer, try to get me drunk. You got all that wine sitting in the fridge, don't you?'

'Actually, I don't think you're my type.'

'Your type? What's wrong with me?'

'Well, for one thing you're straight – correct?'

'Damn right. Got a problem with that?'

'No, no, many of my best friends are. It's just that I respect Tudi a lot even if she did call me a twit and I don't think I'd ever fool around with someone she might be—'

'Cut the crap.'

'Well, and then there's this other guy I'm interested in and besides, wouldn't you sort of beat me to a pulp if I tried anything?'

'Damn straight. You'd live to regret it.'

'Then how can you expect me to make a pass when you yourself admit—'

'What kind of chickenshit are you? Someone like me should be worth the risk. I tell you, man, Dusty must be right about you. You're not really a homo at all.'

'Dusty? You mean Tudi.'

'Yeah, like I said – Tudi.'

'Well, I'm sorry you all have to feel that way. I've been trying to be as honest as I could and—'

'Get out of here.'

'Yes, well – 'Night.'

With a muted sigh, Mr. Norris shut the door. He was crawling back under the leopard when he paused to consider something.

'Mr. Supervia?'

The man was stuffing shrimp into a plastic bag. 'Don't try to prove anything now, buddy. Too late. I won't believe a thing you do.'

'No, no,' Mr. Norris said from the bedroom door. 'This isn't a pass. I'm just wondering, did you by any chance ever try out for Chippendale's? Did they reject you five or six times?'

'Screw you.'

'No, no, as far as I'm concerned, well, you should've got in, really. But I was asking because—'

'So what do those assholes know? My body–fat ratio is ten times lower than those prisses they let in.'

'You've been going out with Dusty, right?'

Mr. Supervia tucked the shrimp into his knapsack, right next to his rollerblades. 'Hey, that's top secret, man. Tudi finds out and I'm dead meat.'

'How can you be going out with Dusty and saying you want to get back with—'

'Look, it's not my fault. I brought Tudi a carrot shake at work one day and while I was waiting for the elevator, Dusty came up and started hitting on me. So what am I supposed to do? You can't say no to a fine-looking chick.'

'You can't?'

'No real man would. Besides, I was teed off at Tudi then. I didn't believe all that rot about you being a homo.'

'Mr. Supervia, do you realize that I'm Dusty's boss?'

'Yeah. She's the one been telling me this queer jag of yours, it's bullshit. Says you've been boffing the bitch that runs the joint.'

'Vigoris?'

'No, some cereal.'

'Special K?'

'Yeah. And she says you keep on trying to feel *her* up, too, the Dustbuster. I tell her she don't have to go whining to some CEO about harasstion. I'd get to the bottom of this myself, find out what the real story is on you. Now I guess I know.'

'Hey, how about some wine, Mr. Supervia?'

'Yeah, right. I'm outta here, buddy.'

'It's real good, expensive. Come on, one little sip.'

'Don't make me laugh.'

'No, I mean it. I paid forty dollars not including tax. Well, actually thirty-nine ninety-five.'

'Outta my way. You tell your girlfriend she's got about the worst taste in men I ever seen.'

The door slammed. Mr. Norris took the glass he had been brandishing in Mr. Supervia's face and filled it to the brim. He would finish the merlot himself, alone.

Chapter Thirty

On Monday morning Mr. Norris called WyTech. Two weeks earlier they had made him an offer to come aboard as an executive vice president in charge of human auditing. This would mean making $10,000 more than he was at NyLo. Plus stock options, bonuses. But Mr. Norris had phoned back and said no. His conscience wouldn't let him accept such an unseemly raise. Instead, he had asked them to please hire Mr. Bruce Powers, a giant in the industry, a real man's man. Three days later WyTech had upped the ante to $15,000. At that point, Mr. Norris had to be blunt. WyTech, after all, did not have the nurturing, nonpaternalistic, family environment that Mr. Norris had grown used to at NyLo. Indeed, WyTech was notorious for its vicious dog-eat-dog mentality. Few women could stand the strain there. And men fell by the wayside just as often. Mr. Norris was certain they would not tolerate a gay man in their executive corps, which the *New York Observer* had described as a paradise for brain-dead white jocks. So Mr. Norris had told them he was a homosexual. A day later, the offer jumped to $20,000.

If Mr. Norris's reputation as a gay man weren't in absolute tatters at NyLo, he would have been able to turn down the $20,000. But Dusty was building a case against him. She was planning to have him up for sexual harassment, he just knew. As if it weren't bad enough that he was supposedly shacking up with Tudi, but then there was that incident in the CEO's office. Ms. Vigoris had told Dusty how Mr. Norris had tried to cop a look up her Armani. Worst of all, Dusty had heard that Mr. Norris's churchgoing was getting out of hand. He had somehow forced a radical lesbian feminist to become a religious nut, an ex-gay. Of course, Mr. Norris did his best to explain himself. But he always had the feeling that Dusty wasn't listening too closely.

Needless to say, Mr. Norris was aware that in a matter of weeks, after a brief honeymoon period at WyTech, he would be exposed as a fraud. WyTech thought they were hiring a wolf in sheep's clothing, one of the most cunning, vicious executives to hit the labeling industry in years. What they were actually getting, though, was a sheep in sheep's clothing. It would be dreadful, of course, to be exposed as a kind, humane, moral human being who hated John Wayne. But Mr. Norris had been sure to provide himself with a golden parachute before climbing aboard. Or at least a silver one. He would be able to float gently into old age after he was fired, with a tidy pension that could be supplemented by a low-stress job – perhaps waiting on tables. In fact, he had already talked to Mario at the steakhouse, told him to keep his ears open.

'Cheers, Mr. Norris.'

Mr. Norris touched the rim of his plastic glass to Walter's. Two ShopRite martinis in the atrium, Walter's idea. He wanted to celebrate Mr. Norris's new job – a nice gesture. Mr. Norris was glad to learn that Walter held no grudges. But he couldn't quite figure out how the man had found out so quickly that he had accepted WyTech's offer. He hadn't told anyone about it yet except for Mrs. Norris. And she had sworn she had said nothing to Walter herself.

'A little bird.'

'Walter, please be serious. Which bird told you? This was all top secret.'

'Dear boy, do you really think you can have secrets from Uncle Walter?'

Luigi, the bartender, was serving an elderly woman. Tomato juice. He poured so deftly, with such grace. Mr. Norris sighed.

'So how's the job going, Walter?'

'What job?'

'Didn't you just get a new job?'

'Oh, that.'

Walter was now supposedly working as a screener for the Leeuwarden. Candidates who had survived an initial interview with the star chamber would be sent to Utensils at Bed Bath & Beyond. As these hopefuls purchased a garlic press or grater, they had no idea, of course, who was waiting on them. Being a man was the perfect disguise.

'Is it hard, Walter?'

'I beg your pardon?'

'Your job.'

'Impossible. I have yet to find a single woman who knows how to comport herself. One actually sported a Kelly bag – I kid you not. Another waltzed in on the arm of a man in moving pictures, an actor, and he wasn't even obscure. Then when I thought I had found someone, a young woman who refused to allow anyone remotely celebrated or good-looking into her building—'

'Co-op?'

'Yes, she's on the board and resigned from the Colony Club when they allowed a supermodel inside.'

'What went wrong with her?'

'She said "enthuse."'

'Oh.'

They both took a discreet sip or two.

'So, Walter, was it Dusty? Did she tell you about WyTech?'

'My lips are sealed.'

'I think she sometimes listens in to my calls. When I was home in Yonkers once, she—'

'Thought you were back in the city.'

'I am, sort of. But Tudi's still not completely moved out. She keeps coming back whenever she and Alan have a fight.'

'Alan?'

'That's her ex-boyfriend. She's camping out at his place until she can find a place of her own. I tried to tell her it wasn't the greatest idea. But it's none of my business interfering in people's love lives and all. Not that I interfere. I just think Tudi could do better, as far as an ex goes. She's a fine young woman.'

'Might as well let her have the apartment, Norris, for all the good it does you.'

'What's that supposed to mean?'

'Ken told me everything about your little supper. He thinks you're off your rocker.'

It was like a blow to the solar plexus. What could Ken mean by discussing such an intimate moment with Walter? Was there no sense of decency, no respect for a person's privacy?

'Just because I don't want to be another of his one-night stands, Walter, does that mean I'm crazy?'

'At your age, yes.'

'I'm younger than he is.'

'But not half as good-looking. It's time you faced facts, Norris. Life after forty is no picnic for a gay man. You take what you can get.' Walter squinted in the direction of the bamboo, as if he were hoping to discern another stalker. 'Here you had a chance to learn something from an expert about pleasuring another man.'

Mr. Norris shuddered. The barbarism grated more exquisitely than anything in Utensils.

'Maybe I want more than that.'

'Than what?'

'More than pleasure, Walter. Not less.'

'You are a greedy son of a bitch. Speaking of which, there's your Beak.'

'What?'

Mr. Monke-Peelston was striding from the elevator bank toward the exit. Like a foil, the umbrella tucked smartly against his thigh was ready to be unsheathed at the least provocation. Yes, there were clouds, but the chance of rain today, according to Dawne's astrologer, was 9 percent.

'Don't call him that, Walter. And stop waving. Sit.'

'He's going to get away.'

'Let him. Now tell me, was it Mrs. Kundaa?'

'I'm saying nothing except go get me another.' He held up his empty glass.

'Was she the one who told you about WyTech?'

'We're not speaking.'

'But she got you that job, didn't she?'

'Behind my back, through friends. She knows how I hate to work, I loathe it. Now are you going to get me that drink?'

'Why should I buy you a drink?'

'Because it's my turn to celebrate.'

'Your job?'

'My love life.'

'I'm very glad, Walter, but I'm not buying you anything until you help me out. It's very important that I make this transition to WyTech as smoothly as possible. I don't want everyone hating me at NyLo.'

'Why not?'

'Because I haven't done anything wrong.'

'Since when has that ever stopped people from hating you?'

'Do people hate me?'

With a finger to his lip, Walter mused.

'Walter, tell me. Who hates me?'

'I was speaking generically.'

'Do you think Mrs. Kundaa will hate me when she finds out? I'm a little nervous about this. Last night I could barely sleep.'

Walter licked a few droplets from the bottom of his glass. 'My impression has always been, Mr. Norris, that you *want* her to hate you.'

'Not hate me. Dislike me. Sort of be indifferent toward me, uncaring, as if I were a stranger on a subway. I don't want her thinking how horrible and ungrateful I am, you know, after all I've done for you at NyLo, you have the gall to walk right out on me, blah blah blah.'

'Disloyalty.'

'Right, because I'm not the disloyal type. My whole life I've done nothing but been loyal to people I don't really like that much. Like Bruce – I know when he finds out I got the job, he's going to think I stole it away from him.'

'Why would he think that?'

'Because after I had turned down WyTech's first offer, I made him call them up and apply himself. And I gave him a great recommendation, too.'

'So how can he think you stole it?'

'Because I didn't tell him that I had turned them down first. I was afraid it would sound like – as if I were boasting, giving him my leavings. I thought he'd have more confidence if he just went ahead without all that baggage attached.'

'So you got his hopes up, right?'

'I tried to make them hire him. But when they told me there was no way, they would never hire him, not even if I said no, that's when I decided I could accept the job. If he'd had a real chance, I never would have.'

'OK, Norris, so you've got Bruce hating your guts, thinking you're a real lowlife. So?'

'So? It bothers me. It's not fair. I know he'll never believe me when I try to explain.'

'Don't worry. I'll always like you – unless you don't get up off that fat ass and buy me a drink.'

Mr. Norris took the glass he held out and brought it to Luigi, who was in the midst of a sale to the elderly woman. She was trying to make up her mind whether to buy a cell phone from him or not.

'What took you so long?' Walter said when Mr. Norris returned. 'I nearly perished.'

'You know, I think Luigi's forgotten who I am. He made me wait forever.'

Walter sipped the fresh martini. 'So congratulate me.'

'Congratulations. What did you do?'

'I think I'm in love again. My whole life is about to be solved.'

Walter's blue eyes beamed with such delight and merriment that Mr. Norris almost winced.

'And it's all because of you.'

Mr. Norris winced.

Walter chuckled. 'Please, Mr. Norris, relax. You're safe as any straphanger could possibly be. I dislike you, I'm indifferent, whatever you want. But I still owe you one.'

'Huh?'

'If you hadn't been so prim and proper the other night, yours truly wouldn't have got lucky.'

'What are you talking about?'

'Ken was so steamed up on Friday, he came bursting into my apartment and took me right there, on the kitchen floor. I was defrosting, and now he's going to move in with me.'

'What?'

'Now that we're both poor, he doesn't mind sharing a place. Aren't you glad?'

'Very glad.'

'You know, it's funny. For years now I've been trying to loosen Ken up, get him potted. I always had a hunch that would do the trick. Men seem to appreciate me so much more when they can barely see straight. And it turned out I was right. You wouldn't believe what that animal did to me. I was standing there wondering what to do with some Neapolitan that was melting, and Ken takes—'

'Please, Walter.' Mr. Norris held up a restraining hand. 'Spare me the details.'

'Well, anyway, you'll have to tell me your secret. Just how did you manage to get him to drink more than a glass? He always stops after one glass with me.'

'Perhaps if you stopped serving from gallon jugs. Now if you'll excuse me.'

'Aren't you going to have another with me?'

'Pearl Fay, dinner, I've got to . . .'

He was halfway to the revolving door when he heard his name shouted out.

'Your briefcase, Mr. Norris! Don't forget your briefcase!'

As Mr. Norris retrieved it, Walter said, 'I wonder why it's called Neapolitan. Why would chocolate, strawberry, and vanilla refer to Naples? Or perhaps it's Nablus the flavors refer to.'

'Nablus?'

'It's a city in Samaria. The Greeks called it Neapolis, which was what they called Naples, too. The new city, so to speak. Maybe mixing all those flavors together, like all the races in a—'

'Walter, I don't have time to stand around and discuss ice cream.'

'You don't hate me, do you?'

'Why should I hate you?'

'For stealing your boyfriend.'

'I told you I'm glad, very glad.'

Mr. Norris made an about-face and marched off.

Chapter Thirty-One

The bed, all rumpled, was empty. Mr. Norris knocked on the bathroom door. 'Hello?' He peered inside. No one.

At the nurses' station, an intern told him she didn't have a clue. When a nurse finally arrived, Mr. Norris asked again.

'McBride? 316B.'

'Yes, I know. But he's not there.'

'He's there.'

'But I just—'

'316B.'

'But—'

'You got something wrong with you, mister?'

'Wrong?'

'Why you make me say everything over?'

If the nurse hadn't been distracted by a question from the intern, a polite young lady with braces, Mr. Norris might have told the man a thing or two. Brooding, he wandered back down the hall. It would serve the nurse right if he reported him to his superiors. The impertinence of such a remark – 'Something wrong with you' indeed! But what if the man's boss thought that Mr. Norris was prejudiced, a racist, stirring up trouble because the nurse was black, a West Indian. Worse yet, what if the nurse claimed that Mr. Norris had been staring at his biceps, big, bulging melons shamelessly on display in that skimpy, sleeveless outfit.

Someone *was* in the room now. But it wasn't the patient. A parishioner, no doubt, who had not only usurped the only chair but also Mr. Norris's *Star*. Actually, it was Mrs. Norris's *Star*. Mr. Norris had found it lying on the backseat of the Taurus when he had driven over to the hospital that afternoon. He was very disappointed that she would spend good money on such trash.

Brushing against a helium balloon – 'Yo, Love Ya!' – Mr. Norris leaned against the wall.

'That nurse out there,' Mr. Norris said after an awkward silence. The man didn't even bother to introduce himself, just sat there reading with his loafers propped on the railing of Father McBride's bed.

'Great guy.' The man licked his finger and turned a page. 'Dad gets such a charge out of him, just loves him.'

Dad! Was it possible? Could Father McBride have a son? After seven years of confessing to him, Mr. Norris realized how little he knew about his parish priest.

'McBride? No. My old man's in the other bed.'

Mr. Norris didn't know why, but he felt relieved. 'I thought you looked a little old.'

The man flipped another page. 'Thanks.'

'For his son, I mean. He's only sixty, see . . .'

Furtively, Mr. Norris whipped out a comb and ran it through his hair. Stinging sleet had made a mess of the $54 styling he had got in preparation for his first day at WyTech.

A nurse's aide stuck his head in the door and with a wink said to Mr. Norris, 'Your daddy be up in a minute.'

Before Mr. Norris could correct him, the young man had hurried off.

'He must've thought I was you,' Mr. Norris said.

'Huh?'

'My father's dead, see.'

'Oh.'

There were some similarities, actually. The man was gray, balding, around the same age. Of course, he did look as if he were a little taller, in better shape.

Mr. Norris winced as a sharp pain coursed up his thigh. In the midst of his divorce, he had been told by his doctor that it was old age, these sudden pains. If his HMO had allowed it, Mr. Norris would have switched doctors right then and there. He didn't need a twenty-eight-year-old telling him about old age just when he was planning to embark on a long-overdue adolescence.

'Do you mind if I sit on the radiator?' Mr. Norris said as he limped past an IV pole. 'I've got to sit down.'

'What radiator?'

'That ledge next to you – isn't that sort of a radiator?'

'Sit on the bed, fella.'

'I'm all wet.' Mr. Norris squeezed past the man's blue jeans to get to the ledge. 'Oh, gosh. Are these yours? I'm sorry.'

The man took the box of Whitman's Samplers that Mr. Norris had squashed when he sat down.

'I'll buy another.'

'Forget it. Dad shouldn't be eating these, anyway.'

'Do you know what's wrong with him?' Mr. Norris asked after refusing a leaking cherry cordial.

'Dad?'

'No, Father McBride. I just drove over to confession a while ago, and they told me he was here.'

The man shrugged his broad shoulders. 'He's new, just came in. The man before him, he had angina.'

'Oh.'

'Died.'

'That's funny. My father had angina. That's what . . .'

Mr. Norris groped in the pockets of his soggy camel hair

overcoat, but before he could find his handkerchief, the man had reached over and handed him a tissue. Mr. Norris blew.

'You OK, fella?'

Embarrassed by the sudden emotion, Mr. Norris asked for another tissue, then wiped his eyes. 'Sorry – it's just that, they all blame me, my family.'

'Your dad?'

Mr. Norris nodded. 'They said the shock weakened his heart, my brothers and sisters did. See, I had to get married. And she was underage, a Baptist. Dad went to Mass every day.'

'Catholic?'

'Knights of Columbus, all that. And then my mother, she had a stroke not long after – when my wife had a miscarriage. My mother suspected it was an abortion, but it wasn't, I swear. She got so worried about me, I mean she thought I was lying, trying to cover up for Pearl Fay. Anyway, she got so worried about my soul, the state of my soul, well, she just went ahead and died.' Mr. Norris blew again. 'Then Pearl Fay and I, we felt so bad we moved as far away as we could. I got into Harvard, see.'

'Harvard?'

'It wasn't so hard to get into back then, not if you were from one of those states like Louisiana.'

'You're Southern? You don't sound Southern.'

'I've been up here awhile, fifteen years.'

The man was glancing at the tabloid again. Overcome by shame, Mr. Norris just sat there, wishing he had kept his trap shut. And yet he wanted so desperately to talk. Why wasn't Father McBride here to listen? He didn't want to go to WyTech. He just wanted to curl up and die.

'Do you know where he might be?'

'McBride? Could be down for an X ray or something. By the way, fella, you think you could give me a lift?'

'Pardon?'

'With this sleet and all, I'll never find a cab. Got to get to the train station.'

'Oh, sure.'

'I'm running a little late as it is – got to make it back to Dobbs Ferry by five.'

'No problem.'

'What are you doing back here, Lloyd? And look, you've got chocolate all over my paper.'

'That's not my chocolate. And I don't think you should buy that paper, Pearl Fay. You should read the *Times*.'

'I need the color photos for my découpage. I'm redoing that cedar chest I was going to throw away. And anyway, I don't need you telling me what I should read. Dawne says the *Times* is totally biased and crazy.'

'Dawne says.'

'And now you're hanging your wet coat right next to my ermine.' She yanked the camel hair out of the closet and gave it a good shake. 'I thought you were going back to the city tonight after confession.'

'I was. But then I had to go to Dobbs Ferry.'

'Dobbs Ferry?'

'This Jesuit needed a ride. I was in the hospital and—'

'What? What hospital?' She was squatting, wiping up some mud he had tracked into the kitchen.

'They told me at Queen of Heaven that Father McBride had to go to the hospital, Our Lady of the Lake. So I drove over and—'

'Is he all right?'

'I guess. I didn't really get a chance to see him. There was a nurse there who was so awful, wouldn't give me any information at all and then Elmo was in a hurry because he had to—'

'Elmo?'

'The Jesuit.' In the Taurus on the way to Dobbs Ferry, Elmo had transmogrified from a possible friend, a date even, into a Jesuit. By then it was too late to drop him off at the train station in Yonkers, which would have been much more convenient for Mr. Norris. So he had driven him the whole way to his church in Dobbs Ferry. 'He had to say the vigil Mass at five today.'

'I don't know why you have to go traipsing around in this weather playing taxi for the Jesuits. Let them pay like anyone else. Believe me, they can afford it.'

He sighed. 'Well, anyway, it's snowing now. There's no way I'm going to make it back to the city tonight.'

'Sure you can. Take the bus.'

'I'm too tired. Besides, I want to call the hospital, see if someone else can tell me about Father McBride.'

'They don't have phones in the city? Look, Lloyd, did it ever occur to you that I might have plans of my own?'

'I'll stay in the den. You go ahead and . . . Not Herbert, I hope.'

'What sort of name is Elmo?'

'Pearl Fay.'

He trailed her into the dining room, which was set for three. She rearranged a pineapple in her centerpiece. 'If I want to have Herbert over, I'll have him over.'

'No, this is impossible.'

'It's very possible, Mrs. Grundy. But it just so happens he's not coming over.'

'I don't know how you can even consider having someone like that in this house.'

'Don't touch the orchids, please.'

'These are orchids? Why must you buy orchids? I told you, Pearl Fay, I'm not going to have this new job for long. We better start saving every penny.'

'My guests happen to be going on a little mini-vacation. To Puerto Rico, Jamaica, something like that. I thought Mrs. Powers—'

'Mrs. Powers? Not Bruce's wife? You're not having them over here tonight?'

'Why not?'

'Because we're even now. We had Bruce over once, and he took us out to dinner once. Besides, when he finds out about my new job, he's going to blow his stack.'

'Exactly. Which is why I'm doing it this way, Lloyd. He's going to get nicely lubricated and eat the best roast suckling he's ever had, and then I'm going to explain how you wound up getting the job at WyTech instead of him.'

'No, no, please don't start meddling in—'

'Would you rather he found out some other way? Dusty?'

'No, but . . .'

It was strange; Mrs. Norris's idea was beginning to make sense.

'They're headed out tomorrow for a wonderful vacation,' she went on. 'He'll have time to digest the whole thing and by the time he gets back, you'll be gone.'

'Well, I . . . I don't know.'

'What's there to know?'

'For one thing, why are there only three places here? What about Dawne?'

'She's got potluck tonight.'

'Not another one of those ex-gay suppers.'

They were back in the kitchen. Mrs. Norris told him to get the charger down from the cupboard. Uncertain what a charger was, he ignored her.

'It gets me so mad, Pearl Fay. To have someone who's never been gay to begin with join a group like that . . .'

'She had a crush on her best friend once, in eighth grade.'

'I'm sorry, but that doesn't count. Girls go through a phase like that.'

'Well, she is pretty mad at men, you got to admit.'

'Why? I don't get it. Her husband sounded like a nice guy. Just because he never yelled at her or beat her up, that's no reason to resent him, say he didn't really love her.'

'Are you going to get that charger? No, that's a trivet. To the left. Now careful. And for your information, don't go telling me what a nice guy her husband was. Do you realize that he left all his money to his mother when he died – not a penny to Dawne, and nearly a million to his mother? For thirty-two years, Lloyd, she was the wife of a millionaire, never had to lift a finger. Now she has to take a menial job so she can get a decent education and support herself.'

'Well, still . . .'

'This is a secret, you know. I'm not supposed to be telling you this. I swore to her you'd never know. But there are limits. When I hear you mouthing off like a bigot about a poor woman who's trying to make friends and—'

'Bigot – me? Pearl Fay, those ex-gays do a lot of terrible harm. They make people think you can have a choice about all this. When you get right down to it, I don't like the idea of that woman hanging around here any longer. It's high time she got a place of her own. Because the next thing you know—'

'Careful. Don't mark the finish.'

They were in the dining room now, where he had set the charger on the gleaming highboy.

'The next you know, you're going to start believing her yourself, Pearl Fay.'

'I'm not that dumb.'

'No, but . . .'

'I just happen to be tolerant. Not everybody has to think the same.'

'Would you be tolerant of Castro if he put me in a concentration camp?'

'Don't be ridiculous.'

'It's not ridiculous.'

'I need a taller candle for the middle. Go down to the basement, hon, and find me a good candle. Who knows? You might finally meet someone there.'

'In the basement?'

'A concentration camp.'

'That's not funny.'

'Lighten up, will you? You're such a drag.'

Chapter Thirty-Two

There is no vase for the rose. Consuelo wanders off to see if a nurse might have something they could use. Marion is left alone at the foot of the bed. The patient has a tube up his nose, oxygen. His eyes flutter.

'Three weeks.'

He glances at the woman next to the room's other bed. Is she addressing him – or talking to herself? The young man she is visiting cannot hear anything. Beneath an oxygen tent, he gasps, eyes closed.

'Three weeks, and no one come to see your friend there, mister. He just lie there alone.'

Her disdain sears Marion. She will not even look over at him. And yet he is innocent. For he is not a friend of this man who is dying. He has even forgotten his name. All he knows is that he is the one who loved Chet. Chet is the man Consuelo wanted to speak to. But when they arrived at Chet's apartment, a woman told them Chet is dead. He has been dead for almost a year. The woman offered them both a cup of tea. She told them she is the

sister of Chet's lover – Amos. Yes, it is Amos – the name comes
to Marion now. Amos, the sister informed them, had been taken
to St. Luke's/Roosevelt.

'Could I use your phone?'

'My what?'

From the chair by the tent the woman points at Marion's lap.
There the phone he did not want Consuelo to buy nestles. Consuelo
bought it from a bartender on the way to the hospital. And right
there, in the lobby of the office building, where they had stopped
to escape the cold for a moment, she had phoned Marion's sister
in Morocco. His sister said yes, she promised to weed the garden.
And yes, she watered every day.

'This phone here,' the woman says, aiming her disdain at the
hospital phone beside her, 'it is no good. I must shout into and
no one can hear me.'

'I hope this is better.' Marion hands her the cell phone.

Her hair thick, luxuriant, she is a most comely woman. Marion
would like to take her in his arms and place his lips on her soft
white . . . He looks away, ashamed.

'I want that coati back in his cage,' she says into the cell phone.
'By the time I get to home, Papi, I better see him back in the cage.
No, I don't want him be free and happy. I come home in one hour
and Señor Magoo better be back in that cage, understand? I do
not have coatis running loose in my apartment no more.'

As she hands the phone back to Marion, Marion looks tenderly
toward the young man under the tent. Disfigured by sores, his calf
seems as thin as Marion's arm.

'Your husband?'

'Grandson. It is the drugs, you know. He share the needle,
that's what.'

She cannot be quite forty yet. Marion, in his sixties, is still not
a grandfather. Though this is not far off for him – another month,
in fact.

'Why you don't visit?' she demands. 'This is terrible. The man
wants the ice cream bar with the chocolate, and me, I have to go

all the way down the elevator and across Nine Avenue because
you not here to get him the bar he want.'

'I don't live here. I live in Morocco.'

The grandmother turns her handsome face away.

'Do you know how far across the ocean Morocco is?'

'Who cares? Go, leave me alone.'

Consuelo returns with the rose in a blue plastic water pitcher.
She places it by a Gameboy on Amos's night table.

'Amos?' Consuelo leans over and whispers. 'Amos, it is Diane.'

Diane is the sister, too terrified to visit. She told Consuelo that
she would not be able to bear the sight. It would kill her.

'Amos?'

A crone's hand reaches out, gnarled, almost fleshless, and grabs
Consuelo's. The eyes stop fluttering. They close.

At Our Lady of the Lake, Father McBride opened his eyes and
smiled.

'I hope I didn't wake you, Father.'

'Just taking a little snooze.'

'I can come back later.'

'No, sit.'

Mr. Norris pulled the chair as close to the bed as possible. 'Did
it go all right?'

'The angiogram? Yes.'

'Will you have to have an operation?'

'I don't know yet.'

'You don't know what I went through, trying to find out what
was wrong, if you were OK. When I called the parish office on
Saturday night, someone said you were in the ICU, and then when
I called here, they asked if I was a relative, and I suppose I shouldn't
have been so honest, because they weren't very forthcoming. It was
awful. I was so worried.'

'Relax, Mr. Norris. I was just there a few hours.'

'In the ICU? And that horrible nurse insisted you were here in
this room.'

'Leeza can be a tough pill to swallow.'

'Not her. This man. Father, I really think you ought to report him to the administration.'

'You don't mean Milton, the guy from Grenada?'

'He was so rude to me, so bossy – and I couldn't have been kinder, more humble. Father, I was a complete doormat. I'm really sick of being a doormat, you know. By the way, would you mind if I went to confession now? I've got something important to confess.'

'Mr. Norris, really, I don't think . . .'

'I missed Saturday. I drove all the way to Queen of Heaven in the sleet and nearly skidded into a carful of nuns. They went sailing right through a stop sign, just blithely ignoring all the rules, talking and laughing. I saw them.'

'Well, they know where they're going.'

'Huh?'

'If they die.'

'Father, please. I'm trying to be serious. I've got to get something off my chest.'

'Couldn't this wait till Saturday?'

'Bless me, Father, for I have sinned. It has been ten days since my last—'

'For heaven's sake.'

'Confession. On Saturday night, Father, I had impure thoughts about my wife.'

'What?'

'I don't mean sexual thoughts – I mean, they were sexual, but not about me. I'm still not attracted to her or anything—'

The priest winced. 'Please watch that IV line.'

'Oh, sorry. Anyway, she had invited this couple over to dinner on Saturday, and since I didn't want to intrude or anything, I went out to eat by myself. There's this Dunkin' Donuts Pearl Fay doesn't like me to go to after Mass—'

'Get to the sin, Mr. Norris. Please.'

'It's part of the sin, Father. I lied to her when I got back and said I hadn't been to Dunkin' Donuts. I had three bear claws. That's got to be a sin, right, eating that junk? Anyway, when I got back home, it was pretty late. See, I had stopped off for a nightcap at this bar at the mall that someone had told me had a gay night. Only the gay night turned out to be Thursday, not Saturday. Saturday is ladies' night. They get all their drinks half price. This truck driver bought me a drink soon as I sat down. I mean, he was drunk, really disgusting. But I was afraid if I turned the drink down, he would beat me up or something.'

'Was it half price?'

'The mimosa? Father, that isn't very nice.'

'Sorry.'

'By the way, do you happen to know a Jesuit, a Father Elmo? He's the son of the man over there, your roommate.'

'That fella's gone, checked out this morning.'

'But did you know the son?'

'Not really. He'd breeze in and out – nice chap. Why?'

Mr. Norris shrugged. 'Anyway, when I got back home, Pearl Fay was furious with me. She wanted to know what I meant by bringing a greasy dirty truck driver into her living room, and I tried to explain how he wouldn't let me stop drinking mimosas and how he decided we were going to be buddies for life, he and I. And how he wanted me to go beat up some fags with him – that's what he calls them – and so I thought it might be prudent to decline the offer and say I had to get home to my wife and fix the mud scraper—'

'Mud scraper?'

'It's this electric thing that's been on the fritz ever since Pearl Fay bought it for our brass anniversary and then the truck driver says he's real mechanical and all and he'll fix it for me. So when Rocco barrels into the living room, there's Pearl Fay on the sofa with Bruce Powers. Well, I just knew something like that was going to happen. I think that's why I got drunk. I just didn't want to face what I was coming home to.'

'Bruce – that's your boss, right?'

'Former boss. Pearl Fay had invited him and his wife over to dinner, only I had a feeling that the wife wasn't going to be able to make it. And it turned out I was right. Vanessa had to go to Indianapolis at the last minute to put siding on some CEO's mansion, so Bruce came alone – and Father, it was awful, I'm so ashamed. I was drunk, see, didn't really know what I was doing.'

'Just what did you do, Mr. Norris?'

'Well, it was more like a sin of omission. I didn't exactly explain to Rocco that Pearl Fay was my ex-wife. So he thought Bruce was fooling around with my wife, and he said no one puts horns on his buddy, and Bruce got mad back at him and said it was none of Rocco's damn business, that Rocco should take his little conniving boyfriend who stole his job away back to the sissy bar they came from, and of course, Rocco wasn't about to take that lying down. He said no one calls his buddy a boyfriend and gets away with it, and the next thing I know they're both going at it right in the living room and break the leg off Pearl Fay's coffee table and then mess up all the CDs on the spinning wheel, and now I feel so awful. Rocco's on crutches now, and Bruce couldn't go to San Juan because he has no hair, you know.'

'Huh?'

'Rocco had him down on the throw rug at one point and yanked off the new toupee Bruce had just bought, a sort of auburn that really looks nice on him, much better than that chestnut he used to have. Anyway, Rocco flushed it down the toilet and for these and all my other sins which I wish you had time to listen to, but I know you're tired, for these I'm heartily sorry. I'll leave now, let you rest if you'll just absolve me.'

'Hold on. Wait.'

'Father, no, I'm not going to smuggle in any cigarettes. I don't think it's right. I already told you that on the phone.'

'Not that, Norris. The IV. Go tell Milton you just yanked it out.'

'What? See, what I told you about him? He's so incompetent.'

Chapter Thirty-Three

'We manufacture labels.'

'For what?'

'Sweaters, vacuum cleaners, soup.'

'How do you put a label on soup?'

'For the can, we design the logo.'

'Oh. Logos.'

Mr. Norris was trying to explain WyTech to the man on his right, Mr. Monke-Peelston. On Mr. Norris's lap was the housewarming gift he had brought to the party. It was a top-of-the-line cappuccino machine that WyTech was obligated to give to each of its vice presidents because of a rider to an amendment in NAFTA. Mr. Norris hated the machine. Even after watching the ninety-minute video – starring an animated cabinet secretary – that explained how to use it, his own secretary had still not mastered the milk part of the operation. Her cappuccino always turned out black.

'Why don't you put that thing over on the gift table?' the woman to his left said, Mrs. Monke-Peelston.

Mr. Norris smiled politely, but kept the box on his lap. Earlier, as he had walked into Walter and Mr. Lewis's new apartment, he had seen a young lady remove a card from one of the gifts on the table and replace it with her own card. Shocked, Mr. Norris tried to pretend he hadn't noticed. But of her own accord, the young woman came up and introduced herself. 'Muffy St. Cushing – I'm Walter's second cousin. You won't mention this to him, will you? See, it's not my fault. Last week someone did this to me, mixed up my card. I had bought my mother-in-law a twenty-four-karat lizard from Tiffany's and I never got the credit for it. So now I'm evening things out, that's all.'

'You mean the person who switched cards on you is here?'

'No. But I still feel I'm owed. I mean, my mother-in-law thought I had bought her an antimacassar.'

'An antimacassar?'

'And it had the price tag on it, a dollar eighty-nine. I was mortified. You can't blame me for wanting some justice now.'

As he sat between Mr. Monke-Peelston and his wife on the futon, Mr. Norris tried not to look disappointed. Walter had not promised a gay party, true. But so far Mr. Norris had not spotted a single stray male.

'Do you know Mrs. St. Cushing?' Mr. Norris asked Mrs. Monke-Peelston.

'Who?'

'The woman who just walked by, over by the window.'

'No. Why?'

'She's pretty, isn't she?'

Mrs. Monke-Peelston frowned. 'I knew it, I just knew it.' She handed Mr. Norris the tuna sandwich that had fallen into her lap from atop the gift. 'Now my dress is ruined.'

'I don't think any tuna got on it. It's just whole-wheat bread.'

'Why must you balance your food on your present, young man? Didn't your mother teach you any manners?'

She struggled to rise from the futon, which was awfully low. Feeling kindly toward her for calling him young, Mr. Norris lent a hand, giving her a little shove or nudge. She gasped. His hand had not landed where he had intended, on the small of her back. Instead, it had somehow ended up farther south.

'Sorry,' Mr. Norris said to her husband, who was gazing at the Spanish peanuts that had rained into his lap when his wife foundered and collapsed back onto the futon. Occupied as he was in gathering his peanuts back onto the napkin atop his box, Mr. Norris did not have to look directly at the wife, who was muttering something about the tuna she had landed on.

'Do you mind?' Mr. Monke-Peelston said as Mr. Norris conscientiously rooted about for every last peanut, including the little red skins that peeled off so easily. 'I'd rather not be fondled in public.'

'I don't really like Spanish peanuts, but I – Oh, hi, Walter. Would you mind taking this?' As Walter relieved him of the gift, Mr. Norris said, 'It's for you and Ken – from me. Nothing really, just a little . . .'

An expensive present would show, of course, that Mr. Norris had no hard feelings. He was glad Walter and Mr. Lewis were now an item.

'Aren't you going to open it?' Mr. Norris said, following his host into a cramped bedroom, where he couldn't help noticing some sort of split-level bed – a trundle bed? – beneath the jumble of alpaca, mink, polyester, camel hair, and lynx. No, not lynx. *Faux* lynx.

'Is *she* here?'

'She?' Walter shoved the box into a corner with his foot, which made a little tear in the Louis Vuitton gift-wrap paper. Mr. Norris's secretary had some LV paper left over from Christmas. Actually, she had bought the paper from a street vendor, a Senegalese who also sold Rolexes. But Mr. Norris didn't know this until the box was already wrapped, when he made her promise never to buy anything on the street again.

'Dawne.'

'Mrs. Schmidlapp is in the ladies', I believe.'

'Why did you ask her?'

'I didn't. Ken did.'

'You got to be kidding.'

'He likes her. They made the sandwiches together this afternoon.'

'But I thought they hated each other. Last time I saw them he was calling her a nut.'

'He likes nuts. And I noticed you also seem to enjoy them – the Spanish kind.'

'What? Help me. Where is my coat – it's a camel hair like this.'

'You're not going?'

'I've got to drop by the office.'

'On a Sunday?'

'I've got a ton of work. Thanks very much, Walter, for inviting me.'

'I wish you'd stay a little longer. Here, this your coat?'

'Thanks. Please tell Ken I really like the apartment.'

'It's not big enough for two. But I'm happy as a clam.'

Mr. Norris managed to escape without running into Dawne. Or Mr. Lewis. But as he was trying to squeeze through the door, blocked by a fresh batch of incoming guests, Mrs. Monke-Peelston asked if he had any seltzer for her dress.

'I'm sorry,' Mr. Norris said as she pressed a napkin into his hand.

When he got to the wretched elevator, which had a maximum capacity of 200 pounds, Mr. Norris gingerly opened the napkin. Expecting tuna, he was surprised to see only this: '555-1415.'

Mr. Norris observed Secretary's Day by taking his secretary to lunch. Human Resources at WyTech had given him a choice of three women and a young man with a Ph.D. in semiotics from Yale. He had picked the blandest of all, someone who resembled Penny, except that she wasn't a Republican. In fact, she wasn't anything. She didn't bother to vote.

'Let's go here, Mr. Norris.'

Since he had been too busy to make any reservations that morning, and since the wind chill was −40°, he was agreeable. But once inside the restaurant, he had second thoughts.

'I don't know, Ms. Joseph.'

'What's wrong? Is it too expensive?'

It was T.G.I. Friday's. That was what was wrong. Mr. Norris hadn't noticed on the way inside because he was blinded by snow.

'I think something a little fancier would be nice.'

'This is fancy enough for me, Mr. Norris.'

'Come on.'

Back on the sidewalk, Ms. Beatrice Joseph's cross-training shoes skidded, and as she grabbed his arm for support, they both lurched into a tourist who accepted their apologies and told them he was from Dolphin Island, Alabama, and asked if there was a place where real New Yorkers ate, not tourists, because he didn't want to go anywhere that tourists went. Ms. Joseph suggested T.G.I. Friday's, but the man said he had seen a whole busload of tourists go in there a few minutes ago, Maltese tourists. Mr. Norris was too cold to suggest anything himself. He just stood there, unable to think.

'This place has food,' Ms. Joseph said to the tourist, who had trailed them all the way to the NyLo building.

'It looks like an office.'

'It is, but they have food in the lobby.'

'Any tourists?'

'No, no tourists, J.T. Let's eat here.'

'OK.'

Mr. Norris tried to say something, but his tongue seemed frozen. Finally: 'No.'

'What?'

'You can eat here, J.T.,' Mr. Norris said. 'But Ms. Joseph and I have reservations somewhere else.'

'Oh.'

* * *

'I hope I wasn't rude to that tourist,' Mr. Norris said after a waiter had brought them the menus.

'I think his feelings were hurt, Mr. Norris.'

'Well, Ms. Joseph, you really shouldn't invite perfect strangers to lunch when I ask you myself, you know.'

'I didn't ask him to eat with us.'

'He thought you did.'

'Is that why you lied and said you had reservations somewhere else, Mr. Norris? Because he was African-American?'

Ms. Joseph, a young African-American herself, did not smile.

'It had nothing to do with that, Ms. Joseph. He could've been Prince Charles himself, I still wouldn't have—'

'But if it had been Prince Charles, Mr. Norris, you would have at least said goodbye. You wouldn't have turned and run like that.'

Having caught a glimpse of Mrs. Kundaa headed for the revolving door, Mr. Norris had indeed hurried off. A week or so ago, when she had apparently learned through the grapevine that Mr. Norris was leaving NyLo, Mrs. Kundaa had E-mailed him. 'Thanks for letting me know. I hope you have a nice life. Mrs. S. Kundaa.' And he had never seen her again.

'Ms. Joseph, when you said you knew of a nice place, I didn't think you were headed for the NyLo building.'

'It's the PlyTex building.'

'I know, but my old office is there.'

'So? It could have been sort of nostalgic for you.'

'I think it takes more than three days for nostalgia to kick in. Anyway, I hope you like steak. They have the best steak in New York here.'

'I don't eat red meat.'

'Look. They have chicken, see. And prawns.'

'It's so expensive, Mr. Norris.'

Yes, it was. Mr. Norris did not want to be here. But after walking away from NyLo, he and his secretary simply could not find a place that didn't cost an arm and a leg. By the time they got to Mary's Ed's Steakhouse, Mr. Norris felt there was no choice left. He had to find the young woman shelter before her feet froze – and him. And there was little chance of running into Bruce Powers. He was spending his vacation in Garden City, according to Pearl Fay. She said Bruce had decided to sell his house there, find something smaller. So he was doing a little repainting, a few touch-ups suggested by the real estate agent.

'That's all you're having, an appetizer?'

'I'm not that hungry, Ms. Joseph. Besides, it's huge, the calamari, more than I can eat.'

Ms. Joseph could not be persuaded to order an appetizer for herself. But she did have the seafood platter. And a crème caramel for dessert. Both she and Mr. Norris drank milk.

'Two hundred seems like a lot for lunch,' she commented as they waited for the hatcheck person to get his cap. 'They shouldn't have charged you full price for the appetizer. That doesn't seem fair.'

Mr. Norris tried not to fume. He could have had a steak for the same price. Why couldn't Mario have told him that?

'By the way, Mr. Norris, there's something I've been meaning to tell you. It's a little embarrassing.'

Oh, Lord, Mr. Norris thought. Please don't let her get personal with me. I don't want to hear that her father really isn't an Episcopalian priest in New Canaan. I don't want to hear that Huey Newton is her real father and she's just posing as . . .

'Can't it wait, Ms. Joseph?'

'No, it's important. That cappuccino machine, I think you better get it back.'

'But you said, you told me Mr. deGroot said it would be all right for me to give it away as a present.'

'Well, actually, it was Mr. deGroot's secretary who told me that. But then Orville checked and found out you've got to have it actually in your office. And if Mr. deGroot doesn't see it there when he gets back tomorrow, well . . .'

'Oh, Ms. Joseph, why do you tell me now?'

'Don't yell at me, please, Mr. Norris.'

'I'm not yelling. But the housewarming was yesterday. Now I'll have to go out and buy one—'

'It's got to be the same exact one, Orville said. They check the serial number, I'm afraid.'

'Oh, Ms. Joseph . . .'

'Thank you for lunch, Mr. Norris.'

'You're welcome.'

'You're not mad at me, are you?'

'No, Ms. Joseph.'

'Orville shouldn't have told me it was OK. I thought he had checked with Mr. deGroot himself, see.'

The tip Mr. Norris gave the hatcheck person cost more than the hat itself – the knit cap he was wearing. Ms. Joseph herself had no hat. As they moved on to the coatcheck station, he told her she should have a hat of some kind in weather like this. Most of the body's heat is lost through the head. And those shoes she was wearing were really quite dangerous on ice. They had no grip.

'I know,' Ms. Joseph admitted. 'But I'm going to the gym after work and I hate changing shoes all the time.'

Chapter Thirty-Four

Mr. Norris didn't telephone first. He just thought it would be better to drop by after work with a new machine in hand, a fait accompli. No long explanations over the phone. As little fuss and muss as possible. Sure, Walter would squawk. But it was better to have one big squawk in person than a preview on the phone.

It was Dawne, though, who answered the door.

'What's that?'

'A housewarming gift. Do you mind if I put it down somewhere?'

'Sure. Come in.'

He set it down in the living room, where swatches covered the futon. Dawne picked up the tape measure on the windowsill. 'The party was yesterday, you know.'

'Yes, I was here.'

'I thought I heard your voice. Why'd you leave so soon?'

Mr. Norris had wandered into the kitchen, but the cappuccino machine wasn't on the counter.

'What are you doing?' Dawne asked as he headed for the bedroom.

'I'm looking for my present.'

'It's in the living room.'

'No, the one I brought yesterday.' He peered beneath the trundle bed.

'Why do you keep on bringing them presents?'

'It's the same present. A cappuccino machine.'

'Please don't mess up the closet, Lloyd.'

He had parted some clothes to see if the box might be on a shelf in back. 'Don't just stand there. Help me, Dawne.'

'Why do you keep on bringing the same present?'

'It's not the same, not exactly. One has problems spraying milk.'

'What?'

'Never mind, will you? I'm in a hurry. I've got a date tonight.'

In a sober brown dress, her hair gathered in a severe bun, Dawne was an unnerving presence. He realized now how much he missed the handsome meter reader.

'A date?'

'Yes, Dawne, with a man.'

Actually, it really wasn't a date. Rocco was coming over to fix the trash compactor, which was jammed. Mr. Norris was a little worried about having the truck driver in his apartment. If the man weren't still on crutches with a cast, Mr. Norris would not have let himself be persuaded that he needed to smush his trash together at all.

'I don't believe you, Lloyd.'

'What?'

'Your face – it's so easy to tell when you're fibbing.'

'Look, you've got a lot of nerve telling me I don't have a date when I have a date.' Actually, Rocco did seem to like him in some strange way. He was the one who had volunteered to fix the trash compactor when Mr. Norris had visited him in the hospital. And now that he thought about it, what a chest the man had. What arms. All natural, too – none of those fake, Nautilus muscles. And Rocco loved Steinbeck. In the hospital he twisted Mr. Norris's arm, literally, until Mr. Norris gave in and promised to read *The Grapes of Wrath*.

'Did it ever occur to you, darling, there might be a good reason why you can't find anyone?'

'Please, Dawne, the box. Help me find that box.'

'I had the same problem, you know. I just couldn't figure out what was blocking me, why I couldn't seem to find any-one, a good woman. Then I woke up. It was all so clear, so simple. It was my conscience. My conscience just wouldn't let me.'

Perched on the edge of the trundle bed, one sturdy leg pumping steadily up and down, Dawne seemed to be hogging all the air. The cramped bedroom had no windows. And those in the living room were shut tight against the bitter cold.

'You're a nice-looking man, intelligent, a little weird, there's no reason you couldn't have a boyfriend if that's what you really want.'

'I'm not weird.'

'Disgusting.'

'What?'

'My thigh, darling.' She had just measured her thigh with the tape. 'Anyway, we all get what we really want.'

'The cappuccino thing, are you going to help?' On hands and knees, he was searching through boxes loaded with dish towels, vases, hair dryers, Duke of Gloucester china, leopard underwear, and sketch pads. 'And don't tell me I get what I want. I've never gotten a single thing I really wanted.'

'You've got friends who love you.'

'What? Who? Name one.'

'Me. And you've got a job now most people would die for. You're making zillions.'

'I'm not making zillions. I'm just paying zillions in taxes and alimony and rent. And I hate my job. Everyone's petrified when

256 *Plain and Normal*

I walk into a meeting. It's like I'm Heather Locklear and Simon Legree all rolled into one.'

'Who's Simon Legree?'

'Why can't people see I'm just about the most bland person on earth? That's all I want. Is it asking too much? From now on, I guarantee I'm not going to have anything but normal friends, plain, honest, bland people. No more of this nonsense where everyone turns out to be royalty or legally underage or rich heterosexual meter readers.'

Dawne stopped dandling the tape on her knee. 'Oh, so she told you, huh?'

'I'm sorry, but yes, Pearl Fay did.'

'All about my mother-in-law?'

Mr. Norris nodded.

'Well, I'm very sorry myself, mister. I'm sorry I'm not plain and normal enough for you. And I'm sorry you've got a wife I can't trust anymore. It's just so humiliating – I could die.'

He stopped rummaging through the boxes. 'Think about it, Dawne. How can you call yourself my friend when you believe in Pat Robertson and Shirley MacLaine?'

'I hate your sin, Lloyd, not you.'

'What about Ken? How in the world does he ever put up with you?'

'Put up with me? I'll have you know I'm wallpapering their entire apartment for free. And I'm choosing their curtains and I just found them a rug for their bathroom at a flea market that costs practically nothing.'

'You're doing all this for people who are going straight to hell?'

'For your information, Smarty Pants, they don't have sex that much. In fact, technically speaking, they almost qualify as ex-gays.'

'Now I've heard everything.'

'You haven't heard anything yet, mister.' On her feet, arms akimbo, she towered over him. 'You are one smug son of a bitch, let me tell you. I know you look down your nose at me. You think I'm some wacko having hot flashes all the time. And Walter, the way you treat him. How can anyone be plain and normal around you? You're the one making everyone into cartoons. Why can't you just see that we're all the same, even if some of us don't go to your highfalutin church every day? Yes, Mr. St. Patrick, while you're there on your holier-than-thou knees, your lovely ex-wife is asking me to make an appointment for her. She has to get an abortion, see, only I'm so dumb and wacko that I don't think it's right.'

Despite the old age pains in his knees, Mr. Norris had almost succeeded in getting to his feet. Dawne yanked him up the rest of the way.

'You're kidding, you've got to be joking.'

'Do I look like I'm joking?'

'This is just great. Pearl Fay has to have an affair with a strict Catholic, no precautions.'

'Strict Catholic?'

Mr. Norris sighed. 'Herbert. He's in Opus Dei.'

'If it were Herbert, you think she'd be getting an abortion?'

Still holding on to her hand, Mr. Norris squeezed it tighter. 'It's got to be Herbert. Who else could . . .'

'Not a clue?'

'No, no, it couldn't be.'

'Afraid so. They got a little reckless after Pearl Fay got back from New Orleans. She was so frustrated, and Bruce, you know . . .'

'I don't want to hear.'

'You're not supposed to hear. Pearl Fay made me swear. But she broke her promise to me – and anyway, I don't like it. She won't listen to me. She's determined to have an abortion.'

'But she's too old, isn't she?'

'For what?'

'To be pregnant. Can you get pregnant at forty-three?'

'Apparently so. Anyway, she just found out the other day, Lloyd. You've got time to talk to her.'

'I don't want to talk to her. It's not my . . . business.'

'Look, are you a Catholic or are you not? Because if you're not, the next time you try to go to Mass you better be prepared to see me coming down the aisle. I'm going to yank you right out of that pew and let everyone know exactly what I think of you.'

Wrenching his hand free, he turned to look again, but forgot what it was he was looking for. 'Don't be silly, Dawne. I'm not responsible for everyone else's morality. You should be saying this to Pearl Fay.'

'She says she doesn't want to be a single parent, she can't stand the thought.'

'So?'

'So, you say you never get anything you want. Well, mister, here it is on a silver platter for you. You got the chance to be Mr. Plain and Normal.'

'I don't under – Wait, hold on, you don't mean . . .'

'Didn't you ever want a child, Lloyd? Think of it. This is what makes life worth living. You'd stop being so obsessed with yourself. You'd be living for someone else for a change. And listen' – she took his hand and squeezed it hard – 'you'd be saving a life. You'd be literally saving a defenseless human being's life, rescuing its soul, an immortal soul.'

'But I . . .'

'Jesus sacrificed his life for you, Lloyd Norris. For you. Do you believe that or not?'

He nodded.

'OK, then. Need I say more?'

'But Dawne, really . . .'

'Oh, darling, I just remembered. There's some junk in the bathroom. I bet your thing is there.'

Outside, waiting for the bus, Mr. Norris could not get warm. He had to stand with his back to the Hudson, which was a shame. If he had turned and faced the wind, he would have seen a spectacular view of Manhattan. Walter and Mr. Lewis could only afford an apartment in New Jersey, an apartment without a view itself. But at the bus stop on the Palisades, you could see the George Washington Bridge spanning the ice-churned river – and on those far cliffs, the massive fortresses of Washington Heights, apartments that had once stared out at an amusement park, long since gone, where Mr. Norris now waited, the box, still wrapped in LVs, at his feet.

Chapter Thirty-Five

'Don't think this is going to make up for your boyfriend,' Pearl Fay said as she took the LV'ed box out of his hands.

'What boyfriend?'

'Wrecking my spinning wheel, my coffee table – you really think this is going to make up for it, Lloyd?' She gave the box an angry shake.

'Actually, that's not for you.'

'What? Turn it on.'

'Turn what on?'

'Must I do everything?' With a fuzzy high-heeled mule, she kicked the switch. The electric mud scraper purred.

'Oh, you found a battery. That's wonderful, Pearl Fay.'

'Yes, wonderful. Now would you come in? You're letting in all the cold air.'

Spiced by her grumbling, the kitchen seemed even more inviting and warm. Thyme and ginger wafted neatly into every alphabetized nook and cranny.

'So this isn't for me, huh?'

'Do you like the wrapping paper? I wrapped it myself.'

'Who's it for?'

'The office.'

'Ms. Joseph?'

'No, for me.'

She looked up from the béchamel she was stirring. 'Well, I knew it wouldn't be long. You've finally gone off the deep end, babe – wrapping presents for yourself.'

'It's not a present. It's—'

'Never mind the explanation. You've always got an explanation for everything.'

'Rocco wasn't my fault. And he's not my boyfriend.'

'What are you doing here, anyway?'

'Why do you always ask me that when I come by? Why can't you just say something nice like, "How are you, good to see you"? Ow!'

'Serves you right.'

He had stuck his finger in the béchamel for a taste. 'I burned my finger.'

'Stick it under the cold tap. No, not my butter. Put that down. And would you please get out of here? I can't think with you hovering like this.'

For privacy, Mr. Norris went upstairs to the master bedroom. With her ears pricked, Mrs. Norris would have been able to hear him if he had phoned from the living room.

'Rocco?'

'Which Rocco you want?'

Sitting on the edge of his former twin bed, Mr. Norris frowned. He had forgotten Rocco's last name. 'Is there more than one Rocco?'

'There's Rocco Junior and Big Daddy Rocco.'

'Uh, well, I guess the Big Daddy one, please.'

'Big Daddy! Get your fat ass over here! They's the phone, some man! How the hell am I supposed to know! Some man, that's all!'

Mr. Norris cleared his throat. 'Uh, hello?'

'Myrtle, this you, darling? You trying to sound like a man again? It's OK. Coast is clear. I love you, sweetcakes. I want to bury my nose in that—'

'Pardon me. This is actually a man speaking.'

'You ain't Myrtle?'

'No, this is Mr. Norris. I decided that it might be better to leave my trash compactor jammed. See, it makes this terrible noise when it works and anyway, it's such a waste of electricity. I think it would be better, environmentally speaking, to have more natural trash, let it hang loose, so to speak, don't squash it . . .'

'Go on, go on. You're turning me on.'

'No, I'm sorry. This isn't Myrtle.'

'Who cares, Miss? You're good, damn good.'

'Is this the Rocco who broke—'

'Big Daddy – call me Big Daddy.'

'Pardon me, but could I maybe try Rocco Junior?'

'What's wrong with Big Daddy? Go on, cupcake, tell me how you like it all squushy and—'

'Cupcake will have to tell you that some other time, Big Daddy,' Pearl Fay's voice came over the line. 'Hang up, Myrtle, right this instant.'

'I *knew* it was you, Myrtle!' Mr. Norris heard as he cradled the replica of Alexander Graham Bell's private phone.

'So he's not your boyfriend,' Mrs. Norris said as she sprayed Lysol directly onto the mouthpiece of a phone he hadn't noticed before, one right next to the refrigerator. With his new job at WyTech, she obviously felt money was no object. A phone here, a phone there . . .

'That wasn't Rocco. I think it might have been his father.'

'What next? His sister?'

'How much did you hear?'

'More than I care to remember.'

'Look, Pearl Fay, if you're going to violate my constitutional right to privacy, then at least do it properly. Listen to the whole darn thing.'

'If I listened to any more, I'd throw up.'

A mule slipped off as she hurried upstairs. He handed the pumpkin fuzz back to her in the sewing room, where a new computerized Singer was furiously stitching a pattern all by itself, some sort of fish, a plump fish.

'From now on, Lloyd – Oh, I hate these!' She tossed the spiked mule into a ruffed wastebasket. The other, kicked into the air, narrowly missed his ear, the one that stuck out a little more than the other. 'From now on, if you have to make these calls, then do it from your own phone. Don't come racing over here to get your rocks off impersonating a woman.'

'I didn't come over here to impersonate a woman.'

'What are you impersonating then – a man?'

'Stop it. Just cut it out.'

'Well, what is it? What do you want from me? Why don't you leave me alone? Let me die, Lloyd. Just let me die!'

Breasts appeared on the fish. And then hair, golden hair. It was so amazing what a machine could do. Mr. and Mrs. Norris stared, helpless.

'I know, Pearl Fay. I'm tired, too. I've had it.'

'You?'

'Yes, me. But we've got someone else to consider now – besides ourselves.'

'What?'

'The baby.'

The mermaid was finished. In the silence that followed, Mrs. Norris clutched the bathing costume.

'I just knew that woman couldn't keep her mouth shut. I just knew she'd blab.'

'Yes, you knew.'

'Don't touch me.' She jerked away from the gentle hand on her shoulder. 'I know what you think of me. You think I'm a slut, don't you?'

'That was Rocco said that.'

'You didn't stop him. You just let him say those things . . .'

'Pearl Fay, please, he was out of control, completely nuts. And he's huge. What could I do? I'm sorry, really. I should never have gone to that bar you told me about.'

'You're right, though. I am a slut. Couldn't even be faithful to Herbert.'

'Pearl Fay, listen to me, darling . . .'

'If it were Herbert's child, that would make sense. But Bruce, why Bruce?'

'Bruce is a good man.'

'Huh?'

'Don't you remember? You told me so yourself.'

'When?'

'When I came over with the check to pay for the broken furniture. You bawled the daylights out of me, Pearl Fay. You called me a judgmental type of person.'

'A "goddamn prig."'

'Well, anyway – and you told me Bruce Powers was ten times more moral than I'll ever be.'

She took the starched handkerchief he held out and blew her nose. 'I was just saying that to make myself feel better. It was so stupid of me. I don't know why I couldn't say no to him.'

'Look, you were trying to help me out, do me a favor. That's why you asked them over, remember?'

'Yes, but I sort of knew . . .'

'OK, but you didn't know for sure Vanessa wasn't going to show up. You only found out that night that they'd been separated. And Bruce was hurting so bad.'

'It's still no excuse.'

'Imagine what he must have felt like all this time, pretending he still had a wife. Think what he's been through, Pearl Fay. First he gets demoted, and then his wife calls him a wimp because he lost the job to a gay person and she—'

'She was pretty mean to him.'

'Not that that's any excuse.'

'What do you mean? The bitch moved in with a CEO in Indiana and now wants half of everything Bruce has got.'

'Yes, I know, but still you two could have—'

'Would you please make up your mind? Am I guilty or not? Here you go saying how horrible she treats him and start helping me feel better, and now when I agree—'

'Well, Pearl Fay, it's still adultery. I'm not going to stand here and tell you it's fine, go ahead and sin all you want.'

'The prig is back, I see.'

'Yes, the prig is back. And the prig wants to know if you'll take him back for good.'

'What?'

'Pearl Fay, you don't have to do this alone. I'll stand by you. I'll do anything to help. I'll even marry you if you – I mean, if you must have a father for the baby.'

'Gee, how romantic.'

'I'm serious. What's the big deal, anyway? We've done this once before.'

'Yeah, babe, and believe me – once is plenty with someone like you.'

'Thanks.'

'Don't look so hurt, Miss Myrtle. I've got a little treat for you.'

With the handkerchief, she dabbed away a tear before reaching into the pocket of the Amish smock that protected her good cashmere sweater set. 'Here, Toad.'

'What's this?'

'He called a few days ago. I was so mad at you I wasn't going to tell you.'

'But—'

'He wants to have dinner.'

'But I can't. He's a—'

'You know what's good for you, buster, you'll go right back into that bedroom and pick up that phone this instant.'

'But Pearl Fay, I told you he's a—'

'March.'

'It's probably nothing – just a . . .'

'I'm counting to three. One, two—'

'OK. OK.'

'Who?'

'Norris, Severinus Lloyd Norris. I gave you a ride home from the hospital in Yonkers. My wife said you called. Ex-wife.'

'Oh, yeah. Wanted to thank you for the lift. Thought we might get together for a bite to eat.'

Mr. Norris's heart thumped. 'Actually, Father, I'm pretty busy these days. I've got a new job and don't have a lot of time . . .'

'Elmo. Call me Elmo.'

'I'm very sorry, Elmo.'

'Too bad. You would've liked my cousin.'

'Your cousin?'

'Yeah, thought you two might hit it off. My cousin's divorced, too, see.'

'Oh, but, Father, I don't think you understand. Your cousin, she wouldn't really like me I don't think.'

'Who said it's a she?'

'It's a man?'

'You're gay, right? I mean, Norris, the way you were giving me the once-over at the hospital, come on.'

Even the roots of Mr. Norris's sparse hair reddened.

'Oh, my God, Norris. I'm sorry, really sorry. I just assumed you were. Well, look – I've got this other cousin, a girl . . .'

'No, Father. You're right.'

'Come on, which is it? Make up your mind.'

'The first one.'

'Gay?'

'Yes.'

'Like pulling teeth. Anyway, Norris, don't get the idea I'm trying to fix you up or anything. That stuff never works out. I really want you to do me another favor.'

'A favor?'

'Yeah, fella. My cousin, see, he's pretty screwed up. Been married twice. Drinks like a fish. Just can't come to terms with it. Like you.'

'I don't drink like a fish.'

'OK, but you are screwed up, right? You and him both.'

'Father, I resent that, I think.'

'Sorry, that's me. I just speak my mind. Can't help observing. You both could use ten years of therapy, then you might—'

'Father, if you don't mind, my wife is—'

'Elmo. And it's your ex-wife, remember? Now look, here's the deal. We've got ourselves a little group here at church for gays and lesbians, and I want you to talk my cousin into joining. It'd do him a world of good, get him back to church, you know.'

'Father – Elmo, I don't believe in that ex-gay stuff. Forget it. And I won't have anything to do with Courage, that no-sex stuff.'

'Hey, who said anything about ex-gay or Courage?'

'You mean . . . ?'

'I said gay, period. It's got a lot of non-Catholics in it, singles, couples. We meet every Wednesday evening for bingo with Rabbi Hirsh and his PFLAGs from the synagogue. So how about it?'

'I live in the city. Dobbs Ferry is a long way.'

'Come on, fella.'

The doorbell rang. Mr. Norris stretched the cord of Mr. Bell's telephone as far as it could go. But he wasn't able to peer out the window to see who it might be.

'Elmo, really, I don't know.'

'It's a good chance for you to meet people. You said you didn't have any friends. Well, here's a chance.'

'I said?'

'In the car, when you drove me, you were blubbering about . . . Now look, fella, I'm a busy man. Make up your mind. You want to do me a favor or not?'

The bell rang again.

'Oh, all right.'

'How's Thursday?'

'That's tomorrow.'

'So?'

'How old is your cousin?'

'I don't know – forty-five, -six. Big fella. Had a bypass last year, nearly died.'

'You mean he's fat?'

'Husky.'

'Is he tall?'

'Hey, what the hell is this? A frickin' dating service?'

'Father, language.'

'Sorry. But you're beginning to get on my nerves.'

'OK, Thursday.'

'That's more like it. You can come here? I don't have time to get to the city.'

Elmo gave him the name of an Italian restaurant in Dobbs Ferry. And the time. Then: 'By the way, you ever read *The Grapes of Wrath*?'

'No, why?'

'You get a chance, give it a once-over. My cousin, he's sort of nuts about the book, you know.'

'Oh, Lord, Elmo. Your cousin's name, it isn't—'

'Look, I got to run.'

'But I—'

'See you Thursday. Bye.'

In a daze, Mr. Norris wandered downstairs.

'Well, how'd it go, Myrtle?'

'Huh?'

'You got him?'

'Yes, I got him. Who was that at the door?'

'Bruce.'

'Oh.'

'He's in the little boy's room.'

'Oh.'

'Where do you think you're going?'

'Home.'

'No way, José. Come.'

In the dining room, he saw the table was set for three.

'Sit.'

'Pearl Fay, maybe you two should be alone.'

The toilet flushed. Mr. Norris's heart thumped painfully.

'He insists.'

'What?'

'Bruce wants you to join us.'

'I can't. It's too embarrassing. I mean after . . .'

'I've spent all day slaving over a hot stove. You're not going to tell me now – Sit.'

'There won't be enough if I . . .'

'I've got a ton of food.'

'But you've got to eat for two, right?'

She put a hand on her stunning, slim waist. 'There's enough for everyone. Now look happy. He's coming.'

'Oh, Pearl Fay, I don't know . . .'

'Goddammit.' She shoved him down into the chair he hovered uncertainly over. 'Sit, Toad. Eat.'

Chapter Thirty-Six

'Don't go in there. That's the bedroom.'

He showed her the correct door and then went back into the living room.

Dr. Bennet hadn't seen Edwina since the funeral. It was unbelievable. The woman looked more like Hermione's mother than her sister. And Edwina was the younger sister – three years younger. Like a pair of clodhoppers, her thick orthopedic shoes clunked with every step – even on the Karastan. Dr. Bennet wouldn't have been surprised if his downstairs neighbors beat on their ceiling with a broom.

'There's no paper!'

Dr. Bennet looked up from the book he was trying to read. He was stuck on page 12. How in the world could a reputable physicist claim that the coastline of any island is actually, when every atom of every nook and cranny is mapped, infinite? How could Manhattan be infinite? Preposterous. Perhaps it was a good thing he hadn't stuck with physics if this was the sort of nonsense they were fooling around with nowadays.

'Carlos, toilet paper! Pronto!'

'Quiet, please! You'll wake them!'

Consuelo and Edgar were taking a nap in the bedroom. Their plane for Casablanca was leaving from JFK in a few hours.

'The sink.' He tried to rise from the Queen Anne chair, but his legs ached horribly. 'Look underneath the sink.'

The door shut again – almost a slam.

It was Consuelo who had invited Edwina over for tea. His mother had bought herself a cell phone and was trying to think of people she could test it out on. To make sure it worked, she explained to her son when Edwina had shown up in Washington Heights with so little warning that Dr. Bennet had had no chance to vacate the premises.

Even so, if it hadn't been his mother and father's last day, Dr. Bennet would have probably excused himself, no matter how rude it might have seemed. Edwina did not like the wafers and goat cheese Dr. Bennet happened to have on hand. She made Edgar go out for jelly doughnuts. And then she had scolded Dr. Bennet for being too chicken to move to Morocco. That was the very word she had used, 'chicken.' And Consuelo didn't even defend him. For some reason, Consuelo seemed to be on Edwina's side that afternoon. And yet all their lives Consuelo and Edgar had looked down their noses at Hermione's family. Now all of a sudden, his mother was making Edwina promise to look after her son. Edwina said she would. She said she expected him to be her guest this very weekend – no ifs, ands, or buts. Incensed, on the verge of exploding, Dr. Bennet had politely accepted the offer. His mother said it would make her so happy. She would not be able to go back to her roses if he didn't say yes.

'Of course you understand, Edwina,' Dr. Bennet said when the woman finally emerged from the bathroom, 'I haven't the slightest intention of spending the weekend with you.'

'Nonsense.' She thumped her blackthorn on the parquet. 'You've already agreed.'

'I only said that for my mother's sake. I don't want her to be miserable because of me.'

'Then you must come.'

'It's impossible.'

'Why is it impossible? Are you a chicken?'

'You must stop calling me that, Edwina. I will not stand for it.'

'Then what's your problem? Why are you going back on your word? I thought you were a man of honor. I thought—'

'Can you please modulate your voice? My parents need their rest.'

'Help lower me. My knees don't seem to be bending.'

'Oh, for heaven's sake.' With a groan, he got up. Or tried to. His legs really ached. 'I'm sorry, I – Oh, now look what you've done!'

'Quiet, your parents,' Edwina said from the unicorn she had landed upon, accidentally. Somehow, because of the odd angle of her descent and the tonnage of her cargo, the ottoman's delicate tapestry had been ripped by a loose fabric bolt.

'Do you realize how much that thing costs?'

'Calm down, Carlos. It costs nothing.'

'Hermione paid—'

'Yes, she paid. It's all paid for. Now it costs nothing, see? We should enjoy using it however we like. What's the sense of having something if you can't enjoy it? You still swim? You'll come out this weekend and get even then. You can think of a way to wreck my pool, throw gravel in the drain.'

'I'm not going to swim during a blizzard. There's supposed to be a blizzard this weekend.'

'That makes it all the more fun. It's heated, you know.'

The horn had ripped right off the poor beast's forehead. Dr. Bennet felt the raw wound. 'Have you no shame, Edwina? No guilt?'

'I'll stitch it up myself – right now, if you want. You have a needle and thread?'

'I'm talking about us.'

'Us?'

'You and me.'

Starting to list to one side, the old woman steadied herself with her knotty blackthorn.

'What about us, Carlos? Speak up, man.'

'After what we did, I can't bear looking at you, much less spending a weekend.'

'What did we do?'

'What did we *do*?'

'Come, Carlos. I'm no good at riddles. Speak plainly.'

'We betrayed Hermione.'

'We did?'

'For heaven's sake, Edwina – don't you remember that morning?'

'What morning?'

'Hermione hadn't come home all night. I was frantic. She had gone to an auction, a charity auction – with Chet.'

'Oh, the hepatitis thing.' She shrugged. 'Carlos, that was a hundred years ago.'

'It was not a hundred years ago. And you, you told Chet about it. You know it meant nothing to either one of us – and you had to go and tell Chet.'

'He swore he wouldn't tell Hermione. I would never have told him if I thought—'

'You knew very well he was going to tell Hermione. Because that's the way they are – those fairies. They can't keep their filthy mouths shut!'

'Carlos.'

'And you, you were so jealous of Hermione, you couldn't stand the thought that she got me, not you. You'd do anything to destroy her happiness, her trust in me.'

'Actually, Carlos, I was just a little randy, that's all. And you sure didn't do very much to remedy that.'

'That's why you're so stupid, such a cow! Because we didn't do

anything – not technically. I was too wrought up to . . . But then
you have to tell Chet. Why? Why was that necessary?'

'Because Hermione already suspected us, Carlos. I was explaining that we were innocent.'

'She never forgave me. I hope you're satisfied. She never forgave me.'

'Now I've had just about enough of this nonsense.'

'Ow!'

The blackthorn had struck him on the shin.

'You think my sister was a dope? She knew all about your
shenanigans. It wasn't just me. Don't try to pin this on me,
brother.'

'But I loved her. I wouldn't have done any of it if she had just
listened to me, if she just stopped seeing Chet.'

'The man was gay!'

'I know. But still, not everyone knew that. People could see
them together and they talk, people talk. It reflected on my . . . my
reputation. She gave me so much pain, Edwina. It hurt so bad.'

'She was never unfaithful, not once. Why couldn't you trust
her?'

'She left him everything.'

Edwina shrugged. 'Well, you made it clear to all of us you didn't
want a cent of her dough. She was just doing what you wanted.'

'I didn't mean for her to leave it to him. I thought it might go
to a hospital or foundation.'

'Stop staring at my knickers.'

'Must you sprawl like that?'

'I'd cross my legs, Carlos, but I might fall off this thing. Anyway,
Chet didn't need her money himself. He was loaded.'

That was what made it even worse. Dr. Bennet just shook
his head.

'He gave it all to AmFAR, Carlos.'

'What?'

'It's AIDS research. Every penny went there. Didn't your mother
tell you?'

'Mother? No.'

'She tried to see him today, you know. She was going to bring him over to tea. Instead, she got the booby prize. Me.'

'Yes, Mother told me. Was it last year?'

'Right, about a year ago. AIDS.'

Dr. Bennet gazed out at the lone fir on the terrace. No bird disturbed the perfect stillness. 'You should've let me know, Edwina. I never knew he'd passed away.'

'Told you? How can anyone tell you anything when you don't answer your phone and have no machine and every letter comes back unopened. There was a perfectly marvelous Requiem Mass for him at St. Ignatius Loyola. The same priest, too.'

'Hermione's?'

The old woman nodded. 'Anyway, you could've gone to that auction with her.'

'What auction?'

'Hepatitis. She wanted to go with you. She always wanted to go with you. But you were too proud. You couldn't buy anything yourself, so you sent her off without you.'

'She didn't have to go.'

'How else was she going to get rid of her money? She had to spend it on something. And it might as well have been for something good. You wouldn't let her spend a cent on you.'

'I earned what we spent.'

'Right – and made poor Hermione feel like a louse. Why didn't you just teach, like you wanted? She knew you hated selling apartments to her dumb, rich friends.'

'Can you please keep your voice down?'

'You had to play the saint, didn't you? Do you realize how miserable it can be, living with a saint? Have one?'

She held out a box of cough drops. He declined.

'Speaking of saints,' she said, popping one into her mouth, 'I've got one visiting me this weekend. It's the real reason I insist you come out.'

'Impossible.'

'You and the Countess would hit it off, I guarantee. She has this curious habit of doing all sorts of good for people behind their back. To their face she's a bitch on wheels. But the minute they're gone . . . You know my boy, don't you?'

'How is Ward?'

'Up until yesterday, terrible. He had passed the bar after six tries and then couldn't get a job anywhere.'

'Is he still in San Francisco?'

'Right, which is the whole problem. There simply is no room for another lawyer in the Bay Area. A couple of years ago the Countess and Ward had a terrible quarrel in my house. She called him a lazy good-for-nothing excuse for a man nearly fifty, and I won't repeat what he said about her in case it might prejudice you this weekend. Anyway, when I told her how Ward was struggling she made a phone call and the next thing I know, he's landed a job at a firm in Berkeley. She has this wonderful way with men, getting them to stand up to her. The minute they break free and stop speaking to her, she—'

'I believe this is one saint I can do without.'

'Well, then, maybe you'd like the nonsaint who's coming this weekend. Hiet deGroot is one of the nastiest men alive, greedy, ambitious, deceitful. He's the CEO of some industrial design factory or something . . .'

Dr. Bennet smiled faintly. 'If you're implying that I would have the slightest interest in meeting a man . . .'

'Relax, Carlos. I forgot that sex was the only thing on your mind. I guess it never occurred to you that there might be other reasons to meet people. Countess Kundaa isn't supposed to be a date, you know. Even though she is poor. I thought you'd feel more comfortable with someone poor. And she's so proud. She made her gardener return the birthday present I gave him. I just couldn't bear thinking what that woman pays him – he has five children, too – so I sent him a little bonus, some Food Stamps. Actually, her garden is so tiny she's being charitable just to have him look in twice a week and pull a weed or two. They don't have big gardens in Sutton Place, you know. Of course, I always slip her maid some Food Stamps whenever I go to dinner. In any case, the Countess is taken. You mustn't have any lewd thoughts about her this weekend. I have a plan to make Hiet propose to her. He's one of those confirmed bachelors, you know. And he adores her. She's the only person alive, male or female, who can tell that man exactly what a nasty beast he is. He'll do absolutely anything she says, too. Why just the other day, she made him – Now who can that be? Is that my jelly doughnuts?'

'You've already eaten your jelly doughnuts. In fact, you've got some powder on your face.'

'Gracious. Why didn't you say something?'

'I didn't want to be rude.'

'Hand me my purse over there. And would you please answer that door.'

'No.'

With his foot, he was able to reach out and hook the handle of her purse. Deftly, he swung it over to the ruined ottoman.

'Just where do you get Food Stamps anyway?'

'What?' Looking into the mirror of a titanium Art Deco compact, she dabbed at the powdered sugar on her plump rouged cheeks. 'I'm entitled, aren't I? I'm a taxpayer. Oh, it's impossible. I can't stand another buzz. Are you going to get that door, or am I going to have to get up and—'

'You're going to have to get up. I'm not expecting anyone. It's probably just the doorman with some dry cleaning, and I don't happen to have anything to tip him with. I spent my last dime on your jelly doughnuts.'

The blackthorn could get no purchase on the slippery carpet. She struggled in vain to rise, and as she did, for a fleeting moment, a look came over her, one of such determination in the midst of everything that is futile, hopeless, that it nearly broke his heart. It was Hermione, right before his eyes.

'Edwina, wait, let me help.'

'Never mind, now. Who is this man? What is he doing here?'

A stranger had walked in. Looking wild, lost, he gazed from the foyer. Dr. Bennet was sure this was it. They would be robbed, beaten, left for dead.

'Please excuse me, Dr. Bennet. I was desiring to get in. I was worried that no one answered, and I am to meet your mother and father.'

'You must be Marion,' Edwina said from the ottoman.

'I am.'

Still perturbed, Dr. Bennet demanded to know how the man had got inside the apartment. Marion explained that Consuelo had given him a key. In case of an emergency like this.

'This is no emergency.'

'But we must leave very soon, Dr. Bennet.'

'You have a couple of hours still.'

It had been so many years since he had seen Marion – and that had been in the Anti-Atlas. With Hermione. The man looked so weary now. He seemed to have shrunk, dried out by the desert air. So much darker.

'Well, anyway, why don't you sit down? Oh, Marion, this is Lady Schuyler-Tuft.'

'Edwina. Call me Edwina. Now Marion, don't be shy. Tell me all about yourself. Consuelo says you are a scholar of some sort.'

'I am a scholar of the Adams family.'

'Dear me,' she exclaimed, clapping her hands together. 'I just adore that show. You simply must get cable, Carlos. It's on every single night now. Oh, Edgar, don't, dear. You're getting finger-marks on Carlos's window.'

'It's Marion,' Dr. Bennet said as the Moroccan withdrew his hands from the sliding glass door. He had gone over to check out the view perhaps. Or to get away from Edwina.

'Edgar, Marion – what's the difference?' Edwina said complacently.

'The difference is between my father and a truly horrible man. I don't mean you, Marion. I mean your namesake. Marion's real name is Charles. But he met John Wayne once and decided to change it. That was Wayne's first name – Marion.'

'Pardon,' Marion said, turning toward them. 'I am not named after John Wayne. I told him to his face that he is a disgrace, a coward. He refused to serve his country during the war, and he deserted his wife, and had not the courage to face history, the facts, in *The Alamo*. Marion Morrison's films, they are a cheap way to feel brave, no?'

'But Marion, I thought—'

'I am named after your grandfather, Edgar Marion Bennet. He was a good friend of Henry Adams.'

'Did he ever meet Morticia?' Edwina asked. 'Oh, someone please help me up. Marion, come here. Do I have powder still?' Marion said no as he tugged. 'Carlos, here you are on a bluff overlooking the Hudson, and your apartment is facing the wrong way. You have no view of the river.'

'It's cheaper. The apartments with a view cost a lot more.'

'Do they still have that amusement park on the other side? Remember when Hermione made us get on that roller coaster? I nearly died. Marion, would you care for a jelly doughnut? Carlos, go get Mr. Wayne a jelly doughnut. He looks too thin.'

'You ate them all.'

'There must be something. Go look.'

In the kitchen an idea occurred to Dr. Bennet. He would pretend there was nothing to eat, no cookies. Then he would suggest that Marion take Edwina over to Broadway for a snack. That would leave him some time alone with his parents. He so much wanted another chance to beg them to stay here with him. He could not bear to see them leave.

'Edwina, there doesn't seem to be any – What's this smoke?'

'Smoke?'

'I smell smoke.'

Still on the ottoman – Marion had not been able to dislodge her – Edwina said, 'This place is like Grand Central Station.'

'What do you mean?'

'Another man just walked in. Marion left the door open, and this man came in.'

'What man? Marion, you can't leave doors open like this in New York. This is terrible. Where is he?'

'In the library,' Edwina said. 'He's looking for a belly dancer. I said that I didn't think you kept a belly dancer in the apartment, but he insisted that Consuelo said he could come get her.'

'Oh.'

'You mean you *do* have a belly dancer, Carlos? Shame on you.'

'It's a statue – ivory.'

Back in the kitchen, Dr. Bennet reached for the Fig Newtons he had hidden in the back of the top cabinet. His heart pounded unmercifully. It ached with hope. After coming all this way uptown, Joe Pollock must be hungry. Surely he would want something to eat.

POLITE SEX James Wilcox

Emily and Clara face bright futures in New York. But youthful hope gives way to wisened weariness as it becomes clear that compromises in love and work are all part of growing up.

'Wilcox observes with acuity, wit and great compassion the poignant and circuitous path towards adult happiness.' *GQ*

£6.99   1 85702 429 X

MISS UNDINE'S LIVING ROOM James Wilcox

When the body of nasty Mr Versey is found under his window one morning, the evidence clearly points to L. D. Loraine, despite the fact that he's 91 and nearly bedridden. Scandal ensues, at the centre of which lurks the old man's niece.

£6.99   1 85702 427 3

NORTH GLADIOLA James Wilcox

For Ethyl Mae Coco, an upright matron in her late 50s, life revolves around her string quartet. But her sedate life is soon to be overtaken by a series of bizarre happenings, and before long the whole family's dirty laundry is being well and truly aired.

£6.99   1 85702 426 5

MODERN BAPTISTS James Wilcox

When Bobby Pickens's half-brother – ex-con, ex-actor and ex-husband (three times) – moves in with him, things don't take long to go wrong. In a matter of weeks Bobby finds himself involved in a theft, a hit-and-run collision, unemployment, a nervous breakdown and a number of fouled-up romances.

£6.99   1 85702 425 7

All Fourth Estate books are available from your local bookshop,
or can be ordered direct from:

Fourth Estate, Book Service By Post, PO Box 29,
Douglas, I-O-M, IM99 1BQ

Credit cards accepted.

Tel: 01642 675137   Fax: 01624 670923
Internet: http://www.bookpost.co.uk
e-mail: bookshop@enterprise.net

Please state when ordering if you do **not** *wish to receive further
information about Fourth Estate titles.*